MURDER IN THE MORNING

"I guess you haven't looked at today's paper yet, Aunt Peg?"

"It's still out by the mailbox. Shall I go get it?"

"No, I can read to you what's in front of me. Sara Bentley's cottage burned to the ground last night, and the body of a young woman was found inside."

"Sara?" Peg gasped.

"It says that the body was badly burned and the police haven't been able to make an identification yet." I stared down at the paper, drumming my fingers on the page.

"What?"

"Where had Sara been for the last week, and why did she suddenly decide to come back? And why on the night that the cottage burned down?"

"Maybe she had something to do with the fire," said Peg, voicing my thoughts aloud. "Does it say what started it?"

"No." I read the official wording. " 'Cause of the blaze has yet to be determined.' That could mean anything."

"Including that the fire marshal knows what happened, and they just haven't released their findings yet." Aunt Peg paused. "Here's a gruesome thought. What if Sara didn't return to her cottage last night? What if she's been dead since she disappeared and the murderer brought her body back?"

"Oh, Lord." It was definitely too early in the morning for me to deal with possibilities like that.

Books by Laurien Berenson

A PEDIGREE TO DIE FOR
UNDERDOG
DOG EAT DOG
HAIR OF THE DOG
WATCHDOG
HUSH PUPPY
UNLEASHED
ONCE BITTEN
HOT DOG
BEST IN SHOW
JINGLE BELL BARK
RAINING CATS AND DOGS
CHOW DOWN
HOUNDED TO DEATH
DOGGIE DAY CARE MURDER
GONE WITH THE WOOF

Published by Kensington Books

Once Bitten

A Melanie Travis Mystery

Laurien Berenson

KENSINGTON BOOKS
Kensington Publishing Corp.
http://www.kensingtonbooks.com

KENSINGTON BOOKS are published by

Kensington Publishing Corp.
119 West 40th Street
New York, NY 10018

All Kensington Titles, Imprints, and Distributed Lines are available at special quantity discounts for bulk purchases for sales promotions, premiums, fund-raising, and educational or institutional use. Special book excerpts or customized printings can also be created to fit specific needs. For details, write or phone the office of the Kensington special sales manager: Kensington Publishing Corp., 850 Third Avenue, New York, NY 10022, attn: Special Sales Department, Phone: 1-800-221-2647.

Kensington and the K logo Reg. U.S. Pat. & TM Off.

ISBN-13: 978-0-7582-8746-5
ISBN-10: 0-7582-8746-1
First Kensington Hardcover Printing: September 2001
First Kensington Paperback Printing: August 2002

eISBN-13: 978-0-7582-8907-0
eISBN-10: 0-7582-8907-3
First Kensington Electronic Edition: July 2013

10 9 8 7 6 5

Printed in the United States of America

PROLOGUE

It's not that hard to recover from a broken heart. I should know. Do you want to hear the secret?

It's this: just breathe. In, out. In, out. See how simple that is? You'd be amazed how much time can pass while you just concentrate on that one thing.

In, out. In, out.

My fiancé, Sam, had left in July. He needed to find himself, he'd said. As far as I knew, he was still looking. Meanwhile, my life had gone on. Now it was November, and I was still breathing. Still doing okay.

What choice did I have? Just because Sam was gone didn't mean I had the luxury of putting everything else on hold. Not even close.

My son, Davey, had turned seven in September and entered second grade. His father, my ex-husband, Bob, had sent a card from Texas. Enclosed, Davey had found a round-trip plane ticket. *Come visit any time*, Bob had written. *I'd love to see you*. Davey seemed intrigued by the thought of his first cross-country trip.

As for me, I was still mulling over the offer. Considering that Bob's input into Davey's life had been virtually nonexistent for most of my son's seven years, I figured I'd be ready to put Davey on a plane to Texas when he graduated from high school or when Poodles grew wings.

Whichever came first.

Ah, yes, the Poodles. They were keeping me busy, too. Until recently, there'd only been one dog in my life: a wondrous Standard Poodle named Faith. Black and beautiful, big, and blessed with a wicked sense of humor, Faith is all anyone could hope for in a pet.

Before my Aunt Peg gave her to me as a reward for a job well done, I'd never had a dog. Never understood how a pair of dark, expressive eyes and a paw laid gently across my knee could open a whole new door to my emotions. Faith came into Davey's life and mine as an exuberant puppy. Now, at the somewhat mature age of two and a half, she has lost none of her *joie de vivre*.

She has also recently become a mother. Or dam, in dog parlance—and Aunt Peg would be the first to correct my terminology. In dog show circles, she is Margaret Turnbull of Cedar Crest Standard Poodles. A breeder and exhibitor of more than thirty years' standing, Aunt Peg has won and done just about everything there is to do in the sport of dogs.

Faith had had a litter of puppies in July. Aided by Peg's expert advice, Davey and I had selected a girl to keep for our own. Davey had already named the puppy Eve when she was born, and I liked the symbolism the name implied. Though I couldn't imagine I'd ever have Aunt Peg's longevity in the breed, I did harbor the hope that this litter would be the beginning of a line that would someday make me proud.

In the meantime, Eve's upbringing was one more thing to wedge into my already tight schedule. Aunt Peg, who insists that her puppies be gotten off to the best possible start, was helping out. During the week when I was working as special needs tutor at Howard Academy, a private school in Greenwich, Connecticut, Peg was keeping Eve at her house to ensure that she received the thorough socializing that all young puppies need.

The only other thing I had to worry about was the wedding.

When Sam and I were still together, we'd thought about getting married on Christmas Eve. Now, as things turned out, there was going to be a Christmas ceremony after all. Just not mine, unfortunately. Instead, I'd gotten roped into helping out with my brother Frank's wedding.

Life is full of little ironies, isn't it?

1

"We're looking for something small," Bertie said. "Cozy. Intimate."

Bertie Kennedy was Frank's fiancée, a professional handler on the Northeast dog show circuit. When I'd introduced the two of them fifteen months earlier, I never dreamed things would come to this.

"Of course it's going to be small," Sara Bentley replied. "You're only giving me six weeks. With that kind of lead time, you'll be lucky if we pull this off at all."

"You'll manage." With enviable calm, Bertie eyed the woman she'd chosen to plan her upcoming nuptials. "You always do."

"No, I don't." Sara's thick, dark curls bounced from side to side as she shook her head. "That's the whole point."

What whole point? I wondered. What did Sara and Bertie know that I didn't?

I sneaked a glance at the legal pad Sara had balanced across her knees. Her Mont Blanc pen was poised to fly across the page, but though we'd been talking for the past fifteen minutes, she had yet to make a single note.

"Don't be silly," said Bertie. "You've had some bad luck, that's all. And maybe some bad timing. This job is going to be perfect for you."

Sara relaxed her shoulders slightly. When she smiled, her whole face lit up. I guessed her to be about the same age as Bertie and me: late twenties, early thirties, but happy—she looked as innocent as a child. "Well, I do have impeccable taste."

"Precisely. And great organizational skills. Not to mention entertaining contacts up the wazoo."

"I do know how to throw a party," Sara admitted.

"And how to close a bar," Bertie mentioned. Clearly there was history between these two women that I was missing out on.

Sara laughed, not offended in the least. She brushed her unruly hair out of her eyes and got down to business.

I sat and watched as the two of them ran through the basics of what Bertie wanted—yellow everything, no quiche, and a really kick-ass band—and wondered what I was doing there. Or, more precisely, since the meeting was taking place at my house, what were they doing here?

When Bertie had called the night before and asked me to sit in on a meeting with her wedding planner, I'd been happy to oblige. I liked Bertie a lot, and I thought she'd make a superb addition to the family. Frank had not only chosen well, he'd also, to my way of looking at things, been incredibly lucky to find someone as great as Bertie who was willing to take him on.

Then again, I'm no expert when it comes to charting the course of true love. Sam's unexpected flight had certainly proven that.

I also know next to nothing about planning a wedding or any other sort of large social function, and so far I hadn't proven any help at all.

"What do you think?" Bertie asked, poking me in the knee hard. "A buffet is a good idea, right? No way people want to have to sit down and eat. Besides, we're going to keep this small and casual. Everyone can help themselves when they feel like it."

"Sure—" A squeal from the next room, followed by the sound of several high-pitched barks, halted me mid-thought. "Davey?"

Sara looked up at the same time, recognizing her own dog's voice as easily as I'd have recognized Faith's. "Titus?"

"Yes?" The single syllable floated in from the kitchen. It was injected with all the innocence a seven-year-old boy could muster.

"Is everything all right in there?"

Before he could answer, Faith appeared in the living room doorway. If she'd been human, she would have been shaking her head. As it was, the urge to tattle could easily be read in her expression. Whatever game Davey had gotten the visiting Sheltie to take part in, Faith didn't approve.

Standards are the largest of the three varieties of Poodles. As Faith approached the armchair where I sat, she and I were almost eye to eye. And of course, her show coat made her look even bigger.

The front half of her body was encased in a long, thick mane of black hair, which was mostly wrapped and banded now to keep it out of her way. In the show ring, that hair would be brushed, shaped, and sprayed into an outline uniquely recognizable as belonging to the Poodle breed.

Faith walked across the room, reached up, and placed both her front paws across my lap. Her body language was unmistakable. She figured Davey and Titus were about to get into trouble, and she intended to be well out of the way when it happened.

"What are you guys doing?" I called.

"Nothing," Davey answered.

As if there's a mother in the world who would believe that.

My son appeared at the edge of the archway between the hall and living room. Titus, Sara's Shetland Sheepdog, seemed to be standing behind him, though the wall was blocking my view. Davey had both hands behind his back and looked as though he was bracing against something. I thought I heard a low growl.

"Titus!" Sara said sharply.

Immediately the dog leapt around Davey and trotted into the room. The Sheltie was a beautiful golden sable color. His ears were up and alert and there was a smile on his foxy face. A long, thickly furnished tail wagged up and over his back as he danced to Sara's side. Clearly he was still ready to play.

"Davey, what do you have in your hands?"

Reluctantly, my son pulled out the Frisbee he had hidden behind his back. With a yip, Titus flew across the room and grabbed the edge of the plastic disk in his teeth. Shaking his head, he tried to pry the toy free.

"Sorry." Sara leapt up and pad and pen scattered. "Titus knows how to behave better than that. It's just that Frisbees are his favorite thing."

"Davey knows better, too," I muttered.

That knowledge didn't seem to have stopped my son from throwing the Frisbee in the house. I could hardly blame the dog, who, after all, had been no more than a willing co-conspirator.

In the few minutes it took us to get everyone sorted out, Sara decided that she had enough information to get started making calls, finding out about availability, and chasing down quotes. She gathered up her things. Bertie and I both saw her to the door.

Sara's blue Mercedes Benz sedan was parked at the end of my driveway. Titus ran on ahead, jumping up to bat his white paws eagerly against the side door. If Sara was concerned that his nails might scratch the pristine metallic finish, she didn't show it.

Instead, she took her time, fishing her keys out of her purse and pausing to kiss Bertie good-bye on both cheeks in the European fashion. Then, to my surprise, I received the same treatment, even though we'd only met an hour earlier.

Bertie glanced at me and rolled her eyes as Sara walked out and got in her car. "Old friend," she said as I closed the door.

"Good friend?"

"At times. Probably more when she needed me than when I needed her."

Bertie reached for the coat rack behind the door, where she'd hung her leather jacket when she came in. I'd already sent Davey upstairs to get ready for bed. He had school the next day and so did I, but I had no intention of letting Bertie leave until I heard more.

I took the jacket out of her hands and hung it back up. "It sounds like there's a story there."

"Believe me, with Sara there's always a story. Her life is one big story."

I headed toward the kitchen and Bertie followed. "She seemed nice enough to me."

"Who said she wasn't nice? Not me. Life around Sara can be a hell of a good time. Fun, fun, fun, as they say." She stopped and frowned. "Who said that anyway, the Beach Boys?"

"I think so. Though to tell you the truth, I'm not up on surfer music." We pulled out chairs at the kitchen table and sat down. My house has a perfectly nice living room, but except when I'm entertaining people I don't know well, I seem to spend my life in the kitchen. "How long have you known Sara?"

Bertie thought back. "Probably seven or eight years. When I was trying to get started as a handler, she was at all the shows. Her mother breeds Shelties. Scotchglen Shetland Sheepdogs. Maybe you've heard of them?"

I shook my head. I've been going to shows for the past two years, which, in most dog people's eyes, makes me a newcomer to the sport. I'm still trying to get the exhibitors in the Non-Sporting group straight. The Herding group, where Shelties were classified, was currently beyond my sphere of knowledge.

"Anyway, Sara and I hit it off and we started hanging out together."

"Was she a wedding planner then?"

"No." Bertie grinned. "I'm not even sure she's a wedding planner now."

I heard footsteps on the stairs, and a moment later, Faith entered the kitchen. She was ready to go outside while I went up and tucked Davey into bed. By the time I returned, she'd be waiting for me on the back steps. When I let her in, the big Poodle would dash upstairs and settle in for the night at the foot of Davey's bed.

Dogs are creatures of habit. So are mothers, when they get the chance. I loved our cozy domestic ritual; loved the thought of my son and our dog cuddling, keeping each other safe and warm all night long.

Bertie saw to Faith while I went up and took care of Davey. Minutes later we resumed our conversation as though it had never been interrupted.

"The thing about Sara," Bertie said, "is that she's still try-ing to find her niche. When I met her, she was going to shows because that's what her mother did. And, I guess, be-cause she genuinely enjoys the dogs. But then she saw what

I was doing and decided it might be a good way to make a living."

"Sara was a handler?"

"More or less. She was never very successful at it. You know what handling's like. It's a twenty-four hour a day job. And Sara wasn't willing to put in the time. Let's just say she was much better at schmoozing the judges than she was at cleaning the crates."

I thought about the shiny Mercedes Sara had parked in my driveway. I'd found my niche, to use Bertie's terminology, and I considered myself lucky to have a Volvo. Who knew searching could be so lucrative?

"Then what did she do?"

"Dog show photographer. For a while, Sara figured that was the perfect choice. She likes taking pictures, plus she got to go to all the shows and visit with her friends."

"For a while?"

"Well, she wasn't really getting hired all that much. The big shows, the established ones, have been using the same guys for years. What Sara should have done was try to drum up business at specialties, or the new start-up dog clubs. But that wasn't where she wanted to be."

"Exit one photographer," I said.

"She still takes a good picture," Bertie admitted. "I used her for some pub shots on a Lhasa I was showing last year and they turned out great. And that stint kind of led to her next career."

"Which was?"

I leaned back in my chair, enjoying the possibilities. I'd become a teacher and a mother young enough to rule out any such frivolity when it came to making choices. Listening to Sara's history gave me a vicarious thrill. I wondered how long it would be before we worked our way around to the wedding-planner gig.

"Dog sitter/pet groomer," said Bertie. "Freelance, of course. Because, as Sara has pointed out many times, she could never work for anyone but herself."

"And that didn't work out either?"

"No, it has. For the most part, anyway. At least she's still doing it. I don't think she has a lot of clients, but there seem to be enough to make her think she's in business."

"Enough to buy her a Mercedes?"

"Oh, that." Bertie waved a hand. "Mummy's money paid for that. Good God, you didn't think Sara was actually trying to support herself with all those jobs, did you?"

"Well . . . yes."

"No, no, no. . . . Sara's mother comes from old money." Bertie pursed her lips and made a face, as if to illustrate Sara's patrician forebears. "Delilah got into showing dogs as a child in the old days, when kennel maids did all the actual work, and ladies, if they showed their own dogs at all, wore white gloves to do so. She was Delilah Cooper-Smith then, Delilah Waring now. Sara's father was the first husband."

"Divorced?"

"Deceased." Bertie smiled, then added mysteriously. "Some say Delilah was to blame."

"Don't tell me he was murdered."

"No." Bertie's green eyes sparkled with "gotcha!" glee. "Heart attack. But Delilah isn't the easiest woman to live with."

I grinned along with her. If your hobby is solving murders, I've found it helps to have a sense of humor.

"So after all these other occupations, Sara became a wedding planner exactly when?"

"Um . . ." Bertie's gaze shifted from mine. "Yesterday."

"Good golly, Miss Molly."

Since Davey got old enough to mimic everything I say,

I've tried hard to give up swearing. Some days that vow is harder to keep than others.

"But she'll do a good job, I'm sure of it. Sara needs the business, and if her friends don't support her, who will? Besides, how many established wedding planners do you think I could find to take me on with six weeks' notice?"

There was that.

"Okay," I said. "But why did you bring her here? What do *I* have to do with any of this?"

Bertie pushed back her chair and rose. "I thought you'd have figured that out by now."

She walked out of the kitchen, heading for the front door. Unfortunately, I hadn't figured anything out. I jumped up and followed.

"What?"

"I need your help."

"With Sara?"

"No, not with Sara. She's all set. That's what I wanted you to see. It's your Aunt Peg I'm worried about. You know how she tends to . . ."

"Meddle?" I supplied. "Interfere? Try to run peoples' lives?"

"Precisely. I want you to get her to let me do this my way."

Fat chance.

"I want you to keep her under control."

No chance.

Believe me, I've tried.

But hey, I thought, welcome to the family.

2

That weekend, I had Faith entered in back-to-back dog shows in Hartford. Having lost a large section of neck hair in the spring, the Poodle had been out of the show ring for most of the year. By October, however, her mane had finally recovered enough to suit Aunt Peg's exacting standards.

I'd started entering her in the shows again, and Faith had quickly picked up the remaining single point she needed. At the moment, she was in the thoroughly unenviable position known as "stuck for a major."

In order to complete its championship, a dog must accumulate fifteen points in competition within its own breed and sex. Unfinished dogs do not have to compete against already finished champions (as they do in England), and the number of points awarded is based on the number of dogs or bitches beaten. The most a dog can win on a single day is five; the fewest, with competition, one. Included in that fifteen must be two "major" wins—shows where the dog has won at least three points, meaning that he has beaten a considerable amount of competition.

The theory behind the rule is sound. It prevents a so-so dog from gaining its championship by piling up singles by winning over sparse or inferior competitors. In practice, however, it often leads to a situation where a good dog, through no fault of its own, spends weeks or even months trying to secure that last, coveted, major win.

Exacerbating the problem is the fact that points are based not on the size of the pre-entry, but on the number of dogs or bitches that actually show up to be judged. It is very possible to get back a judging schedule that lists a major entry, only to arrive on the day and find that half the competition has stayed home. Other factors, including time of year, availability of good judges, and whether or not area breeders have puppies that need to gain experience in the ring, also combine to play a role.

Faith had accumulated eleven points, including one major, before she lost her coat in the spring. Her first weekend back, she'd won another single. But though I'd entered her every weekend since, the shows had only drawn enough Standard Poodles for one or two point competition. This was the first time the possibility of a major had been offered.

I was tired of waiting, and I was tired of throwing away money on useless entry fees. I planned to go to both shows, and I was hoping like mad to win.

Aunt Peg, however, had had major reservations.

"Derek Hunnicutt?" she'd said in dismay when she heard that I'd sent in entries. "You entered that bitch under Derek Hunnicutt? Whatever for?"

"Because I think he'll draw a major."

"Of course he will. He'll draw every professional Poodle handler in the Northeast. They all love him, and with good reason. They're the only ones he ever puts up."

"At least I'll have a shot. It's better than sitting home because there's no major to even try for."

"That's what you think now. If you think waiting for the right judge and the right major is frustrating, just see how you feel after having done all the work of getting her ready and taking her in the ring and then watching it come to nothing."

"But Faith's a very pretty bitch—"

"And you think Derek will notice? He'll be much too busy looking for recognizable faces at the other end of the lead to worry about a little thing like that."

Politics. As is true in so many facets of life, the dog show world is rife with them. Some judges really want to judge dogs, and they're good at it. Some would like to do a good job, but they've applied for and been approved to judge more breeds than they are actually familiar with. And then there are those who seem to care only about keeping the all-important handlers with their big strings of dogs happy.

Because Aunt Peg had overseen Faith's career up until that point, she had been entered only under Poodle specialists or other judges who had a real affinity for the breed. So though I'd heard plenty of horror stories about careless or incompetent judging, I had yet to experience it for myself.

Aunt Peg had sighed. "Who's doing Sunday?" she asked in a disgruntled tone.

"Sondra Fleischman."

"Well, at least that's something."

"You approve?"

"Clearly it's not up to me to approve or disapprove."

Now, it seemed, was the point where I was meant to apologize. I didn't, which meant that the silence lingered.

"I'll see you there?" I said.

"Of course you'll see me there! Who else is going to hold your hand when Derek ignores you entirely?"

Good old Aunt Peg. She never disappoints.

* * *

Saturday dawned clear and cold. And I mean dawned. With a late morning judging time and more than an hour's drive to the show site, Davey and I were up before daybreak. My son loves this sort of adventure. Me, I'd rather stay in bed. But the thought of a possible major lured me like a siren's call.

By November dog shows in the Northeast have moved indoors for the winter. The good thing about that—especially in a breed that depends as heavily on coat and presentation as Poodles do—is that you don't have to worry about the weather. The bad thing is that indoor venues are often smaller than optimal, with cramped rings and grooming areas that quickly become crowded to capacity.

Though we left home at an early hour, I knew we'd be far from the first to arrive at the arena where the show was being held. As I entered the building holding Davey's hand and dragging crate, grooming table, and tack box on a dolly behind me, the room was already mostly full. I scanned the side that had been set aside for grooming. Empty space or a familiar face, I'd have taken either one.

"Over here!" cried Aunt Peg, waving her hand over her head and drawing the attention of everyone in the vicinity. "We've saved you some room."

Davey's fingers slipped through mine as he ran on ahead. His aunt leaned down and scooped him up into her arms.

Even without the theatrics, I'd have had an easy time picking Aunt Peg out. At six feet tall, she has always stood a full head above most women of her generation. She turned sixty-one on her last birthday, but no one who knows her would dare to think that something as mundane as chronological age might ever slow Peg down.

She was Faith's breeder and had kept a puppy from the

same litter herself. Hope, Faith's sister, had finished her championship in the spring and was now "cut down" and enjoying her retirement from the show ring. That it was taking me a good deal longer to accomplish the same feat with Faith had escaped neither of us.

"Whose setup is this?" I asked, pulling the dolly up the narrow aisle. Aunt Peg was busy rearranging the equipment: stacking crates, pushing tables together, and rolling a hair dryer out of the way to free up some space. "Are you sure there's enough room?"

"It's Bertie's stuff. She won't mind a bit," Peg told me, a general well in command of her troops. "She's off showing a Yorkie, but as soon as she saw me come in earlier, she told me she'd save you a spot."

I'd just bet she had. Obviously Bertie was hoping I'd keep Aunt Peg off her back. The question was, what made Bertie think I wanted her on mine?

"This will suit perfectly," said Peg. "I can help you get Faith ready for the ring and tell Bertie about some thoughts I've had all at the same time."

As I kicked out the legs on my grooming table and hauled it up into position, I wondered whether Bertie was actually busy in a ring somewhere, or if she'd simply tucked the hapless Yorkie under her arm and run for the exit. The answer to that question probably depended on how long Aunt Peg had been there before my arrival.

"Here comes Bertie now," Peg said, beaming as the slender redhead hurried toward us up the aisle. "Did you win, dear?"

A strangled sound came from deep within my throat. Faith, who'd just been hopped up onto the tabletop, cocked her head in my direction. The Poodle is very adept at picking up my moods, and I knew she sensed my astonishment.

Dear? Aunt Peg was calling Bertie dear? That couldn't be a good sign.

"Third in a class of three," Bertie grumbled.

"Too bad. You'll do better next time."

Sheesh, I thought. When I lost, Aunt Peg enjoyed listing everything I'd done wrong in graphic detail. When had she turned into such a Pollyanna?

"Melanie?" Directed at me, Aunt Peg's tone sharpened. "Don't you think now might be a good time to start brushing that bitch? I can see you've let her trim go. I'm going to have some serious scissoring to do."

I opened my tack box and got out slicker, pin brush, and wide-toothed comb. Next I hung a spray bottle of water from the tabletop, for misting Faith's coat to tame static. Ready to go to work, I laid the Poodle flat on the table, left side down. The left side is the show side, that is, the side that faces the judge in the ring. For that reason it's always worked on last, to make sure that the finish is fresh.

Aunt Peg considered my efforts with a critical eye as I started line brushing Faith's mane coat. Davey had climbed inside Faith's crate and was amusing himself by barking at passing dogs, none of whom seemed overly impressed by his performance. Bertie slipped the leash off the Yorkie, did a quick wrap job on its hair, and put the dog back in its crate. Judging by the expression on her face, she was just biding time, waiting for the boom to fall.

It didn't take long.

"Poinsettias," said Aunt Peg. "I think they're very pretty, don't you? Especially around Christmas time."

"Beautiful," I agreed. "Vibrant. *Red.*"

Aunt Peg speared me with a suspicious gaze. "What's wrong with red?"

"Nothing. It's just that I believe I heard Bertie mention that she wanted the flowers at her wedding to be yellow."

"Wedding?" Peg said innocently. "Did I say anything about a wedding?"

"Not yet . . ." I muttered.

"I'm bored," Davey stood up and announced.

Usually I greet that pronouncement with a sigh. Today it sounded like music from heaven. Maybe Aunt Peg could be convinced to step in and provide my son with some entertainment. The two of them often enjoyed browsing around the shows together and scoping out the best concession stands.

Just as I'd hoped, Peg heard her cue and held out her hand. "Come with me, young man. Let's go have an adventure, shall we?"

"What did I tell you?" Bertie said as soon as they walked away. Bertie is one of the most competent people I know. The fact that Peg could reduce her to desperation was actually pretty interesting. "You can see why I need your help. Frank and I just got engaged and your aunt's already called me half a dozen times. You just heard for yourself what she's like. I'm not sure how much of this I can take."

"So she likes poinsettias," I said, shrugging. "She'll get over it."

"Not that! Who cares about the stupid flowers? The other thing. She called me dear!"

Aha. Light dawned. I began to grin. "So she did. She never calls me dear. Maybe she likes you better."

"Don't mess with me, Melanie. This is serious. That woman is formidable enough when she's acting like a dragon. You know, normal. That's okay, tough I can deal with. It's all this unexpected niceness that's killing me. What am I supposed to do about that?"

"Enjoy it while it lasts?" I suggested. "Trust me. I know Aunt Peg better than you do. She won't be able to keep it up for long."

By the time Aunt Peg and Davey returned, Davey's arms were filled with new toys for Eve, and I'd already finished brushing Faith and put in her topknot.

Faith wears the continental trim, which is one of two approved show cuts for adult Standard Poodles. She has a mane coat of long, thick hair on the front half of her body, puffs of hair known as bracelets around each of her ankles, rosettes on her hips (more rounded puffs of hair), and a pompom at the end of her tail. All of this hair must be studiously shaped before she goes in the ring.

I'm getting pretty good at the job, but Aunt Peg is a master. While she and Davey were gone, I'd started scissoring Faith's bracelets. Peg didn't comment but she did take the scissors out of my hands, lift the hair with a comb, and deftly smooth out a straight edge I'd left.

"Hold her nose," she instructed, referring to Faith.

In order to get the lines right, the Poodle must be posed for grooming exactly as it will be seen in the ring. That means that the dog's head must be high in the air. Even well trained dogs, which Faith was, have a hard time holding that pose for long periods of time. My function, therefore, was to hold it for her, easing the strain on her head and neck at the expense of my own arm and shoulder.

"Bertie's hired a wedding planner," I mentioned. Having little else to do besides stand there with my hand in the air, I blithely ignored Bertie's sudden look of dismay and frantically shaking head. "Did she tell you?"

"No, I don't believe she's had a chance to mention that yet." Peg's gaze swung from me to Bertie, who smiled weakly. "Who did you get?"

"Sara Bentley. She's going to do the whole thing."

The scissors flew up and over Faith's mane coat, opening and closing like the wings of a hummingbird as Aunt Peg considered the news. "Sara Bentley. That name sounds familiar, but I can't quite place it."

"She used to show dogs," I said. Aunt Peg's knowledge of the dog show world and the people who inhabit it could fill an encyclopedia.

"Of course. Shelties. Delilah Waring's daughter. Little Sara. Used to show in Junior Showmanship. Delilah would dress her up for the ring like she was a porcelain doll. Little Chanel suits, can you imagine? She must have had them made."

"She's not little Sara anymore."

"Certainly not. That was years ago. Before . . ."

Peg's lips pursed, but that wasn't what tipped me off that she was thinking about something important. Her hand stilled; the scissors stopped moving. This had to be serious.

"Before what?" I asked.

Even Bertie was paying attention now.

"Before Sara got herself in a load of trouble by poisoning a competitor's dog."

3

One thing you have to say for my aunt, she sure knows how to liven up a conversation.

"She what?" Bertie gasped.

I just stood and stared.

Aunt Peg considered our stunned expressions for a moment, enjoying our undivided attention. Casually, she resumed her scissoring. "It's really a very old story. It goes back to Sara's junior days. I imagine she's put it all behind her now."

"Just my luck," Bertie muttered. She opened one of her stacked crates and took out a MinPin. "I've hired a murderer to plan my wedding." Her glance slid my way. "I'm not sure how, but this is probably your fault."

"My fault? I never even met the woman until a couple of days ago, and you were the one who introduced us. She's *your* old friend."

"Now, now," Peg broke in. "In the first place, Sara was quite young when this took place. I'm sure she's changed since then. And in the second, who said anything about murder?"

"You did," I said, and Bertie nodded her head in agreement. "You said she poisoned someone's dog."

"As I recall, the dog didn't actually die. I hate to admit it, but I'm somewhat sketchy on the details. Of course in deference to Delilah's feelings, none of us talked about it much."

"At least not when she was within earshot," I said, well acquainted with the ways of dog show gossip. "But I'll bet you all had a field day with it when she wasn't around."

"Some of us," Aunt Peg sniffed, "are above such things."

"While others of us get a real kick out of them," said Bertie.

What a great addition to the family she was going to be, I thought. If nothing else, she'd give Aunt Peg another direction to sling her barbs. Once Peg got over this whole unexpected niceness thing.

"There must be more to the story," I said. "If Sara was known to have poisoned someone's dog, how did she ever manage to become a professional handler?"

"That must have come later," said Bertie. "Sara's here at the show today. If you want, you can ask her."

Sure, I thought, make me look like the one who's rude and nosy.

"What's she doing here?" asked Aunt Peg.

"She has Titus entered in obedience. I believe she said he needs one more leg for his CDX."

Many, if not most, dog clubs run obedience trials concurrently with their dog shows. Unlike their conformation counterparts, obedience dogs are required to perform a series of precise exercises that demonstrate their ability to learn and obey. Also unlike breed competition, they do not have to beat everyone in their class in order to do well.

Instead, each of the exercises is assigned a numerical value, with all of them together equaling a perfect score of two hundred. If a dog accumulates at least 170 points and does not flunk any one of the exercises outright, he is awarded a green qualifying ribbon. Three qualifying scores, under three different judges, earns a degree.

CDX, short for Companion Dog Excellent, is the second title a dog would compete for after earning its CD. In order to gain a green ribbon, Titus would be required to do such things as heel off-leash, retrieve a dumbbell, navigate a high jump and broad jump, and remain in the position he'd been left (either sitting or lying down) for up to five minutes with his handler out of sight.

Known for their high degree of intelligence and willingness to work, Shelties make excellent obedience dogs. Poodles do, too, for that matter. Now that Faith had nearly finished her championship, I harbored the secret ambition of taking her to a few obedience classes and seeing how we both liked it. As soon as I found some spare time, that is.

"Down," Aunt Peg said firmly.

Obediently I dropped my arm.

"Not you, Faith." Brushing my hand out of the way, Peg gently tugged the Poodle's front legs forward. Familiar with the cue, Faith lay down on her haunches. "Melanie, are you paying any attention at all? If we don't get this bitch sprayed up soon, you're going to miss your class."

"Gotta run," said Bertie. "Good luck to you two." With a scant five minutes of preparation, the low-maintenance MinPin was ready to go. She tucked the little dog under her arm and strode away toward the rings.

I checked my watch. We were running a little late. "While you spray, I'll check the ring and get my number."

Applying hair spray to a Poodle's coat is, like scissoring, an art. Illegal under A.K.C. rules, which prohibit showing a dog with any foreign substance in its coat, the rule is flouted with impunity by competitors. The problem is that hair— even dense, correctly textured Poodle hair—does not stand straight up by itself. It's simply impossible to achieve the dramatic outline that Poodles flaunt in the show ring without the copious use of hair spray.

This practice is abetted by those who judge the breed, most of whom enjoy a flashy presentation and reward for it accordingly. In deference to the A.K.C. dictates, Poodle exhibitors have learned how to apply the majority of the forbidden substance to the base of the hair, achieving stiffness and height without telltale stickiness.

Since I was still working on perfecting my technique, I figured this made a pretty good division of labor, and Aunt Peg agreed. I fished Davey out of Faith's crate and tucked his hand in mine. Together we headed off in search of ring eight.

Our judge, Derek Hunnicutt, turned out to be a florid man with thinning hair and a squinty gaze that peered out at the dogs in his ring from behind a pair of thick glasses. His hands, like the rest of him, were large. As he stepped over the table to examine a Maltese, I saw the toy dog flinch at his touch.

Like all the other bits and pieces of information about judges that came my way, I filed that one away for the future. *Don't bring the man a puppy.* No matter how good a job a judge does in other areas, if he doesn't have a kind hand on a dog, certain precautions must be taken. Seasoned campaigners can handle a heavy touch; sensitive puppies who are learning what the show ring is all about must be treated with more care.

Davey and I walked over to the gate and waited our turn to talk to the steward. In the ring, Hunnicutt was judging Best of Breed. He took the entry shown by well-known professional handler Crawford Langley and placed it at the head of the line.

Mindful of what Aunt Peg had said, I wondered if the win

was deserved. Unfortunately I didn't know enough about the Maltese breed to have a useful opinion on the subject.

Standard Poodles were next to be judged and most were already gathering at ringside. By the time I'd gotten my armband, the Open Dogs class was being judged. Watching as I waited, my first impression was that Hunnicutt was fast, and perhaps not as thorough as I'd have liked, in evaluating the dogs before him.

Some judges think that rolling along at a speedy clip shows decisiveness and command of the entry. Some exhibitors wonder if what it actually shows is a need to move judging mistakes out of the ring quickly.

"There's Aunt Peg," said Davey as I rolled my armband over my sweater and secured it with a pair of rubber bands. "She brought Faith to us."

Good thing, too, because by that time the puppy bitches were in the ring. Peg waved us over, quickly tucking a long comb into one of my pockets, then patting the other to make sure that it already contained a handful of dried liver and a squeaky toy.

"Sorry." I took Faith's leash from her, balling most of it up in my hand. "I didn't realize he'd go so fast."

"He always does. About the best thing you'll be able to say for today's judging is that it was mercifully brief."

As usual, when she was standing ringside, Aunt Peg kept her voice low. Especially now that she had applied for her own judge's license and had received provisional approval, Peg had no intention of stating such rude, if truthful, opinions for an audience.

Her first judging assignment was scheduled to take place in two weeks. I knew Aunt Peg was well aware that there would be critics standing ringside as she performed her duties, too.

Before I could reply, the steward called the Open Bitches into the ring. With a major entry, the class was large. Ten Standard Poodle bitches—seven black, two white, and one apricot—formed a line that filled two sides of the matted arena.

Hunnicutt had requested "catalogue order," which eliminated the need to jockey for the prime position at the head of the line. Instead, the handlers found their places according to the numbers on their armbands. Faith and I were right in the middle.

The judge began his examination of the class by standing in the center of the ring and letting his gaze slide down the line, pausing briefly on each dog in turn. Having stacked Faith with her front legs square underneath her and her hind legs slightly extended, I used one hand to support her chin and the other to hold up her tail.

Surreptitiously I glanced up and down the line as well, checking out the competition. To my admittedly biased eye, Faith was the best bitch there. Not only that, but she'd already beaten most of the other entrants at earlier shows. I felt my stomach drop, however, as my casual assessment revealed something else.

I was the only owner-handler in the ring.

That didn't bode well.

Though Poodles are predominantly a professionally handled breed, there does exist a small core of talented amateurs who compete regularly against the pros and win. The fact that none of them had chosen to show under Derek Hunnicutt indicated that Peg was probably right: I didn't stand a chance.

Hunnicutt lifted his hands and sent the line once around. Keeping Faith positioned squarely on the mats meant that I ran beside her on the more slippery floor. Not only was the footing bad, but the ring was too small to hold ten trotting Standard

Poodles. We started, clumped, bumped, stopped, then started again before finally completing a listless circuit of the ring. I was beginning to feel annoyed that I was even there.

"Psst!"

Aunt Peg was leaning over the thigh-high barrier, gesturing in my direction. "What's the matter with you?" she demanded in a stern undertone as I approached. "Quit moping around in there or you're going to defeat yourself."

"It doesn't look as though I have much of a chance anyway."

"You're here, aren't you? And thanks to me, you're holding the prettiest bitch in the ring. Of course you're not going to win—I already told you that, didn't I? But the least you can do is put some effort into it and make me proud."

A pep talk, Aunt Peg style. But it had the desired effect. Maybe we were going down, I decided, but it wouldn't hurt to do so in style.

Like most Poodles, Faith is a natural clown. She loves performing for an audience. Some dogs grudgingly allow themselves to be shown; Faith adores it.

Which was a good thing because, by the time the class was over, about the only thing we had to show for our efforts was the fact that Faith had enjoyed herself enormously. Ribbonless, she trotted out of the ring just as happy as she'd gone in. It was her owner who was looking distinctly grumpy about the whole experience.

"If you say I told you so, I'm not going to be happy," I grumbled as we headed back to the setup.

"I wouldn't dream of it. Now that you've got that out of the way, you can look forward to tomorrow's show. And since Faith is already bathed, clipped, and scissored, it'll be a breeze."

First she was calling Bertie "dear." Now she was ignoring the fact that I hadn't even placed in my class and telling me to look on the bright side. Briefly I wondered if aliens had stolen my aunt and replaced her with a cheery six-foot impostor.

"What's up with you?" I asked as I hopped Faith back onto her table and began gently to pull apart her topknot.

"Up?" Peg said innocently. "I don't know what you mean."

Davey giggled. "You know what up means, Aunt Peg. It's the opposite of down."

"Down?" She pulled her nephew into her arms and pretended to consider. "Isn't that the fluffy stuff they take off geese and put inside pillows and comforters? How can that be the opposite of up?"

Davey howled with laughter. He's reached an age where puns and word-play are among his favorite things. "There's a girl in my class whose name is Fluffy. Do you think she's made of down?"

"It's entirely possible," Peg agreed. Releasing her nephew, she pointed him toward Bertie who was working at the other end of the aisle. "Go see if Bertie has time to join us for lunch, okay?"

"Okay!" Davey skipped off.

"I'll tell you what's up," I told Aunt Peg. "You're entirely too cheerful. You're beginning to get on my nerves."

"And you're entirely too morose. So Sam left. Guess what? Bad things happen. It's about time you got over it and moved on. Get a life."

"I have a life."

"Not one that's good enough, apparently. For God's sake, Melanie, it's been nearly four months and you're still wandering around like a lost lamb. Sam will come back when he's ready. In the meantime, I'd like to think that my niece has something better to do than put her whole life on hold and wait for his return."

That stung, as it was obviously meant to. Even worse, there might have been the tiniest bit of truth to her words.

"I haven't been that bad, have I?"

"You've been worse," Peg informed me. "I'm trying to soften the blow."

Not very hard, apparently.

"I have to admit, I've been worried about you. And so has Frank."

"Frank?" My carefree younger brother had never worried about anyone but himself in his whole life.

"He even asked Bertie to keep an eye on you, maybe get you involved in the plans for their wedding."

Wasn't that just like a man? I thought. Somehow it hadn't occurred to my brother that the best cure for being dumped by my own fiancé might not be helping out with someone else's wedding.

"Wait a minute." My eyes narrowed. "That's not what Bertie told me. She told me I was supposed to baby-sit you."

Aunt Peg spun around. "Baby-sit me? I'll have you know I'm entirely capable of taking care of myself."

And any other hapless individuals who happened to wander into her sphere of influence.

"Baby-sit me?" Peg repeated. "We'll just see about that!"

Drat, I thought. I knew I shouldn't have spoken so fast. Double drat.

If things kept up like this, I was going to have to cultivate a whole new crop of swear words.

4

"Lunch?" Bertie said, coming back down the aisle with Davey. "You must be kidding. I have thirteen dogs to show, and at least two are going on to the groups. The only food I'll get today is going to be on the fly."

"Why didn't you say so?" I asked. "Faith's all done and she doesn't mind hanging out in her crate for a while. Aunt Peg and Davey can go get something to eat and you can put me to work."

"You don't have to do that, Melanie."

Despite her words, I could tell Bertie was considering the offer. Fiercely independent, she had built her business over the years through sheer talent and determination. During most of that time, she'd had nobody but herself to depend on.

Being a professional handler isn't an easy job for anyone, much less a young woman alone. The days start and finish in the dark, and the work is often arduous. Week-ends demand constant travel, driving to out-of-the-way places, often in less-than-ideal weather. And even on a handler's day off, the dogs must still be cared for.

Not only that, but the pressure to win, to produce results for your clients, is constant. I knew the sacrifices that Bertie had made, and I knew how much of her life she'd dedicated to succeeding in the sport of dogs. But until she'd mentioned it just now, I hadn't realized that her string had grown so large. Bertie must have been running from the moment she arrived at the show hours earlier.

"Come on," I said. "Give me a dog to do. It will be good for me to learn something besides how to brush a Poodle."

"Well . . . I've got two Shar Peis, a class dog and bitch, going in about fifteen minutes. I've been wondering how I was going to juggle that."

"Extra hands." I held mine up and wiggled my fingers. "At your service."

"We'll bring you back something," Peg promised as she and Davey left. Actually, considering the caliber of most dog show food, missing lunch wasn't a hardship.

"I had no idea you had so many dogs now," I said, leaning back against the edge of a grooming table as Bertie sorted through her tack box, looking for the Shar Peis' leashes. "You ought to think about hiring an assistant."

"I've considered it. And of course, Kate worked out great for a while."

Kate Russo was one of my former students at Howard Academy. The teenager's love for dogs and her boundless energy had combined to make her seem like the perfect helper. I'd introduced her to Bertie a year earlier, and Bertie had taken Kate on as an unpaid apprentice.

"How come she's not still working for you? Did she quit?"

Bertie nodded. "This fall when she started high school. Her mother really wanted her to concentrate on her studies and I could understand that. Besides, Kate wanted to sign up for the debating team and try out for JV basketball, so her time was really limited.

"Having her around was great while it lasted. This many dogs *is* a lot for one person to handle, but you know how these things go. I'm half afraid that as soon as I hire someone, all my clients will disappear and I'll be overextended financially. Working around the clock isn't my idea of fun, but it seems like less of a gamble."

Bertie handed me a show leash and pointed to two medium-sized wooden crates, each at the bottom of a stack. Chinese Shar Peis, the breed famous for their loose, wrinkled skin, are not terribly tall, but they're heavy for their size. Bending down, I braced myself as I opened the crate and the Shar Pei came bounding out into the aisle.

"You've got the bitch," said Bertie. "Her name is Ping. Mine's the litter brother."

"Don't tell me. Pong?"

"How'd you guess?" She smiled. "They're both in Open. Pong's the only male, so with any luck I can pick up two points by beating the bitch for Best of Winners. Ping's going to have a harder time of it, but if she does win, I'll need you to show her for me in the breed."

Things went pretty much just as Bertie had predicted. Though Ping had to settle for Reserve Winners Bitch, Pong did indeed get two points. Not only was he Best of Winners, but he also won the red-and-white ribbon for Best of Opposite Sex.

Making the win even more gratifying, the litter mates' breeder-owner was standing ringside to watch her Shar Peis compete. Judging by the woman's jubilant expression, this was one client Bertie wouldn't be losing any time soon.

On our way back to the setup, Bertie suggested that we detour past the obedience rings. "I looked at the schedule," she said. "Open A was supposed to start at noon, so I'm pretty sure that Sara and Titus will be hanging out. With so little time before the wedding, I just want to make sure she's on top of everything."

"It's only been three days since we got together at my house," I pointed out.

"And I've only got six weeks to pull this whole thing together. Let's hope Sara's been busy."

Like the rest of the show, the obedience area was crowded. Inevitably, casual spectators are drawn to these arenas. It takes years of study and a skilled eye to sort out the difference between the winners and the losers in breed competition; obedience is much more straight-forward. Even a novice can usually tell whether a dog has followed his owner's command or not. Plus, the exercises are fun to watch.

Each obedience class requires different obstacles to be set up for the competition. For Open, it was a high jump built of solid planks and a broad jump placed on one side of the matted floor. It only took a moment to locate our ring, which was at the far end, currently occupied by an exuberant Border Collie.

As we headed that way, I gazed around the area, looking for a sable Sheltie. Yes, I know, most people would have looked for Sara. But I'm a dog person; we tend to do things differently.

"There she is." Abruptly, Bertie stopped walking.

I managed not to crash into her, but Ping, following closely behind her brother, wasn't so lucky. She and Pong went down in a heap, then apparently decided that was a great opportunity to engage in a wrestling match. Almost immediately, they had their leashes tangled, in part because Bertie wasn't paying any attention to their antics.

"Uh oh," Bertie said under her breath.

"What?" I looked up, leaving the playful dogs to their own devices. At least they didn't have any hair to muss.

Sara was standing somewhat away from ringside beside a wire mesh crate that held Titus, sleeping, inside. She wasn't alone; an older man was standing next to her. From where we stood, it looked as though they were arguing.

"Who's that with Sara?" I asked. Ping, pushed by her brother, rolled into my legs and nearly knocked me over.

"Grant Waring. Her stepfather."

"They don't look too happy."

"Unfortunately, that's not unusual. Sara doesn't come from a close family. Hell, they're not even a normal family. I guess Delilah must be showing something in Shelties. Grant hates dog shows. He never comes unless Delilah drags him along."

Bertie was too distracted to notice, but people were beginning to stare at us. In a setting where everyone took enormous pride in their dogs' training and deportment, our tussling Shar Peis stuck out like a pair of circus clowns at the opera.

"Let's give her a minute," she said. "I don't want to intrude."

"Good idea," I agreed. "Besides . . ."

I lifted my hand, intending to gesture toward the problem at our feet. Unfortunately, Ping chose that moment to lunge once more at her brother. With a snap, the end of the short show lead flipped out of my fingers and ricocheted down to slap the Shar Pei on the flank.

Ping's first reaction was surprise. Delight quickly followed as she realized she was free. Before I could grab her, she'd taken off.

"Oh, criminy!"

I jumped over Pong's prostrate body and ran after her, zigzagging between spectators toward the ring. Luckily the class was now between competitors and the stewards were adjusting the jumps. Otherwise, I'd have committed the cardinal sin of allowing my dog to disrupt another's performance. As it was, Ping and I were merely providing something akin to halftime entertainment.

Grant Waring was a fit, good looking man in his fifties, sporting a full head of steel gray hair and a tan that had to have been acquired somewhere other than Connecticut in November. His blue jeans were snug; his loafers, polished. A bulky fisherman-knit sweater hinted at an admirable physique beneath.

"That is not an option," I heard him say as I scrambled toward him, trying to grab Ping's leash.

"It is if I say so," Sara snapped. "It's my decision, and you can just—"

Grant stumbled forward as the galloping Shar Pei barreled into him from behind. With considerably more grace than I'd have shown under the circumstances, he recovered quickly, reaching down to snag Ping's leash and pull the dog to a halt.

"Well," he said, "what have we here?"

"Sorry. She got away from me." I took the lead from his hand and hauled Ping back.

The Shar Pei was now jumping up and trying to wrap herself around Grant's leg. To his credit, he didn't look too perturbed about the situation.

"Don't worry about it," he said. "Happens at my house all the time."

"Hi, Sara, Grant." Bertie materialized behind me, leading the other half of our dynamic duo. For safekeeping, she took Ping's leash from me and added it to the other she held in her hand.

Grant's brow furrowed as he studied Bertie with a slight frown. Bertie is one of the few women I know who are truly gorgeous. She has thick auburn hair, a wonderful complexion, and the kind of tall, athletic build that looks good in anything she chooses to wear.

Most men don't frown when they look at her. In fact, they usually fawn all over her. It's a good thing my brother isn't the jealous type, or he'd have to buy himself a shotgun.

After a second, Grant's expression cleared. "Bertie, right? I'm afraid it's been a while."

"Too long," Bertie agreed easily. "Sara and I have been out of touch, but she's recently agreed to work on a project for me."

"Really?" Grant glanced at his stepdaughter with the same sort of quizzical expression he'd just trained on Bertie. "May I ask what kind?"

"I'm getting married over Christmas. Sara's planning my wedding for me."

"Then congratulations are in order. Who's the lucky groom?"

One look at Grant Waring and I knew he was the type of man who moved in a tightly contained social circle where everyone belonged to the same clubs, sent their children to the same private schools, and wintered at the same Florida coastal town. Good manners required him to ask after Bertie's betrothed, though there wasn't a hope in hell that the two of them had ever crossed paths.

"His name is Frank Travis. He owns a small business in Stamford. In fact," Bertie added, suddenly remembering my presence and performing an introduction, "he's Melanie's brother."

"Please pass along my best wishes," Grant said smoothly, taking my hand in his. His eyes were a warm shade of brown. For the moment that they focused on me it was as though nothing else in the world was more important to him.

"I'll do that."

"Sara." He turned back to his stepdaughter. "I'm sure you and your friends have a lot to talk about. I *will* see you at home later."

"Yes." Sara didn't look happy about it.

"Everything okay?" Bertie asked as Grant strode off.

"Sure, fine." Sara glanced at me. "Don't mind Grant. He's always like that."

"I thought he was charming."

"He can be. That's one of his better qualities. Don't get me started on his bad ones." Sara looked back at Bertie. "Were you looking for me, or is this just a coincidence?"

"Looking," said Bertie, glancing at her watch. "Though now I'm running out of time again. I just wanted to find out if you were making any headway with the plans."

"Of course. I've made tons of calls. What do you think of leasing one of the dining rooms at the Greenwich Country Club? Imagine the terrace that overlooks the golf course, trimmed with fairy lights and filled with flowers."

"It sounds wonderful. There's only one problem. I'm not a member of the Greenwich Country Club."

"I am and I've already spoken to them about it. If it meets your approval, I'll go ahead with the arrangements. See?" Sara patted Bertie's arm reassuringly. "Headway. There's more, too, but you probably don't have to discuss it all now. You were right—I *am* good at this. In fact, I think I'm really going to enjoy it."

"Phooey," I said as Bertie and I walked the Shar Peis back to the setup. "We forgot to ask her about that story Aunt Peg told us."

"That's all right. With Grant around hassling her, this probably wasn't the best time. Don't worry, I'm sure I'll be seeing plenty of Sara over the next few weeks. I'll find out the scoop if you want."

Aunt Peg and Davey were back at the crates, waiting for

us when we returned. The hamburgers they'd brought for us were flat and cold in their soggy, grease soaked buns. Fortunately, the half-dozen brownies Peg had also piled into the cardboard carry box had survived the wait better.

Munching, Bertie, Peg, and I readied Bertie's last three class entries: a Keeshond and two Chinese Cresteds. Then, satisfied that she had everything under control, I got Faith out of her crate and began to pack up. The Poodle's long black topknot, done up now in wraps and bands to keep it out of her way, flipped and bobbed as she danced on the tabletop.

Damn, I wished she had finished today. I was really looking forward to the day when I could cut off her hair and let her live like a normal dog, one who knew what it felt like to have her owner scratch the top of her head, or to run full tilt through the woods.

"It's getting to be about time," I whispered to Faith.

Pressing my nose against hers, I cupped my palms under the sides of her jaw and rubbed back and forth over her lips and teeth with my thumbs as I stroked her cheeks with my fingers. Faith leaned forward into me, wiggling her body with delight and enjoying her favorite non-hair-invasive caress.

"Tomorrow," Aunt Peg said firmly. She'd been eavesdropping on our private conversation.

"What about tomorrow?"

"Get up, get in the car, come back here, and do it all over again."

Showing dogs, in a nutshell.

Some days it was just like having a job.

5

There are times when it seems like nothing goes the way you planned.

Late Saturday afternoon, when Davey and I got home from the dog show, there was a car parked in our driveway. A screaming red Trans Am with Texas plates. It took me a few seconds to make the connection. It took Davey even less time than that.

"Daddy!" he shrieked. I braked hastily as my son threw open his door and scrambled out. "Where did you come from?"

Good question, I thought, parking the Volvo as Bob climbed out of his car and stood in the driveway. I hate surprises; have I mentioned that? My ex-husband knows it, or he would if he ever stopped to think about such things. Unfortunately, taking my wishes into consideration has never been a strong suit of his.

Bob swooped his son up off the ground and swung him around in an exuberant circle. "I came from Texas, where do you think? I'm here to visit my two favorite people in the whole world."

Watching Davey's legs fly by above her head, Faith jumped up and tried to join in the fun. Her barking was loud enough to alert the entire neighborhood that the Travis family was home. And in case anyone missed the point, Davey's high-pitched screams of glee provided the final punctuation.

It was only a matter of time before someone called 911. Either that or a psychiatric facility.

"Let's move this sideshow indoors." I started up the steps, hoping everyone would follow.

"Good idea," Bob agreed, rallying the rest of the troops.

Though a year and a half had passed since I'd seen him last, it didn't look as though much had changed. His sandy brown hair was cut a little shorter and looked as though it might be thinning on top. The creases around his eyes had deepened, probably from squinting into the Texas sun. But he still handled himself with that appealing self-confidence and easy grace that had made my heart pound a decade earlier.

At the door, Bob stopped and carefully wiped his cowboy boots on the mat before coming inside. That was new.

"Your two favorite people?" I said as Davey and Faith ran on ahead to the kitchen.

"Sure, why not?" Bob leaned forward and brushed a kiss across my cheek.

I stepped back before he could add a hug. "What about Jennifer? Your new wife?"

The one who'd finally reached voting age in the spring, I could have added but didn't. I was taking my new, mature attitude out for a test drive.

"It didn't work out."

I peered at Bob closely, looking for signs of sadness or maybe remorse. I found neither. "How come?"

"She decided to go back to college."

So help me, I almost laughed. So much for the new maturity.

"I'm sorry," I managed to say instead.

"Don't be, I'm not. It obviously wasn't the best decision on either of our parts and we parted pretty amicably."

I pulled off my jacket and hung it on the coatrack. Making himself at home, Bob followed suit. I waited until he turned back to me, then asked bluntly, "Bob, what are you doing here?"

"What do you mean?" He seemed genuinely surprised by the question. "Frank invited me. I came for the wedding. I'm going to be an usher."

"The wedding is six weeks away."

"So I'm a little early."

As soon as Bob tilted his head to one side, adding that boyishly innocent look that I suddenly remembered from years gone by, I knew I was in trouble. He was hiding something. That, and hoping to cajole his way past my questions until he was ready to let me in on his plans.

I wondered what it was this time. Last time he visited unexpectedly, he'd been hoping to gain joint custody of his son.

"Don't you have things you need to be doing in Texas?"

"No."

"A job?"

"I've made some good investments."

This was said with becoming modesty. Eighteen months earlier, my accountant ex-husband had seen his oil well come in. Literally. I guessed things had been going pretty well for him since then.

Bob started to follow Davey toward the back of the house. I put a hand on his arm to stop him. Before we continued our conversation in front of our son, I needed a clearer picture of what was going on.

"So what are your plans?"

"Plans? Who needs plans? I thought maybe I'd just hang loose for a while."

"Hang loose?" The skeptic in me nearly added a snort.

Bob put his hand on top of mine and patted gently, like a cowboy trying to soothe a skittish filly. His fingers felt warm and solid against my own. "Don't worry, darlin'. Everything will be fine."

Not in this lifetime, I thought.

Just as Aunt Peg had forecast, the next morning I got up, got in the car, drove back to the show site, and did the whole thing all over again. With one small exception. This time I had Bob with me.

"Dog show?" he'd said the evening before, when I informed him that Davey and I had plans for the following day. "Sounds like fun."

The man was lying through his teeth.

The only time I'd ever seen him pay any attention to Faith, he'd compared her to a bear. And I knew for a fact that he thought her elaborate trim was downright silly. Add to that the fact that he wouldn't know anyone at the show or understand what was going on. But if Bob wanted to make himself accommodating, far be it from me to discourage him.

Once again, Poodles had been assigned a late morning judging time; once again, we had to leave early. The Bob I had known liked to sleep in. He must have suspected that if he wasn't ready I'd leave him behind, because he was standing by the front door, jacket on, holding two steaming cups of coffee five minutes before the appointed hour.

He'd made one for me, too. Darn it.

Then again, I thought, how hard was it to get to the door

on time when you'd only been sleeping at the top of the stairs?

Last time Bob had visited, he stayed in a motel. This time he was planning to bunk with Frank, but the drive had taken less time than he'd anticipated. My brother wasn't expecting him until after the weekend, and so he'd come to our house first.

It hardly made sense for him to leave, sleep for a few hours, then come right back, Bob had argued the night before. Why not just let him stay?

All I can say is, I must be getting soft in my old age.

Our small house only has two bedrooms, as Bob knows perfectly well since he lived here for two years of our marriage. He'd glanced in my direction hopefully. The glare I sent back could have melted sludge.

Nothing if not able to read the subtle nuances, he'd switched his attention to our son. "How about it, sport? Want to share your room with me? I'll bet you have a sleeping bag stashed somewhere. Can I borrow it and sleep on your floor?"

We ended up with Bob in the bed and Davey, to his delight, on the floor. I somehow forgot to mention ahead of time that Faith sleeps on that bed, too. As I was closing my door I heard a startled yelp—human, not canine—followed by a fit of giggles from Davey, and I figured that they'd gotten things sorted out.

"Sleep well?" Bob asked now, as we walked out into the cold November morning.

"Very." An expedient answer, if not entirely true. Not that the truth was any of his business.

I'd left the Volvo in the driveway the night before, parked behind Bob's Trans Am. Since our one-car garage was crammed with enough junk to host a rummage sale, lately I'd gotten in the habit of leaving my station wagon outside.

Most mornings recently, I'd had to allow a few extra minutes to scrape the frost off the windows.

But now, to my surprise, not only were the windows clear, but the engine was running. A steamy cloud puffed out of the exhaust pipe. The car was already warm.

"I got the keys out of your coat pocket," Bob said. He opened the back door and got Davey and Faith inside and belted up. "I hope you don't mind."

Mind? A warm car on a frigid winter morning? That was a luxury, not an imposition. Whatever was going on around here—and clearly there was much I still didn't understand—I decided I didn't hate it.

In contrast to the dog show scene of several decades ago, cluster shows—where several kennel clubs get together to hold back-to-back events at the same venue—have now become the norm. I'd left most of my equipment at the show the day before, so that morning we had nothing to unload. My things were just where I'd left them, on the edge of Bertie's setup.

She, like the other professional handlers, would have gotten to the arena at dawn to feed, water, and exercise her string of dogs before the competition began. By the time we arrived, however, breakfasts had been eaten and ex-pens had been folded away out of sight. The business of putting on a show was once more in session.

"Good morning!" Aunt Peg sang out cheerfully as we approached. "Isn't this a glorious—"

The words seemed to die in her throat. Actually, judging by the expression on her face, it looked as though a bone might have gotten stuck there. A large one. And she was staring right at Bob.

Bob and I have had a chance to talk our past problems through. He and Aunt Peg aren't so lucky. I suspect she's never forgiven him for abandoning me and Davey, leaving us young and alone, with no visible means of support, while he went off in search of a life that looked a little easier.

"Bob," she said, her voice just this side of civil. "What a surprise."

"For me, too," I said, hopping Faith up onto her table. "We got home last night and there he was. Imagine that."

"Daddy stayed all night!" Davey added helpfully. "It was lots of fun."

"Indeed."

Deliberately I turned away and reached for my tack box. I hauled it out and opened it up, getting out the brushes and combs I was going to need. Call me cruel, but Bob was on his own now.

"Nice to see you again, Peg," he said jauntily.

He leaned toward my aunt, but if he thought he'd succeed in kissing her cheek, he was sorely mistaken. At six feet, she looked him straight in the eye, guessed his intent, and evaded him nimbly. Bob should have been chastened. Instead he grinned.

Uh oh, I thought.

"Just passing through, I assume?" Peg asked.

"Actually, I thought I'd stay a while. Frank invited me to his wedding. I figured I'd come a little early and lend him some moral support."

"Because you have so much experience in being a good husband," Peg mused. "How's your new wife?"

"Gone," Bob said cheerfully. "Pffft!" He waved a hand through the air. "You know how these things—"

"Bob." My tone was pleasant; the warning was in my eyes. Goading Aunt Peg is not a game.

I could feel her mounting displeasure from across the aisle. Even Faith was getting edgy. Only Bob seemed oblivious.

"Bob and Jennifer have separated," I explained.

"Divorced," he corrected. "Mexico."

"Even better." Aunt Peg smiled. "Then you're free as a bird. You could go anywhere . . . else."

"I like it here." Bob leaned against a bank of wooden crates, signaling his intent to stay put. "With my family—"

Abruptly my ex-husband straightened. His jaw fell.

Two guesses, I thought. Either someone had run an electrical charge through those crates, or Bob had just spotted Bertie.

I turned and had a look. Right the second time.

Shar Peis must have been scheduled earlier on Sunday, because Bertie was heading back toward the setup leading Ping and Pong. According to the ribbons in her hand, she'd repeated her wins from the day before.

Bertie's face was lit by a happy smile. Her hair bounced on her shoulders as she walked. A navy silk dress, fitted through the bodice, looser below so she could run in it, swirled enticingly around her long legs.

"Hot damn!" Bob said appreciatively.

"No swearing in front of Davey."

Now my ex-husband was speechless. His eyes, however, were huge. I wondered if Bertie ever got tired of having this effect on men.

"She's headed our way," Bob managed.

"Of course. Those are her crates you're leaning against. Would you like me to introduce you to Frank's fiancée?"

"*That's* Bertie?"

His expression alone was worth a chuckle. "Didn't Frank ever describe her to you?"

"Sure. He said she looked good."

One word here. Men. You know what I'm talking about.

"Hey," said Bertie. Her gaze flickered toward Bob, then back to me. "I could have used your help again with these guys."

"It looks as though you won anyway."

"The judge liked cleavage," she confided in an undertone. "One of the few who'd notice."

"I can't imagine anyone wouldn't notice you," Bob said.

I'm sure he didn't mean to sound obnoxious. Bertie and I both grimaced anyway. I guessed she did get tired of all the attention.

"It happens." Her tone was dismissive.

"Bertie, I'd like you to meet my ex-husband, Bob."

"You're Bob?" She took a minute to have a good look at him. "I thought you might have horns."

"They're in back," said Peg. "Under the hair. Though now that I check, there seems to be less—"

"Aunt Peg!"

Bob flinched slightly. "You people are tough. What's a guy have to do to catch a break around here?"

"Maybe take Davey for a walk around the show?" I suggested.

"So you can talk about me while I'm gone?"

"Something like that." I reached out and squeezed his arm. Probably not the show of support he was hoping for, but all I was ready to offer. "Go sit ringside and let Davey explain to you how dog shows work. You'll have fun."

"Sure we will. Davey and I always have fun together. Don't we, sport?"

"Right, Daddy."

For the briefest moment, Bob leaned closer. His cheek brushed my hair; his lips hovered next to my ear. I could feel the warmth of his breath against my skin.

"We used to have fun, too, Mel," he whispered, his words meant for me alone. "Think about it."

6

"What was that all about?" Bertie asked.

Brush in hand, dog on table, I was standing perfectly still, watching Bob and Davey walk away. "I don't know."

"What did he say?"

"Nothing."

"It didn't look like nothing." Aunt Peg removed the pin brush from my hand and began to work. Bertie put both the Shar Peis in their crates. "You've gone absolutely pale."

I sucked in a deep breath and slowly let it out. "Bob reminded me that he and I used to have fun together, too. And he told me to think about that."

"That's not good." Bertie shook her head. "Not good at all."

"What do you suppose he meant by it?"

Aunt Peg and Bertie both stared at me as though I was nuts.

"I should think that's perfectly obvious," said Peg.

"He wants you back," said Bertie.

"Don't be ridiculous. Two minutes ago, he was all but drooling over you."

"That's just testosterone. A knee-jerk reaction. It doesn't mean a thing. But a man who comes all the way from Texas to see his ex-wife—"

"And his son," I interjected.

"Now *that* means something," Bertie continued as if I hadn't interrupted.

"He came for your wedding. That's what he said."

"And you believed him?"

"Well," I conceded, "he is a little early."

Aunt Peg flipped Faith over and went to work on her other side. "Six weeks early! You don't suppose we'll have to put up with him all that time?"

"He told me he was planning to stay with Frank." Since Peg was busy brushing, I got out the comb, knitting needle, and tiny colored rubber bands we'd need to put in Faith's top-knot.

Bertie looked thoughtful. "Frank hasn't mentioned anything about that to me."

"Bertie? I've got something for you, sweetheart!"

The voice, high-pitched and dulcet, belonged to Terry Denunzio, friend, gay guy, and assistant to professional handler Crawford Langley. He strutted up the aisle, a small blue envelope held aloft in his hand. Terry doesn't seem to know how to walk, but he does sashay beautifully.

"Kiss! Kiss! Kiss!" he sang, inclining his face toward each of ours in passing.

"What is it?" asked Bertie. "Someone's passing me notes now? Have we gone back to high school?"

"Maybe you have a secret admirer," I said. If the note was from Bob, I was going to kill him.

"No secret," said Terry. "It's from Sara Bentley. She was

here earlier, showing that little dust mop Tidy Bowl in obedience."

"Titus," I corrected.

People who show in breed often think obedience dogs are inferior specimens. People who show in obedience tend to look down on us. Go figure.

"What*ever*," Terry sniffed. "She had to leave, but she asked me to pass this along to you when I got a chance."

"Thanks. It's probably something about the arrangements for the wedding."

"And since I'm here anyway," Terry continued, "Crawford would like you to know that Wanda Francis is judging like a woman who wants to be first in line at the lunch buffet. Her ring is running early, and if your MinPin misses its class and breaks the major, your name will be mud."

"Yikes!" Bertie grabbed the envelope and stuffed it into her tack box, then flicked open a crate door and beckoned out a small red dog. "I'm on my way."

"As well you should be." Terry grinned after her. There's nothing he enjoys more than shaking things up.

Reaching down, he cupped a hand under Faith's jaw. She gazed up at him adoringly. Like all the best handlers, Terry has a wonderful hand on a dog.

"Pretty girl," he crooned. "Sondra likes pretty. Today's going to be your day."

"Don't say that!" Aunt Peg wailed. Dog shows are the one thing she's superstitious about. "You'll jinx us."

"Not a chance." His gaze slid in my direction. "Besides you've been working on finishing this nice bitch for so long, even the rest of us are beginning to root for you. Ta!"

Terry sauntered off. I couldn't decide whether his parting shot had been meant as insult or encouragement, which was about par for the course where Terry was concerned.

Between us, Aunt Peg and I put up Faith's tight show ring topknot, using a knitting needle to part the long, silky hair, and fingers and comb to arrange the bubble of hair over her eyes. Then I sprayed while Aunt Peg scissored. Again. It's a never-ending process. Meanwhile, Faith had the best job. All she had to do was stand there and pose.

Finally the Poodle was ready. I stepped back and had a look. Gorgeous, I decided. My child was going to be the prettiest debutante at the ball.

With great care, Faith was lifted down from the table, allowed to shake once—lightly—then taken to ringside. The entry had grown since the day before. All the owner-handlers who'd known enough to avoid Derek Hunnicutt were now out in force.

While Aunt Peg primped and worried, defending her charge zealously against anyone who might dare to step into their space and jostle the precious hair, I went and picked up my number. Bob and Davey had found seats on the far side of the ring. Davey waved; Bob flashed me a thumbs-up followed by a self-conscious shrug. He didn't have any idea what was going on, he seemed to be saying, but whatever it was, he was behind me all the way.

My ex-husband might have been confused, but my Standard Poodle was not. She'd been in the show ring, off and on, for nearly two years now, and she knew exactly what was expected of her. Be pretty, have fun, catch the judge's eye. And hold it.

And Faith was well up to the task.

Judging dogs is a highly subjective process, and there are many reasons why a particular dog might win on a certain day. Some of them simply have to do with being in the right place at the right time. It's often hard to tell whether or not the best dog has won since nine out of ten knowledgeable ringsiders generally won't agree on which dog in the ring is the "best."

However one thing judges and exhibitors do agree on is that some dogs have a certain indefinable quality that sets them apart. A sparkle, a verve, a "joie de show ring" that makes them stand out from the others like single stars shining more brightly than the rest of the constellation.

"He was asking for it," you'll hear judges say afterward. "I couldn't deny him the win." Truly great show dogs do exactly that. They watch the judge, they play to the audience, they refuse not to be noticed.

That day, under Sondra Fleischman, it was Faith's turn. She not only asked for the win, she demanded it as her due.

From the moment we walked into the crowded ring, Faith owned that class. She knew it was hers, and it only took Mrs. Fleischman a minute or two to figure out the same thing. As for me, I wish I could take credit for the Poodle's superb performance, but I was just along for the ride.

And what a ride it was.

The first time Faith and I won a class against competition, I just about fell over. This time, I was ready to be called to the head of the long line. I accepted our blue ribbon with thanks, then hurried Faith back into position for the Winners Bitch class. This was where the points would be awarded. Until she had defeated the winners of the earlier Puppy and Bred-by-Exhibitor classes, all we'd really won was a scrap of blue ribbon.

Mrs. Fleischman gave the three of us a moment to get organized. Usually, at that point, the judge will take another good, long look. She'll move the class winners as a group, then separately. She'll consider her decision with care.

Not that day. That day the choice was so clear that the judge had already made up her mind. She simply walked to the head of the line and pointed. At Faith.

A tiny gesture worth four glorious points. And I was holding a new champion.

Elation poured through me, setting off tiny sparks of sensation that felt like a burst of adrenaline run amok. For a moment, I actually went weak in the knees.

Dimly I heard a shriek from ringside. Aunt Peg, I thought, though behavior of that sort is usually beneath her. Davey was laughing and clapping his hands. Bob fitted his fingers to his lips for a whistle that all but stopped the show in its tracks. My family was proud of us, bless their faithful, long-suffering hearts.

Then I realized that they weren't the only ones making noise. Terry was there, too, applauding happily even though I'd just beaten his boss for a major that I knew he'd miss somewhere down the line. Bertie had also managed to catch the end of the judging. I saw her slap Aunt Peg on the back. As breeder, Peg was basking in the moment, too.

Even Crawford Langley, leading his Open Bitch back into the ring to try for reserve winners, paused to stick out his hand. "Well done."

"Thanks."

I grabbed Faith and scooted over to the marker, anxious to grab my purple ribbon before the judge changed her mind. Or I woke up and realized it had all been just a dream.

"You have quite a cheering section," Mrs. Fleischman said, handing me my prize. "And a lovely, lovely bitch."

"Thank you," I stammered. "You just finished her."

"Owner handled?"

"All the way."

"Good for you. That makes it even better."

There was scarcely time to pause outside the ring before I had to go back in. Winners Dog and Winners Bitch both compete with the champions for Best of Breed (or, in the case of Poodles, Best of Variety). Crawford was back, too, of course, with a white Standard specials dog that he'd done a tremendous amount of winning with.

This time, it was my turn to stand second to him, but Faith and I didn't mind a bit. Crawford's dog was Best of Variety. Faith won Best of Winners and Best of Opposite Sex. All in all, it was a perfectly delightful way to finish her show career.

Back at the setup, Bertie gave me a big hug, slipped Faith a yummy piece of dried liver, consulted her schedule, and began grooming a Bichon. Davey and Bob swooped in, offered copious congratulations—though Bob still didn't look entirely clear on what had happened—and disappeared again.

Aunt Peg, meanwhile, was busy schmoozing with the other breeders, accepting good wishes from her peers, all of whom knew from personal experience just how hard it was sometimes to get even a good one finished.

As for me, I had Faith up on the table. My face was buried in her coat, her nose was nuzzling my ear. I felt her solid body beneath the silly hairdo and smelled her wonderful clean dog smell and told her, over and over, what a good and patient Poodle she'd been.

"Champion Cedar Crest Leap of Faith," I said, rolling the title off my tongue. The words had a magical sound. Champion Faith. My first. My best. What a wondrous animal she was. Faith wagged her tail obligingly, pom-pom thumping up and down on the rubber mat.

"Now you'll have to start thinking about Eve," Bertie said, watching our love fest with a smile.

"She's not even four months old!"

"That's not too young to start her training. Just think, as soon as you get Faith's coat off, you'll have another to grow in."

"Bite your tongue." Still high from what I'd just accomplished, I had no desire to contemplate starting over again.

Instead, I changed the subject. "Hey, did you ever open that note from Sara? What did it say?"

Bertie put down her comb. "You know, I forgot all about it. Let me have a look."

The light blue envelope was just where she'd left it, wedged in behind some leashes hanging in the lid of her tack box. Bertie drew it out, slit the flap with her thumbnail, and drew out a single sheet of light blue paper.

Her eyes skimmed quickly down the page.

"How odd," she said.

"What?"

Bertie glanced back at the envelope, flipping it over and checking both sides. Nothing was written on either. "I wonder if Terry delivered this to the right person."

"What's the matter?" I asked.

"For starters, it's not about the wedding. And on top of that, it doesn't make much sense. Listen to this."

She held up the sheet and read:

> *"You've always been a good friend. I know I can count on you, perhaps better than you can count on me. Whatever you hear about me, don't believe most of it, and don't worry. I'll be in touch. Sara."*

7

"That is odd," I agreed. "Read it to me again."

Bertie did, stopping to add editorial comment as she went along. "What does she mean, 'you've always been a good friend'? No, I haven't. Sara and I have known each other a long time, but we've never been what I would call good friends. And then she says, 'I know I can count on you.' Count on me to do what?"

I had even less idea than Bertie did what the note meant. "It's the next line that bothers me: 'Whatever you hear about me, don't believe most of it.' I wonder what Sara's been up to that she expects us to hear anything at all."

"Maybe it's a joke," Bertie decided. "Sara has always had a warped sense of humor. I guess I'll have to call her tonight and find out what's going on."

Looking annoyed, she tossed the envelope back in her tack box and returned to the Bichon she'd been grooming. At least we weren't talking about Eve's coat anymore.

"How's my new champion?" Aunt Peg asked, walking up the aisle. She stopped beside Faith's table and chucked the

Poodle under the chin. "I'll have you know that was a very popular win."

"So it seemed. Apparently I've been working at it for so long that the other exhibitors were beginning to feel sorry for me."

"Pish," said Peg. "Finishing a first show dog of any breed—much less a Poodle that's owner-handled—is a big deal. Of course it takes time. There's a lot of learning you have to do along the way."

"I was lucky to have a good teacher."

"Yes, you were," Aunt Peg agreed, not above taking her share of the credit. "And a very good Poodle."

I paused, plastic wrap in hand, as something occurred to me. "You know, she's finished showing now." The reality of what that meant was just beginning to sink in. "I don't even have to wrap this ear if I don't want to. I could just cut the hair off."

Aunt Peg's hand shot out and grabbed the scissors that were lying on my tabletop. "Don't even think such a thing. You may have won all the points you need, but Faith's championship isn't confirmed yet. It will take the A.K.C. several weeks to put a certificate in the mail. In the meantime, don't you dare touch a single hair, just in case."

"She's right," said Bertie. "You wouldn't believe how many horror stories I've heard. A handler will send a dog home and the client goes ahead and cuts the coat off. Next thing you know it turns out the judge forgot to sign her book, or marked someone absent who was really there, so the win doesn't get recorded as a major. It's amazing how many things can get screwed up. I always tell my clients to wait, too."

Outvoted, I sighed and went back to my wrapping. After all the time I'd already spent caring for Faith's coat, another couple weeks wouldn't kill me.

"Dinner's on me tonight," Aunt Peg said happily. "A celebration. Everybody at my house. I'll call Frank and tell him. Bertie, can you make it?"

Bertie combed through the Bichon's long, silky tail, then flipped it up over the dog's back. "As long as it's not too early. I'm hoping to have to stay for groups."

"No problem. Come whenever you can."

"Bob, too?" I asked.

Peg's smile dimmed. "I'd forgotten about him. Wishful thinking on my part. What do you suppose he's up to this time? I have to admit, it worries me, having him show up unexpectedly like this."

"Me, too. But so far, he hasn't done anything but make himself agreeable. And if he hooks up with Frank tonight, he can move in with him instead of staying with me."

"I guess we'll have to include him, then. Everybody likes Chinese food, right?"

It was strictly a rhetorical question. Aunt Peg cooks for her dogs. Human visitors, if they're lucky, get takeout.

"Love it," Bertie and I agreed.

We knew the drill.

It was after seven o'clock by the time we all got ourselves assembled at Aunt Peg's sprawling home in backcountry Greenwich. Bertie stayed for the groups, placing with a Tibetan Spaniel, then drove home to Wilton to unload the dogs she had with her, check on the dogs she'd left at home, and do evening feed and ex. Frank came over from Stamford.

Though he lives in Cos Cob, a small shoreline town next to Greenwich, a year earlier my brother had opened a coffee bar just north of the Merritt Parkway in Stamford. By all accounts (Bertie's being more reliable than Frank's), the business had really taken off. Since my brother had spent nearly a decade trying to decide what he wanted to do with his life, I was delighted to find that he'd been working on a Sunday evening. Bertie's stabilizing influence, no doubt.

As for Davey, Bob, and me, we had it easy. We simply loaded up our gear at the show and drove directly to Aunt Peg's. She'd beaten us there by a couple of minutes. The joyous barking of her house dogs, running loose in the fenced meadow behind the house, attested to their recently attained freedom.

"There's Eve," cried Davey, pointing out our puppy as the cavalcade of black Standard Poodles came racing past the fence near the driveway. "And that one's Zeke!"

Zeke was Eve's litter brother. Both puppies had been born, along with four other brothers and sisters, in my bedroom in July. Davey had been in attendance for part of the whelping and he felt a proprietary air toward the litter.

"Who?" Bob's head whipped from side to side as the Poodles streaked by. The man was trying, I had to give him that. "Which one? Where?"

Faith meanwhile, shot out of the car and threw herself up against the fence, annoyed that she was missing out on all the excitement. "Soon," I told her, wrapping my arms around her neck and pulling her back. "Another couple weeks and you'll be right out there with them, running and pulling hair to your heart's content."

"There!" Davey pointed again for Bob's benefit as the bunch swung in a wide, galloping circle and came back around. Poodles love to entertain. These dogs knew they were the best show in town, and they enjoyed putting on a performance for our benefit. "That one, right there."

"They all look alike. How do you expect me to pick one out?"

He did have a point. The Cedar Crest line of Standard Poodles was incredibly uniform, both in looks and temperament. Aunt Peg had devoted three decades of her life to achieving just such a goal. Watching the family of beautiful dogs gambol around the field filled my fledgling breeder's heart with joy.

Not Bob's. Once again he was lost.

"Try and pick out the two little ones," I advised as the wild bunch zoomed by a third time.

Bob just shook his head. When we went inside a minute later, he was leading the way. You didn't have to be a teacher to see that he probably hadn't enjoyed pop quizzes in school either.

Aunt Peg had gone through the house to let her dogs in the back door at the same time we came in the front, and the Poodles met in the hallway. Predictably, pandemonium ensued.

Ordinarily I would have stepped in and quelled the raucous greeting for the sake of Faith's coat. That night, I let her tear around and have some fun. I guessed Aunt Peg was pretty pleased about Faith's finishing, because she didn't say a thing.

"Now," Bob said to Davey, when things had finally begun to settle down, "show me which one is Eve."

That was easy, especially since my son was sitting on the floor with the floppy almost-four-month-old puppy in his lap. "She's right here!" Davey giggled.

"Where's her head?" Bob leaned down for a closer look. "I don't think she has any eyes. All I can see is a big ball of black fur."

Automatically Peg reached over and smoothed back the puppy's short, silky topknot, revealing her long, tapered muzzle. As with all Poodles intended for the show ring, the hair on the top of Eve's head had never been cut. At her young age, however, it wasn't quite long enough to fit into the banded ponytails that kept Faith's topknot out of her way.

"A little Dippity-Do will address that problem," Aunt Peg said. "Let's go find some, shall we, Davey? You can help me put it on."

He scrambled up and followed Peg toward the room near her kitchen that she'd recently outfitted as a grooming room. Eve hopped up, too, and she and Zeke trailed along after them.

"Cute puppies," said Bob. "Davey told me they're Faith's?"

"Yes, we bred her in the spring. The litter was born last summer in my bedroom. It was quite an experience."

"The bedroom? I thought dogs had puppies in the garage."

"Not Aunt Peg's dogs." Not by a long shot. "The whole thing was pretty nerve-racking. Luckily, I had expert assistance."

"Peg, of course."

"Actually, no." I almost sighed, but squelched the impulse just in time. "Aunt Peg didn't get there until the next morning. Sam was the one who helped me whelp the litter."

"Driver," Bob muttered. "We met the last time I was here. Davey said the two of you were engaged."

"We were." I stopped, then corrected myself. "Maybe we still are."

"Don't you know?"

"Not exactly, no."

He lifted a brow at that. "Your brother told me that Sam's disappeared. Up and left for parts unknown."

I reached down and tangled my fingers in Faith's warm hair. The Poodle pressed her body against my leg. The contact made both of us feel better. It always does.

"That pretty much sums it up."

Bob took my hand and led me into the living room.

Together we sat down on the couch. Faith, knowing she was invited, hopped up and draped her front legs across my lap.

"You guys must have been pretty serious. What happened?"

"I don't know." I gazed at my ex-husband and shrugged. "I honestly don't. Sam's ex-wife died and it threw him for a loop. He decided there were some things in his life that he needed to work out on his own. So he left."

"Last summer?"

"Yes."

"And you haven't heard anything since?"

"A postcard in August with a picture of Mount Tamalpais and an address in San Fran. 'Missing you and Davey,' it said. 'How are the puppies?' I didn't write back."

"Why not?"

Bob's fingers squeezed mine. Abruptly I realized he'd never given me back my hand.

And that I'd never taken it.

"At first, I couldn't think what to say. Then I realized there was nothing *to* say. Sam will come back when he wants to. Or he won't."

I squared my shoulders, hoping the small gesture made me look stronger than I felt. "But if he thinks that I'm going to give him the illusion of a relationship by mail in the meantime, he's crazy. If Sam wants to know how Davey and I are doing, then he can damn well come and see for himself."

Bob's index finger began to move slowly, stroking the soft skin of my palm. "Frankly, I'd say that you and Davey are managing just fine without him."

"We are." I slid my hand from his. "Just like we did when you left."

He didn't react to the rebuff. Instead, his hand reached up and cupped Faith's muzzle, his fingers finding and scratching exactly the right spot behind her ears.

Just what I needed, I thought. Another man who knew how to get to me through my dog.

"That was a long time ago," Bob said slowly. "You married a boy; you needed a man. I'd like to think I've changed since then. Grown up. You loved me once—"

The doorbell rang, loud and insistent.

I jumped up off the couch as if I'd been shot from a gun. Who'd have guessed it was actually possible to be saved by a bell?

Faith began to bark and ran from the room. Almost immediately, the rest of the Poodles appeared from various parts of the house. The canine welcoming committee was out in full force. Vastly relieved by the interruption, I went to join them in the hallway.

"Dinner," my brother, Frank, announced when I opened the door. He held up his hands to display two heavy, fragrant bags. "Aunt Peg called. I picked up. And Bertie just checked in. She should be no more than a few minutes behind me."

"Perfect timing," Aunt Peg said.

Her discerning gaze swept over both me and Bob. Bob looked disgruntled—I was sure of it. As for me, I was probably pale again. Gosh darn it all.

"I see I can't leave you two alone for a minute," she said in an undertone as the two men greeted each other and headed for the kitchen.

"Then don't," I snapped.

Peg sighed. Heavily. Theatrically. I didn't need to look at her to know that she was probably rolling her eyes.

We didn't even have a chance to close the door before Bertie's van came pulling into the driveway. Aunt Peg went out to greet her. Delighted to be welcoming someone normal to her house for a change, no doubt.

Bertie and I set the table while Frank and Bob unpacked the food and ladled the dishes into serving bowls. Faith, guest of honor at our celebratory gathering, was given a giant Milk-Bone to chew while we ate. Of course that meant each of the other Poodles had to have one, too. Halfway through the meal, Frank and Bob let the rest of us know we'd been talking about dogs too long by starting a loud conversation of their own.

Poor things, who could blame them really?

So we all took a deep breath and started over. Bertie brought us all up to date on her plans for the wedding. Frank regaled us with stories from the coffee house. Aunt Peg asked how things were going at school and got answers from both Davey and me.

Bob and I never got another moment alone, which suited me just fine. Better still, I got to send my ex-husband home with Frank at the end of the evening.

"I'll drive him back to your place so he can pick up his car, and he can follow me home," Frank said, sounding perfectly pleased by the arrangement.

It was Bertie who looked a bit chagrined. Frank's apartment is quite a comfortable size for one person; two would probably find it cozy. The addition of a third adult, however, would just about eliminate any possibility of privacy.

I resolved to check back with Bertie during the week and make sure that Bob's presence wasn't too much of an imposition. Having him at Frank's place made my life simpler, but I had no intention of turning my problems into hers.

November brings midterms to Howard Academy. Though I don't teach any courses—my job is to tutor those kids who are having trouble keeping up—there was still plenty for me to do in the high-pressure atmosphere of exam time.

Another weekend was approaching before I even remembered my vow to get back to Bertie. And then, to be perfectly honest, I only remembered because she called me on Thursday night.

"I think something's wrong," she said.

Guilt socked me like a blow. I knew I should have been keeping tabs on things.

"It's Bob, isn't it? Don't say another word. I'll pick him up and take him to a motel."

"Bob?" Bertie sounded surprised. "What's the matter with him?"

"I don't know. I thought you'd tell me. Isn't that what you're calling about?"

"No. It's Sara. Sara Bentley. She seems to have disappeared."

8

"Sara Bentley?" I'd been so sure Bertie was calling to complain about Bob that it took me a moment to switch gears. "Where did she go?"

Bertie's answering snort conveyed what she thought of that inane question. "That's the whole point. I don't know and neither does anyone else. Remember that strange note she sent me at the show? I figured I'd give her a call and find out what was up. Except that Sara hasn't been home all week. Her machine is piling up messages, and her cell phone goes straight to voice mail.

"I called a couple of mutual friends and nobody's heard from her. Sara's a social butterfly—not that her idea of who's currently in favor doesn't change with the wind—but it's unlike her to be out of touch with everybody. A few minutes ago, I even tried Delilah and Grant. They haven't seen her either."

I thought for a moment. "Maybe Sara has a batch of new friends that you don't know anything about."

"I doubt it. If she did, we would have heard about them

last week when we were at your house. As I'm sure you noticed, Sara likes to talk, mostly about herself."

"Maybe she's just been really busy. After all, it's only been four days."

"You don't understand. For Sara, four days is a lifetime. She's met a guy, fallen in love, gotten engaged, and broken the whole thing off in less time than that."

"Okay." I was beginning to see her point. "So now what?"

"Brace yourself," said Bertie. "I need your help."

Let me set the record straight. I think Bertie's great. I've always wanted a sister and I loved the fact that she was about to become part of my family. But whenever someone tells me they need my help, things never seem to work out the way I hope they will.

"Doing what?"

Bertie must have heard the suspicion in my voice. Lord knows, I made no effort to hide it. It didn't even slow her down.

That was not a good sign.

"The way I look at it," she said, "we've got two options. I hired Sara to plan my wedding, and now she's gone. Vanished into the wild blue yonder. It seems to me we've either got to find her, bring her back and make her get the job done like she promised, or we've got to plan this shindig ourselves."

We? I thought. We who?

"Go ahead," Bertie invited. "Your choice."

"My choice? When did this become my problem?"

"About a week ago." Bertie paused for effect. "The day your ex-husband blew into town."

For the second time, she'd managed to surprise me. Sheesh, I thought, I needed to be quicker on the uptake. When I assumed we were talking about Bob, we weren't. And when I assumed we weren't, apparently we were.

"What's Bob got to do with this?"

"He wants you back, babe."

"No, he—" I stopped.

There was no point in denying it just because the news was unwelcome. After all, that certainly seemed to be what he'd been leading up to at Aunt Peg's on Sunday. Probably the only reason he'd never finished his pitch was because I hadn't given him the chance.

Then again, aside from his speaking on the phone with Davey several times, we'd barely heard from him since—which had left me as confused as I was relieved.

"It's not going to happen," I said firmly. "Besides, you could be wrong. As it happens, I haven't heard from him all week."

"As it happens," said Bertie, "you have me and Frank to thank for that. We've been running interference on your behalf. Frank even has Bob filling in over at the Bean Counter."

"Oh." Well, that explained a few things. "Thank you."

"You're welcome, but actually I was hoping for more than words. I'm thinking along the lines of compensation. How about this? I'll continue to keep Bob out of your hair, and you find Sara for me."

Of all the sneaky, underhanded offers.

I hated to admit it, but Bertie was going to fit into our family just fine.

"That's extortion."

"Just what I was aiming for," she said cheerfully. "Do we have a deal?"

I let her wait half a minute, ratcheting up the suspense. Yeah, right, who was I kidding?

"You know we do."

I heard Bertie chuckle, savoring her success. But then she quickly sobered again. "I'm really worried, Mel. Sara can be capricious at times, but once she makes a commitment to a friend, she honors it."

I wondered if that meant she hadn't counted all those ex-fiancés as friends.

"Also, she was really psyched about working on the wedding. She told me so. I just can't imagine she just suddenly disappeared of her own volition."

"I guess we'll find out. And I do mean we. You're going to have to help me, you know. I don't know Sara at all. I don't even know where she lives."

"New Canaan," Bertie said. "She lives in the guest house on her parents' estate. Gorgeous place. I'd go down a cup size to be so fortunate."

While others of us might have counted ourselves fortunate if we'd had a cup size to spare.

"What are you doing tomorrow afternoon?" I asked. Howard Academy had early dismissal on Fridays, and I could probably convince Frank to pick Davey up at school and take him over to the Bean Counter for a couple of hours.

"Getting ready for the weekend shows, but I can free up some time."

"Good. Why don't we meet at Sara's place? Maybe we'll get really lucky and find her there."

"Maybe," Bertie agreed, but she didn't sound very optimistic.

New Canaan is one of my favorite towns. Located east of Stamford and north of Darien, New Canaan has worked hard to retain its charm and New England ambiance in an area that's teeming with growth. While most of the surrounding Fairfield County towns have allowed chain stores, fast food outlets, and, in some cases, skyscrapers to change the unique flavor of their landscapes, New Canaan continues to resist such advances nobly.

The downtown area is small and picturesque. Nearby Waveny Park draws joggers, kite flyers, and scores of soccer players; every Fourth of July the town hosts a gala fireworks celebration there. Strict zoning laws insure that once you leave the center of town, you see more greenery than houses. As in Greenwich, estates abound; many of them fine old, stone homes, built to last and situated on a sumptuous amount of acreage.

Following Bertie's directions on Friday afternoon, I took Weed Street out to West Road and found that Grant and Delilah Waring lived in just such a manor. From the street, the main house wasn't even visible. Instead, all I could see was a post-and-rail fence enclosing a vast meadow, a long tree-lined driveway, and a copse of tall trees in the distance.

Bertie had gotten there ahead of me. Her maroon Chevy van was parked just inside the gate. I pulled up beside her and she rolled down her window and waved.

"There's a back way around to the guest house," she said, gesturing toward a spot a hundred yards up where the driveway forked. "Actually it's the service entrance, but Sara always uses it so she can come and go without her parents knowing what she's up to."

"I'm surprised she doesn't find it restrictive, living at home at her age. I know I would."

"Sara seems to manage pretty well. And once you see this place, you'll know why she isn't in any hurry to leave."

I waited while she pulled out in front of me, then followed her up the driveway. Even approaching from the back, the Warings' estate was impressive. The house wasn't huge, but it had beautiful lines. Built of red brick that had weathered to a soft shade of rose, the home had three parts: a main section and two ample wings that angled outward at either end. A grotto-like swimming pool was nestled within their embrace.

A garage big enough to accommodate at least half a dozen cars was on the other side of the driveway. Beyond lay a tennis court and a kennel building, with banks of covered runs jutting out from either side. Following Bertie's van around behind the garage, I saw that the long driveway forked again, leading into another small grove of trees. Almost immediately we came upon the guest house, which turned out to be a delightful ivy-covered cottage nestled in a private clearing.

"What a gorgeous place," I said as I parked beside Bertie's van and got out.

She was already starting up the flagstone walkway. "Told you."

"I guess I can see why Sara wouldn't want to move. She's pretty far removed from her parents out here, too. In fact"— I turned around and had a look—"I bet they can't even see back here from inside the house."

"Supposedly, that was the idea. This guest house was added to the property by Roger Bentley, Sara's father and Delilah's first husband. According to Sara, he used it as a hideaway to meet with his various mistresses when Delilah was busy with her dog shows or her bridge club."

"How old was Sara when her father died?"

"I'm not sure," said Bertie. "Thirteen? Maybe fourteen?"

As she stepped forward to knock on the door, I found myself picturing Sara as a little girl, sneaking out of the big house and following her father into the woods. I imagined her pulling herself up and gazing in the cottage's darkened windows. What a way to lose your innocence.

"No one's home," Bertie announced. Unlike me, she was concentrating on the business at hand. "If Sara was here, we'd have heard Titus by now. Somehow I knew it wouldn't be that easy."

"Me too," I admitted. "Let's go inside and have a look around. Do you have any idea where Sara might keep an extra key?"

"The cottage isn't locked. It never is."

"You're kidding."

New Canaan isn't a high-crime area, but it's still a place where front doors are expected to be secure.

"Nope." Bertie turned the knob and pushed the door open. "What can I tell you? That's just the way Sara is. She always wanted to be a flower child, but unfortunately, she was born too late. The hippie movement had already gone by. Peace, free love, good karma. That's Sara all over. She claims not to believe in the ownership of material things."

I wasn't impressed. "Easy for someone who grew up rich to say."

"I'm sure that's probably part of it. Nearly everything she does seems to be a conscious repudiation of her mother's values and lifestyle. Some might say that she's carried the notion of teenage rebellion to its absolute extreme."

I walked past Bertie and stepped into the cottage. A table next to the door held a small, blue porcelain bowl. Inside was a stack of mail and a cell phone, turned off.

"There's one reason you haven't been able to reach her," I said, pointing to the phone. "Wherever Sara went, it looks as though she wanted to be out of touch."

"If she had a choice," Bertie said ominously.

The living room was to our left. In keeping with the rest of the cottage's cozy dimensions, it wasn't very large. Still, the room looked comfortable and well lived-in.

A stone fireplace dominated one wall. There was a tall pile of ash beneath the andirons, and three fresh logs had been stacked on top. The kindling was already in place, and a box of long matches sat ready for use, as if Sara had laid the fire and intended to be back any minute to light it.

Lifting my gaze, I saw a collection of silver-framed photographs on the mantelpiece. All were of Sara and many included Titus. Other than the Sheltie, however, her partners differed in almost every picture. Sara had been captured, smiling happily, with nearly a dozen assorted men. Bertie was right: the woman must have had a very full social life.

The matching chairs and couch in the room were made of dark burnished leather. Bertie walked over to the closest one and sat down, sinking deep into the plump cushion. "This is a dead end. I'm wondering if we ought to call the police."

"It isn't dead yet. We haven't even begun to snoop around. Besides, what are you going to tell them? That your adult friend, who by the way is known for her flightiness, has been out of touch for a few days? Somehow I don't think they'll be too concerned."

"I don't care," Bertie said stubbornly. "Something's not right. Sara must be in some kind of trouble, or she wouldn't be missing. And what was up with that note anyway?"

"I have no idea." I stepped in closer to have another look at the photographs on the mantelpiece. "Who are all these guys up here? Do you know?"

"Old boyfriends, I think." Bertie got up and came over to see for herself. "With maybe a few ex-fiancés thrown in for good measure."

She stopped in front of one frame, her finger reaching out to poke at the glass. "That one's Josh. Funny she'd keep a picture of him around."

"Who's Josh?"

"My cousin. Actually I was the one who introduced them. At the time it seemed like a great idea. But what started as a hot romance ended up fizzling pretty quickly."

"Flattering photo," I said, picking it up. Josh was a good-looking guy. His fair coloring and chiseled features provided a pleasing contrast to Sara's darker, more exotic looks. The picture had been taken on a sailboat, probably out on Long Island Sound. "Sara seems to have chronicled a whole bunch of romances up here. Why are you surprised she'd keep Josh's picture?"

"I don't know." Bertie shrugged. "What I heard was mostly Josh's side, so I guess my feelings were colored by that. But I know he thought things ended badly, and he was pretty bitter about it. Let's just say you won't find any pictures of Sara, flattering or not, sitting out at his place."

I glanced back down the row of photos. "I wonder if any of these guys are more current. Do you know if Sara has a boyfriend now?"

"Probably. Only because there always seems to be somebody. But as to who it is, I wouldn't have any idea."

"Maybe we'll find an address book," I said, walking out of the living room. A small kitchen, with a dining area off of it, was in the rear of the cottage. Passing a narrow staircase that led up to a sleeping loft, I headed that way. "Or if we're really lucky there'll be a message on the answering machine."

"Declaring undying love and leaving a phone number?" Bertie laughed. "Only if you lead a charmed life."

The first thing I noticed about the kitchen was that nearly the entire back wall of the room was made of glass. A large picture window looked out over the clearing, and several bird feeders hung from the branches outside. Considering that it was November, business was brisk: some sparrows and a blue jay were currently enjoying Sara's largesse.

The second thing I noticed were the dog bowls on the floor. There were three altogether, one for water and two filled with dry kibble. Though Titus probably weighed less than half what Faith did, his stainless-steel bowls were huge—easily larger than the ones I used to feed my Poodle.

Bertie followed the direction of my gaze and guessed what I was thinking. "Who knows? Maybe Sara leaves food out like that all the time so she won't forget to feed him."

"Forget?" It was hard to keep the censure from my voice. I'd no more forget to feed Faith than I would Davey.

Bertie gestured toward the back door. "I know she had that doggie door installed so she wouldn't have to be bothered letting him in and out all the time."

Aunt Peg would have been happy to tell Sara that dog ownership was a privilege, not a bother. Since neither of them was there, however, I decided not to comment.

"At any rate, it looks as though Sara must have taken Titus with her. That's probably a good sign, don't you think?"

"Maybe." Bertie still wasn't convinced. She walked over to the answering machine on the counter. Not unexpectedly, its light was blinking. "That's strange."

"What?"

"I left several messages on this machine, and I know there were a bunch of others. It's one of the older models. You can tell how many messages there are by how long you have to wait for the beep."

"So?"

"It says there's only one message on here. I called Sara on Monday and Tuesday, then left a third message yesterday."

Diverted from the dog bowls, I walked over and had a look. "Well, either the machine is broken or else someone has come in and wiped the messages clean."

"See?" said Bertie. "I told you something was wrong."

I reached over and pushed the play button. "Unless Sara's been here since yesterday and deleted them all herself. Let's see who this one's from."

The tape began to spin and almost immediately an angry voice rang out. "Sara, you creep, this is Maris. Call me, do you hear? I'm tired of being the one who always has to bail you out, and I'm not going to stand for it anymore. It's Friday morning now. Get back to me today or you'll be sorry."

9

"Maris," I said, turning to Bertie. "That's an unusual name. Any ideas?"

"Maris Kincaid. Lives in Norwalk. Breeds Soft Coated Wheaten Terriers and shows a few every now and then. She has a grooming business that she runs out of her basement to pay the dogs' expenses. She and Sara are friends." She glanced down at the machine and grimaced. "Or not."

"I wonder what Sara did to her."

"Who knows? One thing I learned pretty quickly with Sara is that it tends to be feast or famine. Either she's your bosom buddy or you want to kill her. At first I thought it was just me, but it seems to be the way she treats everyone."

"Didn't you tell me last week that Sara was doing some grooming, too? She must have records around here somewhere. I wonder if any of her clients have heard from her this week."

"There's a desk up in the loft," said Bertie.

"Computer?"

"Laptop. We can take a look, but if it's not here, she probably took it with her."

Upstairs, in the top drawer of Sara's desk, we found her business records, such as they were. Actually what we found was a calendar, with names and times stuffed into some of the date boxes and an occasional arrow pointing out to the margin, where several phone numbers had been scribbled.

"You must be insane," I said to Bertie. "*This* is the woman you hired to plan your wedding? No wonder all her businesses have fallen apart."

"Sara's usually very organized." Bertie sounded defensive. Also annoyed. I would be, too, if this was what I had to defend. "Her businesses fell apart because she didn't take them seriously. I'm sure Sara has better records than that somewhere. She has to. They're probably on her laptop."

Which was, as we'd suspected it might be, missing.

I flipped through the calendar to the second week of November. "Sara was supposed to groom three Poodles, a Maltese, and two Cockers this week. Plus, she was pet-sitting a Siamese cat in Rowayton. I may as well call these people and see if any of them heard from her. Maybe one of them can give us a lead on where she went."

"Good idea."

Bertie crossed the room and opened the door to Sara's closet. The small cupboard was a mess. Its hanging bar and shelves were jam-packed with a jumbled assortment of shoes and clothing.

"It figures." She sighed. "I was hoping we might be able to tell if she'd packed some things, but with this much junk, how would we ever know if anything was missing?"

I tucked the calendar under my arm and headed for the bathroom. "Maybe we'll have better luck in here."

The bathroom off the sleeping loft was utterly charming, with a claw-footed bathtub, half a dozen hanging plants, and a lace-curtained window overlooking the clearing. It didn't, however, reveal any clues to Sara's whereabouts. A toothbrush sat in a holder next to the sink, and I found deodorant, moisturizer, sunblock, and dental floss in the medicine cabinet above.

Would Sara have taken those things with her if she'd left of her own volition? I had no idea. It could be that, like some people I knew, she kept a toiletries bag packed with doubles of everything for travel.

"Hey!" yelled Bertie.

"What?"

"Come here."

Her voice sounded muffled, and when I walked back out into the bedroom, I saw that it was empty.

"Where are you?"

"In the stupid closet." A loud thump punctuated her words. "Open the door, would you? There's no knob on this side."

Quickly I strode over and drew the wooden door open. Face flushed, hair disheveled, Bertie shoved aside the tightly packed hanging clothes and emerged from the back of the closet.

"What were you doing in there?"

"There's a shelf deep in the back. I thought that might be where Sara would keep a suitcase, so I pushed my way in to have a look. But then the door swung shut behind me and I couldn't get it open."

"Find anything interesting?"

"No," Bertie admitted, smoothing her hair back off her face. "You?"

"Not really."

Together we trooped back down the stairs.

"If you really want to find Sara," I said as we walked outside, "you ought to consider hiring a private investigator. Someone like that would have access to all sorts of information that I don't. For example, they could find out if she's

been using her credit cards, and if so, where the charges
were made."

"And they'd charge me a bundle in the process." Bertie
pulled the door shut behind us. "I can't afford help like that.
Whereas, as long as Bob hangs around, you're—"

"Free," I muttered.

"Exactly," Bertie concurred happily.

Sometimes being wanted is a double edged sword.

Saturday morning, I awoke to the unaccustomed sensation that I wasn't alone in bed. I could feel another warm,
solid body pressing against mine through the tangle of covers. Deep, even breathing matched my own. It took me a moment to get oriented.

When I had, my hand crawled out from beneath the duvet
and reached out to stroke a long, fuzzy muzzle. Immediately
Eve's head came up and her tail began to wag. Sharp puppy
teeth nipped playfully at my fingers as she bounced to her
feet.

"You're up! You're up!" she seemed to be saying. "Let's
play!"

Faith has finally come to understand the ritualistic pleasure of waking up slowly on a Saturday morning. Not so, her
daughter. Eve is a ball of fire from the moment she senses
that my eyes are half open.

Faith sleeps on Davey's bed and always has. During the
week when she's with Aunt Peg, Eve spends her nights in a
crate. To be honest, Peg is under the impression that the
puppy sleeps crated at my house, too. I figure what she doesn't
know won't hurt either of us.

"You need to go out, don't you?" I asked.

Only a dog owner who was truly clueless would wait for

an answer to that question. Any puppy, awakened from sleep, needs to pee right away. Hence the beauty of keeping them crated overnight. Letting Eve sleep on my bed at her young age was the equivalent of putting her on the canine honor system.

Of course, I was doing my part, too. Basically that consisted of waking up, getting up, and running directly to the back door. No slippers, no bathrobe, just bare feet on the cold wood floors and a puppy who seemed to enjoy playing the game of "chase mom down the stairs."

The commotion we made awoke Faith as well. Business attended to, Eve was investigating the frost, which had left a thin, shimmering coating on the backyard overnight, when Faith came sauntering into the kitchen. I opened the door and stood in a draft of cold winter air as the Poodle took her time stretching before strolling outside.

Mother and daughter touched noses briefly. Eve's front end bowed down, leaving her haunches high and tail beating from side to side, a clear invitation to play. Having been in all night as well, Faith had more pressing things to attend to.

Rebuffed, Eve picked up a tennis ball and tossed it for herself. No flies on this girl. Already it was easy to see she was going to be a live wire in the show ring.

Much as I loved Eve's temperament, however, that was only one of the criteria by which she had been chosen from her litter of six. The others had to do with her conformation, her movement, and even that indefinable characteristic known as presence. Aunt Peg was the one who had picked her for me, and as far as I was concerned, she had chosen well. Best of all, the puppy seemed to be adapting readily to her schedule of living in both our homes.

I had stopped by Aunt Peg's to pick Eve up the afternoon before on my way back from Sara's house. Peg likes to set a good example for us poor minions who try to follow faithfully in her footsteps. As always, she'd had the puppy freshly brushed out and ready to go.

When Eve came dancing over to the door to greet me, I reached down to pat her, then snapped my hand back. "What on earth have you done to her head?"

The puppy was wearing two tiny ponytails, one above each eye. Each colored rubber band held only a small amount of hair that was so short that it stood straight up before fanning out like a small, delicate flower.

"They're called puppy horns." Aunt Peg flipped one ponytail to the side so I could see how she'd put it in. "I realized the other night when Davey and I were applying gel that she just might have enough hair to reach. As I recall, we didn't do this with Faith, but Eve's topknot is thicker. Check on them a couple of times a day. Redo them each morning. Not too tight, or you'll undo any gains you might have made. Vigilance is everything."

It seemed to me I'd heard that before.

"Speaking of the other night," Aunt Peg said casually, "are you seeing much of that ex-husband of yours?"

"Almost nothing," I said to our mutual delight. "Among other distractions, Frank has apparently put Bob to work in the coffee house. I'm on my way over there now to pick up Davey."

"After coming from where?" Aunt Peg hates to be out of the loop.

"Bertie and I were at Sara Bentley's place."

"Doing what?"

"Looking for Sara. She seems to have disappeared."

"No!" said Peg, but her eyes were gleaming. There's nothing she enjoys more than a good mystery. "Since when?"

"Bertie and I both saw her at the show last Saturday. And we know she was there Sunday, because she left a note for

Bertie with Terry." I quickly recounted the note's contents. "But as far as we know now, that's the last anyone saw of her. Bertie left several messages for Sara during the week and finally talked to her parents. They hadn't seen her either."

Aunt Peg frowned. "Didn't you tell me that Bertie had asked Sara to take over the planning for her wedding?"

"Yes. That's one of the reasons Bertie's so anxious to find her. If she doesn't get some arrangements nailed down soon, we may find ourselves eating chicken fingers in your backyard."

"Heaven forbid." That heartfelt sentiment is about as close as Aunt Peg comes to swearing. The last time she'd thrown a party, one of the guests had been murdered the following day. "I suppose you'd better find her, then. Is there anything I can do to help?"

"Just keep your ears open. Maybe you'll hear something at the show next weekend."

"I doubt it," Aunt Peg said sternly.

The Tuxedo Park Poodle specialty would be her first judging assignment, and Peg was prepared to take the task very seriously. Though she wouldn't admit it, I knew she'd been nervous for weeks. First over the prospect that she might not draw—an issue that had already been satisfactorily resolved, since her entry had majors in all three varieties. And second, that she might not do a good enough job.

"Horse feathers," I'd told her.

Aunt Peg had not been reassured.

"Nobody will talk to me," she said now. "I'm the judge and that's considered to be very bad form. Besides, the A.K.C. rep will be watching, so I don't dare talk to anyone either. If there's any snooping around to be done, you'll have to do it yourself."

Like that was a surprise.

* * *

I let both Poodles back inside and ran upstairs to shower
and dress. I thought I heard the dogs barking while I was
washing my hair, but by the time I stepped out of the shower,
the noise had stopped. No doubt Davey had taken charge of
the situation.

Not having any brothers or sisters, my son tends to treat
the Poodles like younger siblings. And though Faith is a
wonderful watchdog, she also feels honor bound to keep an
eye on a multitude of things that I don't think bear watching.
Like squirrels in the backyard, a UPS truck making deliver-
ies at the neighbor's house, or joggers on the sidewalk in
front of our house.

Obviously, I should have taken her warning more seriously, because when I walked into my bedroom a few minutes later, one towel wrapped around my body and another in
the process of wringing moisture out of my wet hair, I found
Bob sitting on my bed.

Shocked, I stopped just inside the doorway. One hand
flew to secure the towel I'd tucked together above one breast.

"What are you doing here?" I gasped.

"Waiting for you." Bob looked almost as surprised by this
turn of events as I was. At least he had the grace to blush. "I
didn't realize you'd be . . ." His hand waved ineffectually.

"Nearly naked?"

A sound gurgled in his throat.

"This is how most people come out of the shower.
Especially when they're not expecting company. Out!"

Bob stood. Slowly. "You look good, Mel."

"Out!"

"I'm sorry. I'm going." The apology might have carried
more weight if he'd made an effort to avert his eyes. Instead,
Bob was staring.

Abruptly, irrationally, I was glad I'd shaved my legs. Vanity, thy name is woman.

"I didn't mean to embarrass you," Bob said, edging past me toward the door. "I only wanted to talk."

"We'll talk downstairs. I'll be down in ten minutes."

It took me less time than that to throw on a pair of black jeans, a heather gray cotton turtleneck, thick socks, and loafers. I used the extra five minutes to run the blow dryer through my hair and wonder what Bob wanted to talk to me about. Whatever it was, I was pretty sure I didn't want to hear it.

"Bagels," Bob said. He was manning the toaster oven when I walked into the kitchen. "I brought breakfast."

"Thanks." I looked around and made a quick decision. Davey, still in his pajamas, was seated at the table. The Poodles were watching hopefully as he smeared cream cheese across a toasted half. "Can I take mine to go?"

"Um, sure. I guess." The toaster pinged. Bob opened the door and slid out two perfectly browned, crunchy halves of an onion bagel. My favorite. Without asking, he began to butter them both. I had to give him one thing, the man had a good memory. "Where are you going?"

"There are some people I need to see today. It's kind of a favor for Bertie. You know, the wedding and all? I was going to take Davey with me, but since you're here, I was thinking I could leave him with you and get an early start."

"If that's what you want," Bob said evenly. "But we haven't seen each other all week. I was hoping we could spend some time together today."

"We will. Later." I was only postponing the inevitable, but I was grasping at any straws I could get. "I'll be back this afternoon." I looked at Davey. "Is that okay with you? Do you think you can manage both Poodles all by yourself?"

"No problem," my son said with confidence. "Dad will help, right?"

"Right," Bob agreed. Outmaneuvered and outflanked, he conceded defeat.

At least that was what I thought.

My ex-husband wrapped my bagel in a paper napkin and brought it to me across the room. He stepped up beside me to hand it over, standing a good deal closer than was necessary. "You look just as good in clothes as you do out of them," he said under his breath.

I snatched the bagel and backed away. I could feel my face growing warm.

"See you later," Davey said cheerfully.

Bob just looked at me and smiled.

Drat.

Double drat.

Ignoring this problem wasn't going to make it go away.

10

I'd spoken with Maris Kincaid briefly the evening before, leaving her, I'm slightly ashamed to admit, with the impression that I was looking for someone to groom my Standard Poodles. That deception seemed preferable to the alternative: trying to explain over the phone that I'd broken into a friend's home, retrieved her messages, and wanted to know why Maris had been making threatening phone calls.

A conversation like that, I'd decided, would go over much better in person.

Maris lived in an area of West Norwalk that appeared to have been developed in the fifties. The houses all had the homogenized look that had been popular in that era: street after street of colonial-style homes placed squarely on wooded one-acre lots. With the specter of world war in the not-too-distant past, Americans had found safety in sameness. Now the look was simply dated.

Whoever had built the development half a century earlier must have been a history buff, for the streets were all named after early patriots. I followed Nathan Hale Road until it ended on Betsy Ross Lane, then took a right and pulled over to the curb.

Except for its fenced yard, Maris's house looked no different from any of the others. Like the neighboring town of New Canaan, Norwalk has stringent zoning laws. There was nothing to indicate from the curb that Maris was running a business in her basement.

She must have seen me drive up because Maris had her front door open before I'd even reached the steps. Her leg, lifted and braced against the door frame, blocked two sandy colored Wheaten Terriers from making their escape as I opened the storm door.

"Watch your step," she said. "These guys are fast."

I slipped inside and pulled the door quickly shut behind me. Maris's approving nod ratified the tactic. She held out a hand and we introduced ourselves.

"I do most of my grooming downstairs," she told me, heading toward the back of the house. "I can also make a house call, if you prefer, but the rates are pretty steep for that. Let me take you down and show you around. Please feel free to ask as many questions as you like. Believe me, I know how hard it is to trust your dog's care to a stranger."

Phooey, I thought as the two Wheatens bounced around us, vying for possession of a stuffed toy. Phone message notwithstanding, Maris was turning out to be a nice person. I hate it when that happens; especially when I've started things off by lying through my teeth.

"I have a confession to make," I heard myself blurt. "I don't really need my dogs groomed."

Abruptly Maris stopped walking. She turned around and crossed her arms over her chest. "Then why are you here?"

"I have to talk to you about Sara Bentley."

"What about her?"

"She seems to be missing."

"I should hope so," Maris snapped. "Otherwise she needs a damn good excuse for yanking me around again."

I couldn't think how to answer that, so I didn't say a thing.

After a moment, Maris frowned. She began to look concerned. "You're not kidding, are you?"

"I'm afraid not."

"Come on." She led the way back to the living room, where we both sat down. "Tell me what's going on. For starters, why did you come to me?"

"I heard the message you left on Sara's answering machine yesterday. You sounded pretty angry."

"I was. I still am." Maris paused, then started again. "I mean, unless there's actually something wrong. What makes you think Sara is missing, anyway?"

I explained about how Bertie had hired Sara to arrange her wedding, and about the note that had been delivered to Bertie at the show. "Bertie's been trying to get in touch with her all week, but Sara's disappeared and nobody's seen her. She's not returning her calls, either. Unless you've heard something . . . ?"

Maris shook her head. "In fact, I left a couple of messages myself. Sara never called me back. That's one of the reasons why I was so mad when I left that message yesterday."

I sat back on the couch. One of the Wheatens came over and rested his head on my knee. After a moment, his front legs, then his shoulders, had insinuated themselves up into my lap. Maris didn't seem to mind, so I let him keep climbing.

"What are the other reasons?"

"I got a message from Sara last Sunday, too. I was at the show, but she left it here on my answering machine. I figured she didn't have the nerve to face me in person."

"What was it about?"

"Business." Her tone was curt. Maris was back to being annoyed. "Sara left me her whole week's worth of clients to take care of. Said something about it being too last-minute to cancel on them and she was sure I wouldn't mind filling in."

"Let me guess. You did mind."

"Of course I did. For one thing, my own schedule was already full. For another, she had me baby-sitting a Siamese cat over in Rowayton." She shuddered slightly. "I'm a dog person. I don't *do* cats. Adding insult to injury, Sara bills her regular clients monthly. I didn't see any money for all the extra work I did, and I probably never will."

I scratched behind the Wheaten's ears and gave Maris a moment to cool off. "Considering she felt free to call you like that, I guess you and Sara must be pretty good friends."

"Most of the time. I'm sure you know what Sara's like. She means well and she's lots of fun to be around, but the usual rules of friendship don't really apply. I mean, no matter what's going on, it'll never be about your life or your problems. In Sara's mind, everything is always all about Sara."

Pretty much the same thing Bertie had said.

"On the other hand, I've never known her to just pick up and disappear. Sara thrives in a social context. It doesn't seem at all like the type of thing she'd do. I hope she's okay."

Maris held out her hand and snapped her fingers. Immediately the Wheaten Terrier left my lap and went to her. "What about Titus? Where's he?"

"As far as we know, she took him with her. He wasn't at her house. Can you think of any reason why Sara might have chosen to run away?"

"No. If something was really wrong, I imagine she would have talked about it. I know she's been going through a bit of a rough patch lately . . ."

"Problems?" I prompted when her voice trailed away.

Maris looked up. She seemed almost surprised to discover that she'd spoken aloud.

"It was nothing Sara couldn't handle," she said firmly. "Having Delilah for a mother, one thing that girl knows how to do is cope."

"Can you think of anyone who might have wanted to hurt Sara?"

Maris stopped to think before answering. In fact, she thought for so long that I began to wonder if I was about to hear about that recent rough patch. Alas, it didn't happen.

"Sara isn't always the easiest person to get along with," Maris said finally. "But for someone to actually want to do her harm? That seems pretty far-fetched. Unless of course you want to talk about Debra Silver. Not that I think she's the violent type or anything, but she hates Sara with a passion. Has for years.

"I think it goes back to something that happened when they were showing against each other in junior showmanship. How anyone could hold a grudge for an entire decade, I have no idea, but you know dog people. Whatever happened, Debra has neither forgotten nor forgiven."

"I heard a story," I said. "Something about Sara poisoning a competitor's dog?"

"Yeah, that's the one. Frankly, it's old news. I don't know the whole story and I never cared enough to chase the rest of it down. If you're interested, I'm sure Debra will be happy to fill you in."

"Thanks." It sounded like a long shot, but it wasn't as if I had any better ideas. "Do you know how I can get in touch with her?"

"Look in the Greenwich phone book." Maris wrinkled her lips in distaste. "Debra married well, and she never lets the rest of us forget it. I'm sure you won't have any trouble tracking her down."

"I'll do that," I said, rising. "I appreciate your taking the time to talk to me."

"You're welcome. Look, when you find Sara, tell her I was worried about her, okay?"

"Sure."

Maris walked me to the door. Her expression was grim. "Yesterday I was so mad at Sara I could have strangled her. Now all I can think is that I hope she didn't do something desperate. She wouldn't just duck out on her friends without leaving word with somebody. If Sara's disappeared, then something's very wrong."

From Maris's house I wound my way across the back roads through Silvermine to New Canaan. Though Bertie had spoken to Sara's parents on the phone, I figured it couldn't hurt to stop by and see them in person. Now that another two days had passed without word from their daughter, maybe they'd be more concerned.

I called ahead from the car to make sure they were home. Delilah Waring sounded surprised, and not entirely pleased, to hear from yet another friend of Sara's; but I kept dropping Aunt Peg's name into the conversation until she agreed to see me for a few minutes. I told her I was on my way.

Ten minutes later, I was parked out front. A housekeeper showed me to the library, where I was offered refreshment and told that Mrs. Waring would be with me shortly.

Another ten minutes passed before Delilah came gliding into the room. I'd expected to hear her coming; assumed that her entrance would be preceded by the sound of Shelties barking, playing, accompanying their mistress in her daily routine. But to my surprise, Delilah was alone. Maybe she was one of those people who didn't like the thought of dogs shedding all over her expensive furniture.

Like a meticulously groomed Sheltie being paraded before the ringside, Delilah Waring presented herself beautifully. Judging by Sara's age, I knew the woman had to be at least fifty; she looked easily a decade younger. Though Delilah was tiny in stature, her presence seemed to fill the entire room. Or maybe she just sucked the air out of it. I could see how Sara might have had a hard time competing with a mother like this.

"How nice of you to come." Delilah's tone was formal. Though we both knew differently, her words implied that my visit had been her idea. She didn't offer to shake hands, but instead waved her slender fingers toward an austere-looking couch. "Please sit down. Polly will bring us tea in a moment."

I'd barely found a spot to perch before Delilah began to speak. "I'm afraid I don't quite understand why you're here. Something about Sara? I try not to get too involved in my daughter's escapades. Whatever it is, I think you'd do better to speak to Sara directly."

Even though I knew it wasn't polite to stare, I couldn't seem to help myself. Bertie had told me she'd talked to Sara's parents. She must have mentioned her concerns. How was it possible that Sara's mother didn't know her daughter had disappeared?

"Mrs. Waring—"

She laughed lightly—a skill that seemed eminently suited to hosting garden parties on the back terrace. "Please, dear, call me Delilah. Everybody does."

"Delilah." I found myself leaning forward in my seat, trying to impart a sense of urgency to my words. "I can't speak with Sara. She's missing and nobody knows where she is. She hasn't been seen or heard from since last weekend."

"Don't be silly." Delilah's smile never faltered. "Sara isn't missing. Oh, good, here's Polly now."

I waited impatiently while the housekeeper set a large tray bearing a silver tea set on the coffee table between us and Delilah poured the tea into two delicate china cups. I don't drink tea if I can help it, but Delilah hadn't asked for my opinion, and I didn't offer it. She handed me a cup and I set it down on the end table beside me.

"Delilah," I said, trying to draw her attention back to the matter at hand. "Do you know where Sara is?"

She raised her head, blinked slowly several times, took a sip of tea, and finally said, "No."

"Doesn't that worry you?"

"Not particularly. My daughter's a grown woman. She makes her own decisions and leads her own life. I try not to interfere."

Not bloody likely, I thought. No doubt the tea was having an effect on my choice of profanity.

"I believe you spoke to Bertie Kennedy a couple of days ago?"

Delilah inclined her head. I took the gesture for agreement.

"Bertie hired Sara to plan her wedding, which is coming up shortly. They were supposed to be in constant contact over the arrangements. Sara had already started to put together some plans when she unexpectedly dropped out of sight."

"Dropped out of sight?" Delilah set down her cup and laughed again. The sound was really beginning to get on my nerves. "Oh please, let's not be dramatic."

"I'm not—"

"It's obvious you don't know my daughter very well. Let me tell you something about Sara. She is a delightful girl with many good qualities, but perseverance isn't one of them.

"She starts well, always has. But she lacks the stamina to go the distance. Believe me when I say we've been through this before. Look around you. This is where Sara grew up. She had advantages that many girls would have killed for. But did she use them to make something of herself? I'm afraid not."

"But still—"

"Let me be blunt," Delilah said. I wondered what she thought she'd been up until that point. "Sara's a quitter. That job she took from Bertie was probably the impetus that made her run away. This isn't the first time she's ducked out to evade responsibility, and I'm sure it won't be the last."

Though I doubted it would pierce Delilah's ironclad armor, I gave things one last shot. "As I'm sure you know, Sara has a large circle of friends. None of them have heard from her all week. Her cottage is empty. Titus is gone. . . ."

Something, the merest flicker in Delilah's eyes, made me pause. "Is Titus gone?"

For the first time since my arrival, Delilah looked briefly flustered. "Now that you mention it, that is a little odd. Titus is here. Out in the kennel. One of the kennel maids found him wandering around the grounds at the beginning of the week."

"Is that unusual?"

"Well . . . not impossible, certainly. It's just that for the most part, he's with Sara. Of course, I had him placed in the kennel for safekeeping. Only for some reason, Sara hasn't been by to pick him up."

11

S ome reason indeed, I thought. If my staring had been impolite, the snort I was tempted to offer now would have come across as positively barbaric. Controlling my baser instincts, I asked instead, "Has anything like that ever happened before?"

"Well, no. Although as I mentioned, Sara can be somewhat . . . unpredictable in her choices. I should think the very fact that she's gone off and left her dog unattended would be enough to tell you that."

"Unless she didn't have any choice."

"Delsy? I'm on my way out." Grant Waring pushed the door open and stuck his head into the library. Seeing me, he abruptly straightened and entered the room. "Sorry, I didn't realize you had company." He strode over and offered his hand. "Hello. We met last weekend, didn't we?"

"Yes, at the dog show in Hartford. I'm a friend of Sara's."

"Another dog fancier." Grant rolled his eyes, but he managed to infuse the gesture with good humor. He turned to his wife. "Enough, darling. I find myself outnumbered already."

"Actually, the visit was my idea," I explained. "I've been looking for Sara. No one has seen her since last Sunday."

"Really?" Grant didn't sound any more alarmed by my news than his wife had been. He turned to Delilah for confirmation. "Is that true?"

"Apparently so. But you know Sara. She's always flitting off somewhere."

"This time she left Titus behind," I mentioned. "All by himself, in her cottage."

Not a dog person, Grant only shrugged at that information. "Sorry to rush off. I'm afraid I have a pressing engagement. Pleasure to see you again."

Frowning slightly, I watched him walk out. No wonder Sara was always flitting off. With parents like these, I could see why she wouldn't want to hang around home much.

"I should be going, too," I said. "Thank you for your time."

"Not at all." Delilah rose from her chair to see me out. "You will remember me to your aunt, won't you? Tell her I expect her to sit beside me at the Belle Haven Kennel Club meeting next month. It's been too long since Peg and I had a chance to catch up."

"I'll be sure to do that. Aunt Peg tells me you have beautiful Shetland Sheepdogs. How did you do at the shows last weekend?"

"Oh, we weren't entered." Too discreet to take a jab at the judge—usually the only reason a hard-core exhibitor would have for missing a nearby show—Delilah only said, "One can't go *every* time, you know. Were you showing?"

Even a week later, the memory brought a huge grin and a rush of pleasure. "I won a major and finished my first Standard Poodle. Totally owner-handled."

"Now that *is* something." Delilah smiled with me, understanding and sharing the source of my happiness. "Congratulations. Peg is lucky to have someone like you coming along to follow in her footsteps. I only wish Sara had felt the same way about my hobby."

"She has a Sheltie," I felt obliged to point out. "And she shows in obedience."

"It's not the same, is it? What a comfort it would be for me to know that there was someone to carry on the Scotch-glen name. Sadly, Sara has made it very clear that it's not going to happen."

Any sympathy I might have felt for the woman's plight was tempered by the realization that, for Delilah, the fact that her line of dogs wouldn't survive her held a deeper emotional significance than did her daughter's disappearance.

Dog people. No wonder regular folks thought we were nuts.

Having run out of excuses, I got in my car and drove home to Stamford. It looked as though Bob was going to get his wish: he and I would finally be spending some time together. I was pretty sure, however, that things weren't going to turn out the way he was hoping.

Driving down the parkway, I rehearsed what I was going to say. *We're different people than we were then. You can't turn back the clock. . . .*

That's right, I thought irritably. Hit him with clichés. See if that helps.

I thought for a moment and tried again. *Just because you've lost Jennifer and I've lost Sam . . .*

I winced, shoulders shifting beneath my sweater. I was *not* going there.

You still look good, too, but . . .

Ouch! Definitely the wrong tack to take.

Maybe I should just wing it, I decided. Go with my gut. Run with the ball. Or something like that.

Then, unexpectedly, Bob saved me the trouble. At least for the time being. When I got home, the house was empty. No humans, no canines.

Instead, there was a note on the kitchen counter. Bob had taken Davey, Eve, and Faith and gone to Frank's place where the "men" (my quotes, not Bob's) were planning to eat pizza, watch a football game, and teach Davey to belch. All right, I'm editorializing here, but you get the idea.

Which meant that I had some more free time. First I fixed a sandwich, turkey on rye, and reveled in the unaccustomed luxury of eating an uninterrupted meal. Then I got back to work.

As Maris had predicted, Debra Silver was indeed listed in the Greenwich phone book. Not only that, but the fact that she had no idea who I was didn't seem to matter. Once I mentioned Sara Bentley's name, our conversation was off and running.

"Let me get this straight," she said. "You're a friend of Sara's?"

"No, not exactly."

"Good, then we have something in common." Debra's speech was fast and forceful. She shot out words like bullets. "Do you play tennis?"

Since I was having trouble keeping up anyway, the non sequitur didn't bother me as much as it might have. "No, not in years."

"Do you know where Shippan Point is?"

"Down by the water in Stamford?"

"Right. I've got a round-robin at the indoor tennis place there at three. Women's league. Why don't you meet me there? I'll be rotating in and out all afternoon. You can tell me all the awful things you know about Sara and I'll do the same."

"Deal," I said.

As I hung up the phone, I decided it was curious that, having spoken so far to Sara's friends and family, I had yet to find a single person who was genuinely, without reservation, on Sara's side. For a variety of reasons, the woman simply didn't engender unqualified support. It would be interesting to hear what someone who called herself Sara's enemy would have to say about her.

Shippan Point is a navigator's nightmare. I got lost twice on the way to the tennis facility; and the round-robin had already started when I arrived. I walked up the carpeted steps, passed the sign-in desk, and stopped in the viewing area overlooking the tennis courts. There were eight courts, all surfaced in Har-Tru. The competition looked pretty cutthroat.

After a minute, I turned my attention to the lounge area. Comfy couches and chairs had been grouped in front of the large windows. The courts were full, and an additional half dozen women were sitting out. Most were sipping bottled water and watching the play. As I approached, one stood up and came to meet me.

"Are you Melanie?" she asked. "I've been watching for you."

Debra's face was flushed and her bangs curled in damp ringlets across her forehead. She wore sweatbands around each wrist, and a flexible brace supported her elbow. Her tennis dress was short and tight. Not that Debra didn't have the figure for it, just that the effort seemed wasted in a women's league match.

"I just came off," she said. "It'll be at least twenty minutes until it's my turn again. Let's go sit down and you can tell me what this is about."

We found a pair of chairs on the other side of the lounge. We could still see the tennis courts, but the other women wouldn't overhear what we were saying. Debra unscrewed the top of her water bottle, tilted back her head, and took a long, deep drink. Her throat, damp with sweat, pulsed with the effort of swallowing.

"We play hard," she said, sinking down into her chair with a sigh. "But don't worry, I'll catch my breath in a minute."

While she did, I told her why I had come. Debra was briefly surprised, then utterly delighted, by the news that Sara Bentley was missing.

"Well, what do you know? Someone finally managed to drive the bitch away. More power to them, whoever they are."

"I guess you wouldn't have any ideas?"

"Me? What makes you ask that?"

"I was told that you and she didn't get along. That there was a problem with a dog when you were both showing in Junior Showmanship."

"Oh for Pete's sake." Debra sniffed. "That was *such* a long time ago. I don't know how people still have the nerve to bring it up." Despite her words, she didn't look displeased by the thought that people might have been talking about her.

"Would you mind telling me the story?"

"Of course not. Do you show dogs?"

I nodded.

"Then you know what junior handling is."

"More or less."

"Briefly, it's a competition where the handler's ability is judged, rather than the dog they're showing. The classes are open to juniors under the age of eighteen, and they can be pretty competitive." Debra stopped and corrected herself. "Make that very competitive. Winning at the big shows really matters, and of course, everyone is trying like crazy to qualify for the all-important Junior Showmanship class at Westminster."

"So you and Sara competed against each other."

"Yes, for several years. We were the same age, and we tended to enter the same shows in the area. Though Sara would never admit it, we were pretty well matched in talent, too."

Debra pursed her lips, thinking back. "Sara always thought she was something special because her mother was Delilah Waring with Scotchglen Shelties, and I was just some high-school kid with an okay Afghan Hound and a mother who didn't mind driving her around to dog shows."

Maris had been right, I thought. Though Debra had to be at least a decade older than eighteen, it didn't sound as though any of her bitterness had faded.

"I heard that Sara may have poisoned your dog."

"May have?" Her eyes flashed. "There was no question about it. Something happened to him and I know she was responsible. It was the Monday of Westminster, the day of the preliminaries for junior show. They hold them in the late afternoon, but we'd been there since morning. Kadu was on his bench in a big wire crate. He was fine when we arrived. My mother and I got him settled, then went out to the rings to watch the show.

"A couple hours later, it was Sara who came and told me that I'd better go check on my dog. She said he didn't look very good. Of course, my mother and I went straight back to see. Kadu was in terrible shape. He had uncontrollable diarrhea. We got a vet right away but there was nothing he could do."

"Did the dog die?" I asked, shocked.

"No," Debra snapped. "Kadu didn't die. But I couldn't show him, could I? I missed the preliminary judging which meant I had no shot at the finals the next night. I'm telling you, Sara got to Kadu. She wanted me out of her way and she accomplished that by taking out my dog."

"Did Sara win?"

Debra's shrug was unconvincingly elaborate. "I don't remember."

Like hell she didn't.

"That happened quite a while ago."

"So?"

"I'm sure there have been plenty of successes in your life since."

"Of course. And I know what you're thinking. That maybe I should have put this behind me by now. Trust me, I have. The only reason I tell that story is to show people what kind of person Sara is. Sometimes people meeting her don't understand. . . . Let's just say she makes a good first impression. And she uses that to her advantage."

That didn't sound so unusual to me.

"Doesn't everyone?"

"Sara uses it to her advantage with men." Debra spoke slowly, enunciating each word as if she were speaking to a not-very-bright child. "She collects trophies. She likes other women's boyfriends."

Ahhh.

"Yours, too?"

"Only one. That was enough. After that, I made sure she never met any of my male friends. Of course, he came running right back as soon as she lost interest. And believe me, Sara *always* loses interest. Sometimes overnight. She enjoys proving how attractive she is to other women's men a whole lot more than she likes having relationships with them."

Debra took another slug of water. She used the back of her wristband to wipe a thin sheen of sweat from her brow. The temperature in the tennis facility was purposely kept cool. The other women who had come off the courts with her were beginning to pull on jackets and cover-ups. I wondered why Debra was still sweating.

"When was the last time you and Sara were in touch?" I asked.

"Let me think." Her gaze wandered out to the courts. She didn't seem to be trying to remember, as much as deciding what to say. "I guess we spoke briefly last week. She called me."

"About what?"

"My husband, Jeff, is a lawyer in Greenwich. He's in litigation, and let's just say that he has a reputation for getting the job done. Sara was looking for a referral. She thought he might know someone. She told me she wanted a real shark."

"Did she say what for?"

"No, and I didn't ask. Frankly the thought that someone else Sara screwed was planning to drag her through the courts didn't bother me one bit. I told her to try Jeff at his office."

"Do you know if she did?"

"No, but if so, I doubt that they spoke. Jeff's never met Sara, but he's heard me mention her. I don't think he'd have taken her call."

The ladies at the other end of the lounge were beginning to stir. One by one, the matches on the courts were ending.

"That's my cue," Debra said, standing. "I've got to go."

"Just one more thing. Can you think of anyone who might have wanted to hurt Sara?"

Excluding yourself, I added silently.

Debra's raised brow let me know she knew what I was

thinking. "Let's see. Sara is a self-centered, totally auto-involved, egotistical rich bitch, who doesn't mind how much trouble she causes or who she hurts as long as she's happy. I'd say that leaves the field wide open, wouldn't you?"

12

For years I've resisted carrying a cell phone. Even now I do so only grudgingly, and mostly for the sake of security. But I have to admit there are times when having instant access to the rest of the world comes in very handy.

Back in the car, I dialed up Frank, told him I was only about twenty minutes away, and asked if he still had custody of my missing relatives.

"Sure do." He sounded happy enough about the arrangement. "Want to talk to them?"

Without waiting for an answer, my brother put Bob on. "It's about time you tracked us down," he said. "Didn't you find my note?"

"Yes, that's why I'm calling—"

"Come on over. The game's great. So's the pizza."

With incentives like those, who could resist?

"And your Aunt Peg is on her way."

That got my attention. "Why?"

"Who knows?" Bob asked blithely. "Peg dances to her own tune. I think this whole wedding thing is making her nervous."

Not Aunt Peg. Solving murders didn't make her nervous. Whelping premature puppies didn't make her nervous. Showing at Westminster didn't make her nervous. I doubted that something as simple as a family wedding could give her the jitters.

"I'm on my way," I said. "Do I need to stop and pick anything up?"

Bob repeated the question to the others and came back with a shopping list that included beer, bean dip and duct tape. Something about an indoor football toss gone awry.

The twenty minutes expanded to forty-five. By the time I reached Frank's apartment in Cos Cob, Aunt Peg's minivan was already parked on the street out front.

Frank lives on the first floor of a remodeled Victorian house. What was originally a large one-family home now holds three smaller apartments, with the house's elderly owner living upstairs. Being young and spry and usually short of cash, my brother pays for part of his rent by doing chores—mowing the lawn, painting, and carrying porch furniture up and down from the basement as the seasons change.

Once he and Bertie were married, however, Frank would be moving to her place in Wilton. There was no way she could bring the kennel-full of dogs that comprised her livelihood here.

"Hey, good to see you!" Frank opened the door, threw an arm around my shoulder, and pulled me close for a hug.

The spontaneous gesture of affection felt good. And I was in no position to take such things for granted. Not too long ago, my brother and I seemed to be continually at loggerheads. Our parents had died eight years earlier, and though we'd both been nominal adults by then, I'd found myself having to step into the role of responsible big sister all too often as Frank wandered aimlessly from one escapade to the next.

Recently, however, everything had changed. Frank had opened his own business, finally finding something he was good at and could actually make a living doing. And Bertie had come into his life.

What had happened next was a revelation. My little brother was in love: joyously, dizzily, head over heels in love. Watching him tumble for the statuesque redhead had been delightful; seeing him now try to live up to the good qualities she saw in him, an unexpected pleasure.

Though I'd been the one to introduce them, I'd never expected them to form a permanent bond. Never had I been so pleased to be taken by surprise.

Frank used the arm he had around my shoulder to pull me inside, grocery bags bumping against my legs as he nudged the door shut behind us.

"Nacho chips!" Davey cried, eyeing the bags greedily.

"Hello to you, too." I leaned down and swiped a kiss across my son's forehead, earning myself a glare filled with all the injured dignity a seven-year-old boy could muster.

Bob and Davey were sitting on the couch facing the TV. Aunt Peg had commandeered the only chair in the room, and it, too, was angled to face the screen.

Eve was snuggled in Davey's lap, but Faith had gotten up to greet me at the door. I reached down to stroke the soft skin beneath the Poodle's chin. She was probably happier than my relatives were to see me. Never let anyone tell you that dogs aren't a blessing.

I shifted the bags to one hand so I could give Faith a better scratch. "Aunt Peg, I didn't know you liked football."

"Let's just say I'm flexible. When in Rome . . ."

Which begged the question of what she was doing in Rome. Or in Cos Cob, as the case might be.

"Let me just put this stuff away," I said, heading for the kitchen. "I'll be right back."

The phone rang as I was pouring the bean dip into a bowl. I picked up and found myself talking to Bertie, calling to check in with Frank before she left a dog show in New Jersey for the two-hour ride home. Most people have weekends off. Not professional handlers, that's when they do the majority of their work.

"Melanie, good," she said, when she realized who she had on the line. "I needed to talk to you anyway. Have you found out anything about Sara?"

"Not much." I gave her a quick run-through of the day's events. "But I did come up with a couple of odd things. First of all, Titus."

"What about him?"

"Remember those big bowls of food and water we saw in Sara's cottage? Apparently they were meant for him. Sara left the dog behind and it looks as though that stuff was supposed to tide him over."

"That makes no sense. Titus went everywhere with Sara. If she had left of her own accord, she'd have taken him with her. And if she didn't, when did she have the chance to fill those bowls?"

"The whole thing is pretty strange," I said. "According to Delilah, someone from her kennel found Titus wandering around the grounds at the beginning of the week."

"And she still didn't think that meant something was wrong?" Bertie sounded outraged.

"Apparently not. Delilah said that Sara makes a habit of running when life gets tough." Leaning against the counter, I fished a chip out of the bag and ran it through the dip.

"Which leads me to my next point. Everyone I've spoken to has mentioned that Sara goes through a lot of boyfriends. That once she gets a guy, she loses interest pretty quickly. I'm wondering if she might have dumped someone who took things a little too personally."

"It's possible," Bertie mused. "But since we don't know who she was seeing . . ."

"You said she was with your cousin Josh last summer."

"Right."

"I was thinking I ought to talk to him. He might know who was next in line, and from there I could trace things up to the present."

"It's worth a try," Bertie agreed. "Let me call Josh and I'll have him get back to you."

"Great. Last thing: Debra Silver said that Sara was trying to get a referral for a lawyer. Do you have any idea what that was about?"

"A lawyer?" Bertie sounded surprised. "No. None. Grant's a lawyer. At least he used to be. I don't think he practices anymore, but if she'd had a problem, I would think Sara would have talked to him."

"According to Debra, she was looking for outside help. Not that it looks as though she found any. Do you think Sara might have run away because she felt threatened by someone?"

"I wish I knew. At least if she ran away, it means she's okay. But if that's the case, why hasn't she called anyone? Her note said she'd be in touch."

"It also said that you weren't supposed to believe everything you heard about her," I pointed out.

"So what have we heard?" Bertie sounded frustrated. "Hardly anything we didn't know already. This whole mess is driving me crazy, Melanie, and time is passing. This wedding's going to happen in some shape or form whether I'm ready or not. Do you suppose you could do me a favor?"

"Probably." When it comes to my family, I never commit without first hearing what's involved.

"Would you possibly have time to stop by a place called Pansy's Flowers? It's in Stamford, so it shouldn't be too far out of your way. Sara told me she thought they'd be the best place for what I wanted. She'd already contacted them about the kinds of bouquets and arrangements we'd need, and they were going to get back to her with prices. Of course, now I'm sure they're wondering whatever happened to us. Could you pick up a price list and let them know that we're still interested in their services?"

"Sure." That didn't sound too hard. "I can probably do it Monday after school."

"Thanks. You're such a help. That makes one less thing to worry about. Is Frank around?"

"Watching football in the other room. I'll go get him."

While Frank talked to Bertie, I grabbed a few moments alone with Aunt Peg. Like Bertie, she wanted to know how things were progressing. "There's something that occurred to me after we spoke yesterday," she said. "That note that Sara left for Bertie didn't make a whole lot of sense."

I nodded and snagged another nacho chip. After a moment, Aunt Peg followed suit.

"Sara said she thought she could count on Bertie, which, under the circumstances, seems backwards. Count on Bertie to do what? Sara was the one who was supposed to be helping Bertie, not the other way around."

"I know."

"Maybe she meant that as kind of a nudge. Maybe Delilah is right and Sara did run away. For whatever reason, she couldn't take Titus with her, but she was hoping Bertie would go to her house and find him."

"Why?"

Aunt Peg aimed a withering look in my direction. "Am I supposed to know everything?"

"Why not? It would certainly make my life easier."

She slid another chip through the bean dip. "All I'm trying to do is broaden your thinking."

"Aunt Peg, I don't need any more questions."

"Maybe you do. Maybe you're not asking the right questions, have you ever thought of that?"

Always.

But that was going to have to be tomorrow's problem. Now I was tired of tracking down answers that only seemed to lead to more puzzles. It was Saturday night, and I was declaring myself off-duty. I popped the top on a can of beer, picked up the chips and dip, and went out to the living room to join my family.

The next morning I was planning to sleep late. I was determined to sleep late. Come on, it was Sunday. My last chance for a whole week.

The telephone woke me up just before seven.

I heard the ringing in my sleep. For an addled moment, it seemed to be part of my dream. Then the dream vanished and I thought I'd set my alarm by mistake. By the third ring, after swatting the clock to no avail, I had one eye open and Eve was dancing on the bed.

I groaned, rolled over, and picked up the receiver.

"Hi, Mel, it's me."

Bob? What could he possibly want at this hour? He'd

been up just as late as I had the night before; our family gathering lasting through an impromptu dinner, followed by a killer game of team scrabble that had my ex and my aunt at each other's throats. Not that this was anything new.

Davey had been asleep on the couch by the time I'd loaded the two Poodles in the Volvo for the trip home. Bob had picked up his son and carried him outside, laying him gently on the back seat and tucking his jacket snugly around the small sleeping form.

When I'd thanked him for his help, Bob had offered to accompany me home. If I wanted.

It wasn't hard to see that he'd been disappointed when I shook my head. Now, a scant eight hours later, here he was again. If he said something suggestive about my being in bed, I was going to hang up on him.

"You there, Mel?" Bob asked. "Are you awake?"

"Not really." I hiked myself up on one elbow and debated how many seconds I could afford to waste before Eve lost control of her small puppy bladder on my comforter.

"You haven't seen today's paper?"

"Until the phone rang, Bob, today hadn't even started for me yet. Damn! Wait! Wait! Hold on!"

Dashing from side to side across the bed, Eve had that frantic look puppies get when they sense that a mistake is about to become inevitable. I threw back the covers, scooped her up, ran downstairs, and put her out the back door. Looking vastly relieved, the Poodle squatted at the bottom of the steps.

I hurried over to the counter and picked up the phone. "Still there?"

"I'm here." Bob didn't sound happy. "What the hell happened? Is everything okay? Do you need me to come over?"

"Everything's fine," I assured him. Awakened by our

hasty descent, Faith came trotting into the kitchen. I opened the door again and she joined Eve in the backyard. "Eve needed to go outside. She's still a baby and her housebreaking isn't perfect yet."

"Thank God." Bob exhaled. "I thought something was really wrong."

Waiting for the Poodles to finish outside, I pulled out a kitchen chair and sat. "Why would you think that?"

"There's a story on the front page of today's newspaper. You know that woman you and Bertie have been looking for? She seems to have turned up dead."

13

Shock bounced me up off the chair. Carrying the phone, I ran out to the front hall. "Bob, what are you talking about? What newspaper are you looking at? How did you know about Sara?"

Cradling the receiver between cheek and shoulder, I fumbled with the lock on the front door.

"It's called . . ." Pages flipped. "The *Greenwich Time*. Frank gets it delivered. It was outside the door this morning."

As if I cared where he'd gotten the paper from. Details! I wanted details.

The dead bolt slid free. I yanked open the door and ran outside. Frigid November air knifed right through my flannel pajamas. Bare feet freezing, I hopped from one to the other on the concrete step and scanned the yard. My paper boy has an erratic arm. Some mornings we're lucky he doesn't break a window.

The Sunday newspaper, rolled up in its plastic sack, was out by the sidewalk. I didn't get the same paper as Frank, but if there was a story, the *Advocate* would have it, too. Still carrying the phone, I skipped down the steps and ran across the dry winter grass. Good thing it hadn't snowed recently.

"Bertie's been talking about Sara all week," Bob was saying. "Frank filled me in on the details. Anyway, it looks like there was a house fire last night. Do you want me to read you the story?"

"No." I reached down, grabbed the paper, and raced back inside. I could only hope it was early enough on a Sunday morning that none of my neighbors had been watching. There are days when it seems like the show going on at my house is better than cable. "In a minute, I'll have it here. House fire? What house fire? Where was Sara?"

"New Canaan, it says. Some big estate."

Shivering, I shut the front door behind me and ran back to the kitchen, where the Poodles were now waiting outside that door. The Three Stooges probably deal with crisis better.

"You mean that whole huge house burned down?"

"No, not the big place. A guest cottage."

I yanked open the back door. The two dogs raced up the stairs, happily anticipating their peanut butter biscuits. What choice did I have but to go to the pantry? On top of that, my feet were still freezing. At this rate, I'd never get the paper opened.

"The cottage burned down?"

"Almost a complete loss. According to the article, it wasn't wired to any sort of smoke detection system, and nobody noticed the flames right away. By the time the fire department arrived, the place was already engulfed. The roof caved in as the first fire trucks were arriving. They never even had a chance to go inside. All they could do at that point was put the fire out."

"But Sara?" Now my teeth were chattering. Delayed reaction, probably. "What does it say about Sara?"

I heard the sound of more pages being turned, as I pulled a couple of large dog biscuits out of the box.

"Here it is." Bob skimmed through the details. "Charred remains discovered by a closet in the bedroom . . . no immediate identification possible . . . medical examiner believes it to be the body of a young woman.

"But listen to this. Here's how it ends.

> *Resident of the cottage, Sara Bentley, could not be reached for comment. According to her parents, on whose estate the house is located, Ms. Bentley's whereabouts are unknown.*"

"Damn," I said, sinking down into a chair.

All at once, I was simply too heavy, too filled with the weight of the bad news, to stand. Despite Bertie's fears, I'd held onto the hope that Sara would turn up. Now it looked as though I'd been wrong.

"Mel, are you there?"

"I'm here," I sighed.

"Don't go anywhere. I'm coming over."

It was surely a sign of how deflated I felt that I didn't even have the energy to argue. Instead, I called Aunt Peg. She's an early riser. I wondered if she'd gotten around to opening up her paper yet.

While the phone rang, I slid the plastic sleeve off my copy of the *Stamford Advocate* and spread the newspaper out on the kitchen table. There isn't a lot of crime in lower Fairfield County. Like the Greenwich paper, the *Advocate* had carried the New Canaan fire as front-page news.

I was scanning the article when Aunt Peg picked up on the fifth ring. It didn't contain any more facts than Frank had already given me.

"Melanie!" Aunt Peg sounded out of breath. "What's the matter?"

Despite the fact that I had other things to worry about, I was still piqued. "How did you know it was me?"

"Nobody calls at seven a.m. unless there's a problem." Her inference was clear: obviously nobody had as many problems as I did.

"I guess you haven't looked at today's paper yet."

"It's still out by the mailbox. Shall I go get it?"

"No, I can read you what's in front of me. Sara Bentley's cottage burned to the ground last night and the body of a young woman was found inside."

"Sara?" Peg gasped.

"It says that the body was badly burned and the police haven't been able to make an identification yet. They're seeking dental records from the owner of the cottage."

"Poor Delilah," Peg said softly. "I'll have to call her and see if there's anything I can do. Have you spoken to Bertie?"

"No, she's showing this weekend. I'm sure she left hours ago. I'll talk to her tonight. I wonder . . ." I stared down at the paper, drumming my fingers on the page.

"What?"

"Where had Sara been for the last week and why did she suddenly decide to come back? And why on the night that the cottage burned down?"

"Maybe she had something to do with the fire," said Peg, voicing my thoughts aloud. "Does it say what started it?"

"No." I read the official wording. "Cause of the blaze has yet to be determined. That could mean anything."

"Including that the fire marshall knows what happened but they just haven't released their findings yet." Aunt Peg paused. "Here's a gruesome thought."

"What?"

"What if Sara didn't return to her cottage last night?

What if she's been dead since she disappeared and the murderer brought her body back?"

"Oh, Lord." It was definitely too early in the morning for me to deal with possibilities like that.

Not Aunt Peg. She was functioning on all cylinders. "I wonder if Delilah and Grant have more information," she mused.

"Aunt Peg—"

"What? It's perfectly natural for a friend to pay a condolence call at a time like this."

"Not if you intend to grill the bereaved about the circumstances surrounding the death."

"Please, dear. Give me some credit for subtlety. Besides, considering the strange things that led up to it, do you honestly think that fire started by accident?"

"Not a chance."

"You see? We're in perfect agreement. I'll let you know what I find out. Bye!"

This time, taking no chances on Bob arriving before I was ready, I hurried through my shower and was fully dressed by the time he got there. I had bacon frying on the griddle and slices of warm French toast stacked on a plate on the counter when he let himself in the front door. By now the Poodles were getting so accustomed to Bob's presence that they didn't even bark at his arrival.

I wasn't at all sure how I felt about that.

"Good morning," he said, walking up behind me and slipping his arms around my waist. His face nuzzled my hair. "Something smells great."

"Must be the bacon." I edged sideways out of his grasp.

Bob's expression closed. "If you say so. Are you okay?"

"Fine. Breakfast's almost ready. All I have to do is go call Davey and get out the maple syrup—"

"That's not what I meant," he said firmly. "And I think you know it."

"I'm fine, Bob. Really, I am."

My voice didn't sound fine. It was skittering up and down. I picked up a long fork and began to turn the slices of bacon. A piece of fat sizzled and popped, shooting off the griddle to land on my wrist.

I sucked in a breath. Bob swore softly. Striding across the room, he grasped my arm and pulled me over to the sink. His other hand turned on the cold water. Reflexively I tried to pull my arm away.

"Quit struggling. This will make it feel better."

I knew that just as well as he did. But it didn't stop me from trying to pull away.

"Fine, she says," Bob muttered under his breath. He held my hand firmly as the stream of cold water did its job. "Everything's fine. Everything's always fine. For Pete's sake, Mel. A friend of yours just died. It's okay to let go a little. It's okay to be upset."

"Sara wasn't really a friend," I said, but I could feel my throat starting to quiver. "We just met for the first time last week."

"No wonder you're feeling stoic then. What the hell are you doing cooking breakfast, anyway?"

"You said you were coming over. I thought you'd be hungry."

And I'd thought the meal would provide a distraction.

"I didn't come because I wanted you to feed me." Now Bob sounded annoyed. He picked up a dish towel from the counter and dried the small red spot on my arm. "I came because I thought you might need me. But I guess that's always been our problem, hasn't it? You don't need me for anything."

"That's not true." I yanked my hand. This time, Bob let it go without protest. "I needed you when we were married. I needed you when you ran away. Once, I'd have given anything to have you with me. But that time is long gone now."

"It doesn't have to be." Bob's hands slid up my arms to my shoulders.

I didn't shrug him off. I could feel the heat of his palms through my shirt. I knew he was going to kiss me. I knew I was going to kiss him back. When he lowered his head, I rose to meet him.

And when the kiss ended, there were tears streaming down my face. Tears of loss, I knew that with every fiber of my being. Though I'd have had a hard time pinning down which loss had prompted them.

"Jeez." Bob tried out a joke. "It wasn't that bad, was it?" His thumb stroked my cheek gently, wiping the wetness away.

I managed a feeble smile. "I guess maybe I'm just not as hard as you think I am."

"I never said you were hard. I said you were strong. There's a big difference."

Behind me, I could smell the bacon beginning to burn. I turned away, swiping away the last of the tears with the back of my hand. "If I'm strong it's because I've had to be, for Davey's sake and my own."

"I know that." Bob pulled several sheets off the roll of paper towels, doubled them, and spread them on the counter so I could lay the bacon out to drain. "You haven't had things easy. All I'm saying is maybe you don't have to go it alone anymore. You loved me once, Mel. And we were good together; you know we were."

He was right, we had been good together. Briefly.

And I had loved him. With the sort of blinding, dizzying

devotion that only first love can bring. I'd grown a lot since those days. I couldn't go back there again. Nor would I want to.

"If you need me," Bob said softly, "I'm here for you."

I spoke without thinking. Words that should have come from my head came from my heart instead.

"I'll think about it," I heard myself say.

14

Aunt Peg never did get back to me on Sunday night. I could have called her, but that probably would have involved admitting that I'd spent the day with my ex-husband. Which was not something I wanted to discuss—or even, particularly, to think about. Especially since I'd enjoyed myself a good deal more than I'd expected to.

We didn't do anything special. In a way, that added to the day's charm. Seeing my son and his father together, engaged in such mundane activities as playing board games, making lunch, and throwing a ball for the dogs, tugged at my emotions in ways I never would have predicted. It was impossible not to see the resemblance between them; everything was right there in the set of a shoulder or the quirk of a brow.

And even though I knew perfectly well that we weren't a real family unit, it was nice, just for a little while, to pretend.

Bob even went so far as to volunteer to drop Eve off at Aunt Peg's on his way back to Frank's place on Sunday night. I thought that might prompt a reaction from my elder relative, but instead, the person I found myself talking to was Bertie.

I'd left a message that morning on her answering machine. She called Sunday evening as soon as she got back from the show. Actually, knowing Bertie, she'd probably already unloaded her van, fed and exed her dogs, then checked their water bowls before attending to her own needs. What she hadn't done yet was see a newspaper.

Briefly, I told her what had happened.

"I don't believe it," Bertie said firmly.

I'd expected shock, maybe anger. Not denial.

"Bertie, it's in today's newspaper. Sara's cottage burned down and they found a body in the rubble."

"How did the fire get started?"

"It doesn't say. I'm sure the police or an arson squad is investigating."

"It couldn't have been an accident." Bertie thought for a minute, considering the possibilities. "Someone did that to Sara on purpose. But when did she come back? And why didn't she call anyone?"

"That's pretty much what I'd like to know. And think about this: since we didn't know that Sara had come home, you have to wonder whether or not the person who set that fire did."

"You mean you think she might have been killed by mistake?"

"It's a possibility."

Bertie swore, loudly and vehemently. I held the receiver out away from my ear and let her blow off steam.

"Sara was a good person," she said at the end. "Flawed maybe, not perfect, but still a good person. This whole thing makes me sick. So now what?"

"What do you mean?"

"You will keep asking questions, won't you?"

"Bertie, it's not just our problem anymore. The police will be asking questions now—"

"And we'll never learn any more about what happened than we can read in the newspaper. Sara was worth more than that. She was a friend of mine and she was counting on me. You've met her parents. You know what they're like. Sara needs someone to be on her side. Come on, just give it a couple more days."

I didn't respond to her plea right away. Instead, I said, "Speaking of Sara's parents, Aunt Peg went to New Canaan to pay a condolence call. She'll probably have the latest news."

"Good. I knew you wouldn't be able to just let things drop." Bertie sounded pleased, as though she figured the matter was settled. She was probably right.

"By the way, I spoke to my cousin Josh. He'd be happy to talk to you about Sara. He's working in Greenwich, and when I told him you were at Howard Academy, he asked if he could stop by there tomorrow afternoon."

As tutor rather than teacher, my days tended to vary. It wasn't unusual for me to have blocks of unscheduled time. On Monday we were in luck.

"Tell him I'm free between one-thirty and two-fifteen. If I don't hear back from you, I'll assume it's a plan."

"Got it," said Bertie. "And Melanie?"

"Hmmm?"

"I appreciate the help."

"You should." I tried for a light tone, but didn't quite pull it off.

I wondered if Bertie was thinking the same thing I was. We weren't looking for a missing person anymore. Now we were hunting a murderer.

Howard Academy is a private school located on a beautiful campus just outside downtown Greenwich. Founded early in the last century by robber baron Joshua Howard, the school's stated aim was to provide the best possible education for children of privilege. Not unexpectedly, in these politically correct days, headmaster Russell Hanover II tries to downplay that aspect of the institution's charter. He has opened registration to all applicants, and a generous scholarship program is in place.

What that means for me is that the children I work with at Howard Academy are a varied and delightful group. My official title is Special Needs Tutor; my purpose, to ensure that every student receives as much individual attention as he or she might need to excel. One of the perks of working in the private school sector is that the administration has some flexibility when it comes to making rules. In keeping with the theory that Howard Academy should foster a child-friendly environment, I'd been given permission the previous spring to bring Faith to school with me.

The kids loved having her around, and I loved the fact that the big Poodle no longer had to wait at home all day for my return. Even the staid headmaster had been known to drop by my room occasionally and bring Faith a biscuit. The arrangement was working out beautifully for all of us.

I had Faith with me when I walked out to the school's front entrance at one-thirty on Monday afternoon. The class bell had just rung and the hallways were full. Even though the kids see Faith every day, she still caused a stir as we made our way through the upper school.

Many of the students who were hurrying by stopped to give her a quick pat or a kind word. Some congratulated me on her new status, which, to my surprise, had been the subject of an announcement at morning assembly the previous week.

"Champion Faith," said a girl named Jane, one of my former pupils, who was now the undisputed star of the girls' field hockey team. She leaned down to brush her hands through the Poodle's hair. "Aren't you something special?"

"Special enough that all that hair is coming off in a few weeks. Pretty soon she'll look like a normal dog."

"I like you just the way you are," Jane told Faith, who wagged her tail happily. The feeling was mutual.

Faith and I reached the reception area just as a green Mazda Miata was pulling up the driveway. Bertie's cousin was right on time. Howard Academy's main building, which houses the administrative offices as well as a number of classrooms, was originally designed to blend in with the other mansions in the neighborhood. Drawing rooms serve as meeting areas, and the front hall is furnished with antiques from Joshua Howard's own collection.

I was waiting there when the Miata pulled into the circle out front and parked beside the wide steps.

The picture I'd seen at Sara's house didn't do Josh justice. Like his cousin, he was a stunner. Tall and broad-shouldered, he unfolded his lanky frame from the small convertible, brushed back his shaggy blond hair, and squinted up at Howard Academy's imposing facade. I had the front door open by the time he reached the top of the steps.

"Melanie?" he asked hopefully, sticking out a hand. "The description Bertie gave me wasn't exactly precise."

I could imagine why. I have light brown shoulder-length hair and hazel eyes, and stand just above average height at five feet six, none of which are the sort of attributes likely to make me stand out in a crowd.

"She was right, though," Josh added. "You do have a great smile."

"Thanks."

"This must be Faith." He leaned down and greeted the Poodle with fingers outstretched for her to sniff.

"Don't tell me Bertie described my dog, too?"

"Of course. Isn't that how everyone does things?"

I wish.

Josh was a doll. It was easy to see why Sara had been interested. I wondered what had brought the relationship to an early demise.

"Come on in." I led the way to one of the drawing rooms. "I really appreciate your coming over to see me."

"No problem. I work on Railroad Avenue. Graphic design. Since you're in school all day, I figured my schedule might have a little more leeway than yours. Bertie seemed to think it was important that we get together. She said you wanted to ask me some questions about Sara Bentley?"

"Yes." I took a seat in a damask-covered arm chair. Josh sat down on a couch opposite. Faith checked out the area thoroughly and chose a place on the rug near my feet that was warmed by sunlight streaming in through the high leaded windows. "I guess you've heard . . . ?"

"About the fire?" Josh nodded. "All I know is what I read in the paper, though."

Monday morning's edition had continued its coverage, though not much information had been added. The fire was now reported to have been of suspicious origin. Positive identification of the body had yet to be made.

"I don't know a whole lot more myself. The reason I got involved is because Bertie had hired Sara to plan her wedding."

"I wouldn't know anything about that." Josh looked uncomfortable. "Sara and I broke up at the end of August. We haven't been in touch lately."

I gazed down at Faith, then let my hand drop, fingers tangling in her long hair. I've found that sometimes people open up more easily when they're not the sole focus of your attention.

"I guess your relationship didn't end too well."

"You could say that. Then again, I'm sure Sara would have a different version. She was the one who ended things. Dumped me flat."

Judging by Josh's disgruntled expression, he hadn't had to deal with much rejection from the fairer sex.

"How come?"

"I guess she found somebody that suited her needs a little better."

"Any idea who?"

"No. I didn't think about that at the time, but afterward I realized it was a little odd."

"In what way?"

Josh paused a moment, getting his thoughts in order. "The thing about Sara was that she liked to talk about herself. A lot. She found her life fascinating and she figured other people did, too. I knew who Sara's boyfriend had been before me. And who the guy was before that. Hell, she not only talked about them, she kept their pictures on her mantelpiece. Like they were some sort of trophies or something."

I wondered if Josh knew that his own photo had been added to the collection.

"So it seemed a little strange that she never did any bragging about this new guy, whoever he was."

"Maybe she didn't want to hurt your feelings," I ventured.

"I guess you didn't know her very well, did you?"

"No."

"When Sara got into one of her moods, hurt feelings were a specialty of hers. When she lashed out, she didn't care who got in the way. Sara wasn't a mean person, but she could be thoughtless. I always figured the problems went back to the way she was brought up."

"I've met Sara's mother and stepfather," I said.

"Then you probably have some idea what I'm talking about. Some people see that big house and all that money and figure she grew up in the lap of luxury, with never a care in the world. Nothing could be further from the truth.

"Sara spent her whole childhood trying to live up to her mother's impossibly high expectations and never quite succeeding. Delilah figured that any child who'd been given as much as Sara had should excel at everything she did. And coming in second in anything was never going to be good enough."

"Do you suppose that's why Sara had so many boyfriends?" I mused aloud. "Maybe she felt she had to find the perfect relationship."

"I don't know. Judging by what happened between her and me, I'd be willing to bet that most of those relationships fizzled due to lack of interest. Sara wasn't really into working to make things come together. She liked having a good-looking guy on her arm to show off, but emotionally she was pretty withdrawn.

"We were together for two months, which I guess is a long time for Sara, but I never got the impression that I was anything more than a convenience for her, a good buddy that she enjoyed hanging out with when it suited her. There was always a certain reserve to Sara, like she wanted you to know that you were only going to get so far with her, and no further."

Josh sounded bitter, and I wasn't sure I could blame him.

"Do you mean sexually?" I asked.

"Hell no," he sputtered. "Though now that you mention it, she was kind of detached there, too. I mean"—his cheeks grew pink—"it's not like I'm some great stud or anything, but I don't usually have many complaints. With Sara, sometimes it was like she was just going through the motions."

Josh sat back on the couch and frowned. "Look, I was upset when Sara dumped me. She's a great girl and when you're with her, life's an instant party. There's always something wild going on.

"But in a way, when we split up, it was kind of a relief. There were lots of times when I got the impression that Sara wanted more, or maybe needed more, than I could give her. I don't want to sound like I'm spouting psycho-babble or anything, but Sara had issues, you know what I mean?"

I was beginning to. "Did Bertie tell you that Sara had disappeared about a week before the fire?"

"Yeah, she mentioned something about it. Frankly, I don't know that I'd have been all that concerned. Sara could be pretty unpredictable. . . ."

Josh stopped speaking. He swallowed heavily and stared at the hands folded in his lap. "I guess Bertie was right to be worried, wasn't she? Judging by how things turned out, Sara did need help, and nobody was there for her."

"There's no way you could have known that," I said gently.

"Maybe not." Josh's eyes lifted and found mine. "But that new guy of hers—whoever he was—he should have. Someone should have been looking out for her. Lord knows, she didn't always have enough sense to look out for herself."

Roused by the anger in Josh's voice, Faith raised her head. I reached down and soothed the Poodle by cupping her muzzle in the palm of my hand and rubbing her lip with my thumb.

"Can you think of anyone who might have wanted to hurt Sara? Anyone she ever talked about having a problem with?"

"Only her mother. But Delilah had no reason to want to harm Sara now. She'd had her whole life to screw Sara up. Anyone could see that Delilah had already done enough damage."

15

After Josh left, I grabbed a jacket from my classroom and took Faith outside for a walk. The Howard Academy grounds are spacious and inviting. My Poodle enjoys taking a spin around the playing fields just as much as I do. She bounced joyously at my side as I headed across the teachers' parking lot and down the hill beyond.

The chill of November in Connecticut was in the air. A carpet of newly fallen leaves blanketed the ground. I burrowed my hands deep in my pockets and kicked up my feet as I walked. Dry leaves crackled and eddied upward in the breeze.

Faith raced on ahead to check out a boys' soccer game, then doubled back to my side. Tail wagging, lips lifted in a grin, she was ready for whatever I wanted to do next. I wrapped her face in my hands, smacked a loud kiss on her nose, then sent her back out to run some more. Gleefully Faith obliged.

Following at a much slower pace, I considered what Josh had had to say. While he'd been talking about Sara, I couldn't help but be reminded of what had happened between Sam and me. Though he and I had been together a lot longer than Josh and Sara, both relationships had come to the same abrupt and sorry end. Josh and I had both been dumped.

Even now, months later, the memory still had the power to make me wince.

Looking back, I still wasn't entirely sure where I'd gone wrong. I'd known Sam for months before I allowed myself to consider the possibility of anything serious happening between us. And once we started seeing each other, I tried to take things slow. I'd worried about Davey's feelings, and hoped desperately that I was doing the right thing.

But somewhere along the way, I'd lost control of the process. I'd fallen in love and found my focus narrowing from a whole world of possibilities to the thought of a life that included only one man: Sam. Once I got used to the idea, it made perfect sense.

It made me perfectly happy.

Right up until the day Sam left.

In the last four months, I'd run through a lengthy gamut of emotions. By turns I'd been shocked, wounded, vulnerable, aching. Oh, yes, and seriously pissed. It had taken me a while to work my way around to that stage, but once it arrived, it felt pretty good. Better than the alternatives, anyway.

And speaking of alternatives, I thought, feeling distinctly grumpy, what was I supposed to do with Bob? I must have been crazy to kiss him. Crazier still to tell him I'd think about what he'd said.

What was there to think about? Bob said he'd changed, and maybe he had. He still hadn't grown up enough to figure out how to make his marriage to Jennifer work, however. Or how to be more than a long-distance father to his son. The last thing I needed was the turmoil of another uncertain relationship.

Why was it, I wondered, that the only men who seemed to find me were the ones who hadn't found themselves yet?

Faith barked sharply, racing toward me across an empty hockey field. She was staring at the upper school building. I glanced at my watch and swore softly. The change-of-class bell had probably just rung. In another minute I'd be late.

"Thanks, sweetie," I said, swooping down to give the Poodle a brief hug. We ran back up the hill, Faith leading the way.

Men. Who needs them when you can have dogs?

After school, I drove home with trepidation. Turning onto my road, I'd half decided that if Bob's car was sitting out front, I was going to keep on driving. I didn't think of it as taking the coward's way out, but rather as a necessary ploy for conserving energy. Some days just keeping up seems to take all I have.

Luckily for me, I didn't have to make the choice. My driveway was empty. I pulled in, unpacked the car, let Faith out back, and had shortbread cookies and a glass of milk ready when Davey's school bus came lumbering down the road fifteen minutes later.

"How was school?" I asked my son, helping him off with backpack and jacket.

"Good." He's reached the age of monosyllabic answers.

"Did you have fun?"

"Mo-om!" His voice rose and fell, its tone conveying the idiocy of the question. "It's *school*."

Right. As if I'd forgotten. Presumably due to the memory loss that comes with advancing age.

"Eat your snack," I said. "When you're done, we have to run downtown to a store called Pansy's Flowers."

Davey scooped up a handful of cookies. "Why?"

His new favorite question.

"I need to run an errand for Bertie. She wants me to check on the floral arrangements for the wedding."

My son's brow furrowed as he chewed. "Dad's coming to the wedding," he said finally.

I'd been standing at the sink, watching Faith through the window. I turned around slowly.

"You're right, he is. Frank asked him to. That's why he's here." Words seemed to sputter out of me in fits and starts.

"He came to see us, too."

"Of course he did." I moved across the room and sank to my knees beside his chair. "Your father loves being with you. You know that."

"Not just me. Dad came to see you, too."

"Well . . ."

"He did." Davey's voice was firm, half daring me not to believe him. "I heard him tell Uncle Frank."

Oh, Lord, I thought. He's only seven, and none of this is his fault. Why does he have to be in the middle?

"Are you and Daddy going to get married again?"

My stomach muscles clenched. Wildly I searched for answers, wanting, needing to say just the right thing. I reached across the table and folded my son's small hand into mine.

"Your father and I both love you very much. You know that, right?"

"Yes." Davey was frowning. "But what about Sam?"

"Sam loves you, too," I said, squeezing his hand.

"When is he coming back?"

For a minute I didn't move at all. There was only one way I could answer that question. The best thing I could do for my son was to tell him the truth.

"I don't know."

"Me either," Davey said matter-of-factly. He reached for another cookie. "I miss Sam."

"I do, too, honey."

"Will Daddy leave when Sam comes back?"

And I'd thought the "why" questions were hard.

"I don't know that either," I admitted. "Maybe before. I think he'll leave after the wedding."

"Maybe Sam will come to the wedding." Davey's tone was carefully neutral, but his eyes were bright with hope.

"I don't think so. He's been gone a while now. He doesn't even know that Bertie and Frank are engaged."

"Yes, he does. Aunt Peg told him."

I sighed and reached for a shortbread cookie. Aunt Peg and Sam had long been pals. I should have guessed that they'd remain in touch. And that she wouldn't see fit to mention that fact to me.

"Does Aunt Peg talk to Sam a lot?"

"Only sometimes. When he calls to check up on us. Sometimes Aunt Peg tells me he said to say hi. But I'm not supposed to tell you."

Undeterred by his lapse, Davey lifted his glass and finished off the last of his milk. Then he slid down off his chair. "I'm full. Are we going to go now?"

"Sure." I reached out and ruffled his hair. Davey scowled and pulled away, as I'd known he would. Sometimes there's nothing you can do but marvel at the resilience of youth.

And the sneakiness of aging aunts.

Pansy's Flowers was a twenty minute drive away, tucked on a small side street off the Post Road in southwest Stamford. I'd been expecting a flower shop. Instead, Davey and I found ourselves at a full-fledged nursery. A high chain-link fence surrounded an acre of land—a generous allotment in that pricey commercial zone. It looked as though Pansy's Flowers was flourishing.

I drove between rows of bundled bushes and trees and pulled into a parking space in front of a glass-and-cedar building with an enormous greenhouse attached along the back. Wind chimes, nudged by the door, jingled as Davey and I entered. Inside the store, the air was redolent with the heady aroma of damp earth and healthy plants.

A profusion of greenery filled the big room. Leaves reached out to brush our faces as we walked. The sound of water trickling in a dozen fountains provided the perfect backdrop.

"Wow." Eyes wide, Davey sucked in a breath. "It's like a jungle in here." His hand slithered out of mine. "Can I go look around?"

I glanced in both directions. Breakable items seemed to be at a minimum. "Okay. But don't touch anything."

I'd barely finished speaking before he vanished, melting into the thick foliage. Verdant hanging fronds slipped silently back into place, leaving no trace of where he'd gone. I hoped I wouldn't have too much trouble finding him again.

A counter ran along the store's back wall. By the time I reached it, a heavy-set woman with gray-streaked hair and a confident stride had emerged through a door behind it. She wiped her fingers on her flower-sprigged apron and offered me a friendly smile.

"Can I help you?"

"I'd like to speak with the person who's in charge of arranging flowers for weddings."

"That would be me."

"Are you Pansy?"

Her smile widened. "Patricia. That's what most people call me now. Pansy was a childhood nickname, just like all this"—she waved a hand to indicate the lush surroundings—"was a childhood dream. When the time came that I could open up the business, the two just seemed to go together."

Made sense to me.

"If possible, I'd like to check on the status of some plans you may have discussed. . . ."

As I was speaking, Patricia reached under the counter, pulled out a box of files, and hefted it up onto the shelf. "Bride's name?"

"Alberta Kennedy."

She began to flip through the copious records.

"The woman you would have spoken to was Sara Bentley. I know she called for information and maybe got some prices, but I don't think she'd gotten around to placing an order. You may not have a record—"

"Honey." Patricia's gaze flickered upward. "I keep records of everything. Here." She slipped some papers from a sleeve. "Alberta Kennedy. December twenty-third. Wedding at St. Michael's, reception at the Greenwich Country Club. Is that the one?"

"That's it," I said, amazed. "We didn't realize Sara had gotten that far—"

"Daffodils, narcissi, and jonquils for the bridal bouquet," Patricia read. She picked up a pair of glasses that hung around her neck and rested them on her nose. "Not too big, she said, nothing flashy. Two floral arrangements for the altar—yellow tulips, if possible. In December, no less. I was going to check on that, and Sara was going to get back to me. We still had the centerpieces for the reception to talk about."

"Um." I cleared my throat softly. "That's actually why I'm here. Sara, the woman who was planning Bertie's wedding, won't be getting back to you. She died over the weekend."

Patricia's hand dropped. Her fingers opened and the pages scattered across the counter. "Oh, I'm so sorry. That poor girl, I just talked to her. She seemed like such a nice person. What happened?"

"There was a fire in her home in New Canaan. Maybe you read about it in the paper?"

"I saw the headlines. But I never realized who it was, poor thing. You just never know when your time is up, do you?" She busied herself gathering the papers into a tidy heap. "And when I spoke to her last week, she sounded so happy, so upbeat. What a sad, sad—"

For a moment I thought I'd misheard her. I held up a hand to stop the flow of words. "I'm sorry, what did you say?"

"Well, you know we'd only met that one time when she stopped in, but she seemed like a sweet girl. And last week on the phone she was so cheerful. I guess it's a kindness, really, that she had no idea what was to come."

"I think you're mistaken," I said slowly. "Sara wasn't talking to anyone on the phone last week. She disappeared the weekend before."

Patricia looked confused. She pushed up her glasses and consulted her notes again. "I wouldn't be mistaken about a thing like that. My memory isn't as strong as it used to be, and in my business I can't afford to get details wrong. That's why I write everything down. Here it is; see for yourself."

I looked down to the place on the top page that her finger indicated.

"It's right there in black and white," Patricia said firmly. "Sara Bentley called me on Wednesday, November tenth. She'd gotten the price list I'd sent her and she okayed some of the flowers we'd spoken about. I don't know anything about a disappearance, but that was her I was talking to, all right."

16

My fingers gripped the edge of the counter as I stared down at Patricia's meticulous records. So Sara had been alive and well last week. Well enough to contact a stranger about plans for Bertie's wedding, apparently, but not enough to call Bertie herself, who'd been frantic with worry over her friend's whereabouts.

"Do you have any idea where Sara called you from?"

"Home, I guess. Or maybe her office, since it was during business hours?"

"Sara didn't work in an office." I was thinking aloud as much as offering an explanation. "And she wasn't at home either. None of her friends had been able to get in touch with her all week."

"Sorry." Patricia shrugged. "I wouldn't have any idea about that. The only thing we talked about were the flowers for the wedding."

Too bad. "What about the price list? When did you mail that to Sara?"

"Oh, I didn't mail it. Sara said she had a fax. That's why I figured she was probably in an office somewhere."

I didn't remember seeing a fax machine in Sara's cottage. "Do you have the number you sent it to?"

Patricia flipped to another sheet. "Right here, with her address and phone number. She gave it to me the first time we spoke."

The address Sara had listed was her home in New Canaan. The phone number had a New Canaan exchange. But the number for the fax began with a 914 area code: Westchester County.

I stared at the number for a minute, thinking about what to do next. Sara had been missing for most of a week, only to turn up dead. I wanted to know where she'd been in the interim.

"You have a fax machine here, right?"

Patricia nodded.

"Do you mind if I send something?"

"I guess not." She produced a pen and a clean sheet of paper, and watched me write out a message.

> *To whoever receives this fax, please contact me as soon as possible. I am looking for information about my friend, Sara Bentley. I'd be grateful for any assistance you can offer.*

I added my name and phone number at the bottom, then walked around the counter and followed Patricia to a small office. The fax machine was on a shelf, beside a desk. I punched out the number and watched the transmission go through. A confirmation slip printed out and fell into the tray.

"Do you think that'll help?" Patricia asked.

"I don't know," I said.

I hoped it couldn't hurt.

When we got home, I got Davey settled at the kitchen table with his homework, then went down to the basement and opened up Faith's portable grooming table. Now that the Poodle had finished her championship, I'd found myself slacking off on the all-important coat care that had taken up so much of my time over the past two years.

As long as Faith's points were in order, it wouldn't matter. The minute I received notification from the American Kennel Club, I planned to put a five-blade on my clipper and run it over her entire body. On the other hand, if anyone's championship could go unconfirmed, it was probably my dog's. Just in case, it was time I paid Faith's coat some much-needed attention.

I'd just hopped the Poodle up on the table when the phone rang.

"I'll get it!" Davey sang out from upstairs.

Talking on the telephone is one of his favorite pastimes, and since my son doesn't get many phone calls, he often tries to snag mine. Unwary callers may find themselves entertaining him for fifteen minutes or more. On the plus side, he's great at taking care of those pesky telemarketers.

This time I gave him five minutes, left Faith lying on the table, and walked up to the top of the steps. "Who is it?" I asked, poking my head out through the doorway.

As usual, Davey was chatting away, his body wriggling with animation as he recounted in minute detail the events of his school day. I had to ask the question twice.

Finally, he turned in his seat, carefully covering the bottom half of the receiver with his hand as he'd seen me do. "Aunt Peg. I'm telling her about social studies."

"Does she want to talk to me?"

"I don't know." As if the thought had never even occurred to him. "I'll ask her."

This involved another several minutes of discussion on both their parts. By the time the issue had been resolved, I was back in the basement brushing again.

It takes two hands to tease mats out of a neglected coat. When Davey called down that Aunt Peg wanted to speak to me, I reached over and put her on the speaker phone. The fact that we had an extension in the basement at all was a symptom of how much of my life I'd been devoting to Poodle hair.

"What happened to you?" I asked.

"What do you mean?"

"I expected to hear from you last night."

"I've been busy," Aunt Peg said huffily. "Am I supposed to check in with you every day?"

Well, now that she mentioned it . . . yes.

"Did you visit Grant and Delilah?"

"Twice," Peg said with satisfaction. "I was there yesterday and today."

Faith flinched as my comb caught in a snarl of hair. I patted her rump reassuringly and began to gently work the knot apart, starting at the outer edge and working in. "How'd you manage that?"

"You're not the only one in the family who can think on her feet. As a matter of fact, I think I find myself rather well suited for this detecting business."

Heaven forbid.

"When I arrived on Sunday afternoon, as you might expect, there was quite a lot going on. Family and friends stopping by to offer support. Some sort of specialized police and fire unit combing through what remained of the cottage. Even the local press was there. Delilah was harried, to say the least."

"Not grief stricken?" Fingers still busy, I had to pull the comb out of my mouth to ask.

There was a moment of silence on the line.

"Everyone handles loss differently," Aunt Peg said finally. "But no, Delilah didn't seem to be overwhelmed by grief. Indeed, if anything, she was behaving like the ringmaster of a rather unwieldy circus.

"Which doesn't mean she wasn't in pain," Peg was quick to point out. "Perhaps taking charge like that was her way of controlling her emotions until she could deal with them in private. Grant, on the other hand, never came downstairs at all. Delilah apologized for his absence and said their doctor had given him a sedative."

"So much for gender stereotypes."

"Delilah's a very strong woman. Make no mistake about that. I know for a fact that she rides roughshod over both the kennel clubs she belongs to, and some would say she's done the same to each of her husbands."

"Not to mention her daughter." I told her about the conversation I'd had with Josh.

"I can't say I'm surprised," Peg said at the end. "Delilah always has been driven. She's the sort of person who knows what she wants and goes after it, and she can't understand how others can lack her determination. After that episode with Sara in Junior Showmanship, there were plenty of people who felt that she'd been pushing the girl much too hard."

"That dog wasn't poisoned, by the way." I gave a final comb-through to the mat I'd been working on and moved to the next. "Only given a laxative so it couldn't compete at Westminster. I got the facts from the other junior handler, who's now grown up, married, and living in Greenwich."

"You see?" said Aunt Peg. "That's what happens when you listen to gossip. Everybody adds a little bit to the story and pretty soon the whole thing gets blown all out of proportion."

Taking the high road, I neglected to mention that it was she, not I, who'd supplied the errant details in the first place.

"How did you manage to finagle another invitation back to the Warings'?" I asked instead. "And what did you find out while you were there?"

"The first part was easy." Aunt Peg sounded smug. "I simply told Delilah that I needed her help. Drawing on the length, if not the strength, of our friendship, I led her to believe that I was nervous about my upcoming judging debut and asked if she had any advice to pull me through."

"I didn't know Delilah was a judge."

"That's because she seldom takes assignments. Delilah would much rather breed and exhibit. Then, too, judging often involves a fair amount of travel. At one time, she didn't seem to mind, but once she married Grant she decided she'd rather stay home. Delilah's been approved for most of the herding breeds for more than a decade. Of course she was happy to give me a few pointers, and I was happy to offer to come back today when things would have calmed down."

Good old Aunt Peg. She didn't miss a trick.

I tapped Faith's flank and she leaned up, then rolled over onto her other side. Once again I parted the hair down the middle of her back. "And?"

"For starters, the fire in the cottage was set deliberately. There's no question about that."

"Do the police have any leads?"

"Not that they've told Delilah about, but she's quite sure they're mounting a very thorough investigation."

"What about . . ." I stopped, sighed, then plunged on. There was simply no delicate way to put this. "What about the body? Do they know for sure that it was Sara?"

"Not yet. At least not by this afternoon. The authorities need Sara's dental records, and for some reason there's been a delay in procuring them. All I know is that it's the kind of bureaucratic screw-up that left Delilah screaming into the phone about the incompetence of hired help. I'm told things should be sorted out by tomorrow.

"One thing they do know for sure," Aunt Peg continued. "The fire *was* the cause of death. So your theory that Sara may have been killed earlier in the week seems to have been wrong."

"As it happens, I found that out for myself today."

"Really? How?"

I brought her up to date on my visit to Pansy's Flowers. "Patricia's absolutely sure she spoke with Sara last Wednesday. They had a perfectly normal conversation about the arrangements for Bertie's wedding."

"How very odd," Peg mused. "So despite Bertie's concerns, Sara seems to have been fine last week if you overlook the fact that she'd left behind dog and cell phone and disappeared."

"Apparently so." I exchanged my pin brush for a slicker and moved on to Faith's bracelets. "But I may have a lead on where she was staying. Patricia faxed Sara a price list earlier in the week, and she knew Sara had received it because they talked about the details on the phone. The fax went to a phone number in Westchester with an Armonk exchange." I'd come up with that last piece by dialing information and asking.

"The police could find out whose number that is."

"I know. I'm going to drop by New Canaan and tell them about it tomorrow after school. In the meantime, I used Patricia's fax machine to send a message to the same number, asking whoever received it to contact me to talk about Sara."

"You did *what?*"

I figured she'd heard me, so I kept right on brushing.

Time, tide, and Poodle hair wait for no man. Or something like that.

"Melanie, dear girl, what were you thinking?"

"Simple. That I might put myself in touch with someone who knew where Sara'd been for the last week."

"Did it ever occur to you that you may have faxed your name to a murderer?"

My hands stilled. "Uhh . . . no."

Her windy sigh reverberated through the phone line. "Not only that, but by using his fax number, you told him you were hot on his trail."

"But I'm not."

"Precisely the problem," Aunt Peg said sternly. "Isn't it?"

17

I didn't get a lot of sleep on Monday night. The third time I got up and went prowling around the house, checking the locks on windows and doors and flipping on the outside lights to scan the yard, Faith slipped down off Davey's bed and came to keep me company. Together we padded through the quiet rooms. As always, the comfort and support her presence offered made me feel much better.

We ended up on the living-room couch: me reading Harry Potter and drinking hot chocolate; Faith resting her muzzle on my knee and snoring softly. I must have begun to doze around dawn. By the time Davey came tearing down the steps in his pajamas at seven-thirty looking for Faith, I'd managed to sleep through my own alarm, which, once awake, I could hear buzzing in my bedroom upstairs.

Oops.

I put Faith outside, told Davey to choose his own clothes, unwrapped a couple of Pop-Tarts, threw them in the microwave, and called it breakfast. My shower took two minutes;

I brushed my teeth even faster. Davey made the bus, but just barely. His outfit was eye-catching: sweater, sweatpants, socks, and turtleneck, all in varying shades of his favorite color, red. Good thing his teacher had a sense of humor.

Of course, I missed the first bell at Howard Academy. Luckily, Russell Hanover wasn't around to witness my transgression. The headmaster seemed to have a sixth sense about things like that. The few times he'd caught me running late were memorable enough for me not to want to make a habit of it.

Still, I knew I was probably doomed to spend the day playing catch-up. Then Bertie appeared unexpectedly during third period and undid all the rest of my plans, too.

When she arrived, a fifth-grader named Sydney Kelly and I were busy outlining a book report. A hellion on the soccer field, Sydney expended more energy lacing her sneakers than she devoted to her school work. Her father was a Wall Street wizard who contributed often and generously to the Howard Academy endowment fund.

Though our esteemed headmaster claimed not to be influenced by such considerations, Mr. Hanover was quite sure that all Sydney needed was a little special attention to bring her grades up to speed. As you can probably tell, what special needs tutor means in the public school sector and what it connotes in the rarefied world of Greenwich private academies are often two entirely different things.

The distinction was probably lost on Bertie, who came bursting into my classroom as though a pack of Bloodhounds was on her trail. I looked up as the door flew open.

"I have to talk to you!"

"Now?"

"Now's good," Sydney offered.

What kid doesn't like to see her studies interrupted?

I stood up from the table, pointing the fifth-grader firmly back toward the book we'd been scanning. Sure, like that was going to work.

"Bertie, what are you doing here? Why didn't the office call me?"

"What office?" Obviously the check-in procedure had been lost on my sister-in-law-to-be. "I parked in the lot and came in through the back door. I've been sticking my head in every classroom I came to."

I closed my eyes briefly, trying not to envision how much chaos that must have caused. When I opened them again, Bertie was still standing there. She was beginning to look impatient.

"Bertie, I'm in the middle of a session right now."

"I can wait," Sydney said helpfully.

I jabbed my finger down on the page. The child didn't even glance at it. Why would she, when the show we were putting on was so much better?

"It's important," said Bertie.

"I should hope so."

"You'll never believe what just happened." She strode across the room, pausing briefly to greet Faith, who was lying on a cedar chip bed near my desk.

"What?" asked Sydney.

Clearly I was losing this battle.

"Sydney, this is a friend of mine, Bertie Kennedy. Bertie, Sydney Kelly, who needs to get at least a *B* on this book report or the coach is going to take her off the middle school soccer team."

"Hey," said Bertie.

"Hey back." Sydney grinned.

Bertie stopped beside the table. Her brow furrowed as her gaze settled on me. "You look like hell. Those pouches under your eyes could hide a baby kangaroo. What's the matter?"

"Late night." I tried to shrug it off. "Early morning."

"Not Bob again?"

"Who's Bob?" asked Sydney.

At least she hadn't commented on the kangaroo thing. A better teacher might have slipped in a quick lesson on metaphors, but right at the moment I wasn't feeling up to it.

"No, not Bob. Other problems."

"You think you've—"

I held up a warning hand. For once, Bertie paid attention. She stopped speaking and glanced at Sydney. The girl was watching us with the same sort of rapt attention most kids reserve for MTV.

"Sydney," I said, "do you think you can work on your outline by yourself for a few minutes?"

"No."

"Can you try?"

"Do I have to?"

"Do you want to play soccer?"

"I guess." The pained expression she managed to arrange on her features didn't bode well for the teenage years to come.

"We'll be right over there." I pointed to the back of the room. "This won't take long."

"That's what you think," Bertie muttered under her breath.

"What?" I asked as we walked away. "What could possibly be so important that you would drive all the way down to Greenwich—"

"Speaking of which," Bertie interrupted, "do you know that your school office doesn't put personal calls through to teachers unless it's an emergency? Like life and death? Which, come to think of it, this almost is?"

Two chairs sat face to face beneath a map of the United States. I pulled one out and sat down. Calmly.

Bertie was exaggerating. She had to be. I decided to concentrate on the first part of what she'd said and ignore the last for now.

"I thought you said you didn't know anything about the office."

Her smile was sly. "Not exactly. What I meant to imply was that they didn't know anything about me. Why do you think I came in the back door?"

I should have known.

"Is this about the wedding? Because if it is—"

"It's about Sara." Bertie sat down, then immediately shot to her feet again as if her news was too exciting to be contained in a seated position. "You'll never guess what happened!"

I hate people who make me guess. I didn't even try.

Looking annoyed, Bertie sat back down. Much more of this and I was going to get seasick.

"She called me this morning."

I heard what she said, but the words didn't make sense. Maybe it was the lack of sleep.

"Who?"

"Sara!" Bertie cast a quick glance at Sydney, who was pretending to read her book, then leaned closer and said, "You'll never believe this—Sara isn't dead. I just spoke to her an hour ago."

"What do you mean she isn't dead? Where is she?"

"Who isn't dead?" Sydney piped up.

"Your English teacher," Bertie said. "So get back to work

before she comes in here, finds out you've been slacking off, and beats your butt."

"Threatening children is out of fashion in today's educational process," I told Bertie.

"Yeah," Sydney agreed, not looking cowed in the slightest.

I gave her the glare. You know the one. She pretended to go back to her book. Bertie shook her head, sucking back a grin. I hadn't known her as a child, but I'd be willing to bet that she and Sydney had a lot in common.

I grabbed my chair and pulled it, scraping across the linoleum floor, until Bertie and I were sitting knee to knee. "What's going on?" I demanded.

"Hell if I know. But whoever that body in the cottage belongs to, it's not Sara, because she sounded fine when I spoke to her an hour ago."

Even on second telling, the news sounded incredible.

"Are you sure it was Sara you were talking to?"

"Positive. And here's the weird thing."

Like the rest of this conversation was normal.

"When I picked up the phone, Sara said, "Hi, it's me,"" like she always does, and started telling me about some bands she was planning to audition. Like nothing was wrong at all."

"She didn't say why she's been missing for more than a week? Or mention the fire that burned down her house? Or ask about her dog that she just about abandoned? Not to mention the dead body that everyone thinks is her?"

"That's what I'm trying to tell you. She didn't talk about any of that."

"Did you *ask?*"

"How stupid do I look? Of course I asked. Sara just kind of sighed and said that there'd been a few complications in her life recently, but that I shouldn't worry about a thing—the wedding was going to be fine."

"A few complications?" Yeah, and Cujo was a misguided puppy. "What about that note she left for you? Did she explain what that was about?"

"It never came up."

"It sounds like a lot of things never came up."

"So sue me." Bertie didn't sound any happier about the situation than I was.

"But if the body in the cottage isn't Sara . . ."

"Who is it?" she finished for me. "And how did it get there?"

"Oh my God," I said abruptly. "You've got to call Sara's parents. Aunt Peg saw Delilah yesterday, and she was trying to get dental records. The Warings still think Sara's dead."

"Sara said she'd been in touch with them."

"When?"

"She was out of town over the weekend. It wasn't until she got back late yesterday that she heard about what had happened. She said she contacted her parents right away."

"Sara's been out of town, or whatever she wants to call it, for more than a week," I pointed out irritably. "Frankly, this whole thing seems really fishy. Did she give you a phone number where you could get in touch with her?"

Bertie shook her head. "She said she'd call me in a day or two when she had more wedding stuff to discuss."

"The heck with the wedding. Did you tell her that you'd been worried about her? Did you mention the dozen messages you'd left on her machine, or the fact that you asked me to look for her?"

"I tried. But every time the conversation veered in that direction, she blew me off."

"She won't be able to blow off the police. Now that she's

more or less surfaced, I'd imagine they're going to want to talk to her right away."

Outside in the hallway, the bell chimed, signaling the end of third period.

"I'd better go," said Bertie.

As if there was even the ghost of a chance that I'd be able to concentrate on schoolwork now.

She said good-bye to Faith and Sydney and slipped out of the room with much less fanfare than when she'd entered. I walked back over to the table where my student, whom I was supposed to have spent the last half hour helping, was gathering up her things.

"I am so sorry," I said to Sydney. "I'll talk to Miss Beck and explain what happened to your report."

"Are you kidding?" The girl's eyes were shining. "That was great. Do you really know someone who's dead?"

"Not exactly." I reached for her notebook. "There's a woman whom everyone thought was dead, but it turns out she's alive after all. That's what Bertie came here to tell me."

"Because you've been looking for her," Sydney prompted.

Nothing wrong with this girl's ears.

"Yes." I flipped through the pages until I came to the one she'd been working on.

"That is so cool."

Before Bertie arrived, Sydney and I had had time to do little more than discuss the outline format. Now the entire page was filled with a perfectly creditable chapter-by-chapter synopsis.

"So is this," I said, handing the notebook back. "Nice job."

Sydney slapped the pad shut and jammed it into her backpack. "It's only schoolwork. It's not like it's that hard."

"That's what I've been trying to tell you. Keep up the good work."

"Sure, Ms. Travis. You too." As she shouldered her back-pack and headed out of the room, I heard her say under her breath, "Looking for dead people. What a great job. That's what I want to do when I grow up."

Good luck, kid, I thought.

18

Frank and Bob had offered to pick up Davey after school and take him over to the YMCA, where tryouts were being held for winter-league basketball. At Davey's age, this part of the process is mostly a formality. The goals of the program are to teach the game, exercise good sportsmanship, and have fun; and every kid who shows up and wants to play gets put on a team.

Frank and Bob had decided between themselves that this was the sort of activity where a boy ought to be accompanied by the men in his family, and I was happy to agree. As a single mother, I'm all in favor of this male bonding thing. Besides, once the league was up and running, basketball games would be held weekly throughout the winter months, so I'd have plenty of opportunities to watch my son play.

Since Sara had turned out to be alive, I decided to table my trip to the police station and swing by Aunt Peg's instead. I figured Sara could explain to the police for herself what she'd been up to, and Bertie's news was simply too good to deliver to my aunt over the phone. Though I've had a modest amount of success uncovering murderers, this was the first time I'd ever had a murder victim return from the dead.

"I've been waiting for you," Aunt Peg said as I got out of the car.

I'd barely turned in the end of her long driveway before her front door opened and half a dozen Poodles came streaming down the steps. Slowing to a near crawl, I nudged the Volvo through the canine welcoming committee and parked beside the flagstone walk. Faith was standing on the front seat beside me, front paws braced against the dashboard, nose pressed to the windshield. When I opened my door, she hopped across my lap and shot out.

I'd expected that. What I hadn't planned on was Eve just as quickly hopping in to take her place. At four months of age, the puppy already weighed thirty pounds. She knocked me back into the seat and thoroughly cleaned my face with her smooth, pink tongue. By the time I'd surfaced, Aunt Peg was standing beside the car.

"What do you mean you've been waiting for me?" I set the puppy on the ground and quickly shut the car door before any of the other Poodles could decide to get in. "How did you know I was coming?"

"I've been thinking about you all day. I figured it was only a matter of time until you showed up. Where's Davey?"

"Basketball tryouts."

Aunt Peg's brow lifted. "Isn't he a little short to be playing basketball?"

"It's a grade school league."

"I should hope so."

Peg waved a hand, whistled once, and headed toward the house. The Poodles came running. Obediently I fell in with the crowd. If I was lucky there might be a biscuit in it for me.

"There's been a development," Aunt Peg said importantly.

She stood at the door, counting noses and tapping her leg with her fingertips to hurry along the stragglers.

"At least one. Sara Bentley isn't dead."

She shut the door and turned. "And here I thought you'd been busy at school all day. How did you find out?"

"From Bertie," I said, feeling seriously deflated. I'd expected my news to cause more of a sensation than that. "How did you know?"

"I didn't," Aunt Peg admitted. "Not for sure, anyway. But Delilah called earlier to tell me that the body had been identified this afternoon and that it wasn't Sara. As I'm sure you can imagine, she was terribly relieved."

The Poodles ran toward the kitchen, pushing and scrambling down the hallway. They knew where the supply of biscuits was kept. Aunt Peg and I followed.

"How did they figure it out?" I asked. "And who was it?"

"Apparently the police got a lucky break. Yesterday they found a car registered to a woman named Carole Eikenberry parked in the woods behind the cottage. While Delilah was getting Sara's dental records, they were attempting to do the same for Ms. Eikenberry. Both sets became available this morning, and the mystery was solved."

"Carole Eikenberry?" The name meant nothing to me. "Did Delilah know anything about her?"

"Only that she believes the young woman was a friend of Sara's."

We reached the kitchen and Aunt Peg paused in front of the pantry. Seven black Standard Poodles milled around her legs in happy anticipation. "You think I'm going to give you a biscuit, don't you?"

Fourteen ears perked at the word.

"Why should I do that? What have you done to deserve a treat? All you did was answer the door." No one, human or canine, offered a rebuttal.

Aunt Peg sighed, opened the cupboard, and pulled out the box. Her Poodles had her very well trained.

While she was busy handing out biscuits, I snagged a box of Mallomars from the pantry and went and sat at the table. "I wonder if Sara knows about Carole," I mused.

"I wonder what Sara thinks she's doing," Peg snorted. "Considering she isn't dead, you'd think she'd have the decency to put in an appearance. And what was that you were saying about Bertie?"

"She spoke with Sara this morning. That's what I came to tell you."

"Bertie saw her?"

"No, they spoke on the phone. Sara called to discuss plans for the wedding."

Aunt Peg sank into a chair and helped herself to a cookie. The Poodles settled at our feet, munching happily. "You must be kidding."

"I'm not. Bertie said she kept trying to steer the conversation toward more pertinent matters and Sara just brushed her off."

"That takes nerve."

Indeed. "Sara told Bertie she'd been out of town and only just found out about what had happened. She said she'd already spoken to her parents and told them she was okay."

Even before I'd finished speaking, Peg was already shaking her head. "Delilah called me with the good news this afternoon. And she specifically mentioned getting the information from the police. She didn't say a thing about talking to Sara."

Considering my own history, you wouldn't think I had a lot of room to cast aspersions. In this case, however, it was more than justified. "Any way you look at it, that is one strange family."

Aunt Peg nodded absently. Like me, she knows all about

strange families. "Sara will have to come back now, that's all there is to it. I'm sure the police will want to question her."

"What do you suppose Carole was doing in Sara's cottage?" I wondered out loud as I helped myself to another cookie. "Did she go there to see Sara, find the place empty, and let herself in to wait?"

"And just happen to get caught in a fire?" Aunt Peg asked skeptically. "I doubt it. More likely she set the blaze herself. But why?"

"Not my problem," I said firmly.

"Don't be a spoilsport."

Another Mallomar found its way into my hands. My third. I guessed I'd be adjusting my portion size at dinner.

"I believe you told your future sister-in-law that you'd help locate Sara."

"And I believe she's been located." I nibbled around the chocolate edge. "More or less."

Aunt Peg didn't look satisfied, but rather than press the issue, she changed the subject. "Speaking of family obligations, I assume you've arranged to take the day off from work on Friday?"

"Of course."

That one was easy. Friday was the day of the Tuxedo Park Poodle Specialty, Aunt Peg's first judging assignment. There was no way I was going to miss it.

"And you'll be there first thing?"

"I'll leave for Tarrytown just as soon as I put Davey on the bus."

We'd both seen the judging schedule. The Puppy Sweepstakes, judged by a club member, started at nine. Aunt Peg's assignment began with Toy Poodles at eleven. There would be a lunch break at twelve-thirty, followed by Miniature and then Standard Poodles in the afternoon. She'd drawn nearly a hundred Poodles, an impressive total for a new specialty show, and a tribute to Peg's reputation in the breed.

"You'll do great," I said, though she hadn't asked for my reassurance. "Look at the size of your entry. The club must be thrilled. Everyone's going to be there."

Aunt Peg stopped eating. "There are some moments when that pleases me enormously," she said slowly. "And others when I think that's exactly what I'm afraid of. I've begun to have those stupid dreams. You know the ones where you show up for the final exam and haven't cracked a book all semester? I think it must be my sub-conscious, trying to tell me that I'm not ready."

"Oh pish!" I borrowed one of her favorite words. "You've been ready for this for years. You're going to have a blast. Besides, if not now, when? You're not getting any younger."

Peg's chin snapped up. "Well *that's* encouraging."

Blithely I plunged on. "Better to take on a new task like this before your memory goes entirely. Not to mention your knees. If you study it the night before, I imagine you can probably manage to retain most of the breed standard. And if not, you know they'll let you take a copy into the ring with you."

The standard is a highly detailed description of the breed in question. It's the bible by which a breed of dog is bred or judged, and these were low blows I was delivering. I could see by Aunt Peg's expression that they were hitting the target.

"My memory is quite sharp," she snapped. "And my knees are perfectly adequate for the job at hand. As to the breed standard, I'll have you know I helped draft the most recent revision—"

"Did you?" I asked innocently. "Then I guess you must be pretty well equipped to do the job."

"Better than most!" Aunt Peg announced.

"That's what I thought." I stood up and gave her a quick hug. "See you Friday."

I love it when a plan comes together.

My next stop was the supermarket, where I picked up the ingredients I'd need for dinner. More efficient women shop with a long list once a week, but I've never been able to get the hang of that system. Besides, planning ahead wouldn't cover contingencies like tonight, when I suspected that I'd be cooking for four rather than two.

There probably wasn't a pair of bachelors on the planet who would pass up a meal of homemade meat loaf, mashed potatoes, and glazed carrots. Just to make sure I had all the bases covered, I threw a six-pack of beer in the cart, too.

Faith had already eaten, and preparations for our dinner were well underway by the time the guys returned. I was setting the dining room table when the front door opened. Davey led the way, dribbling a basketball up the steps. A rumpled gray sweatsuit, bought big enough to fit for more than a few weeks, pooled around his waist and ankles. His face was wreathed in smiles.

"Hey, Mom!" he cried. "I made the team!"

"That's great. Did you have fun?"

"Uh huh." His head bobbed enthusiastically. "And guess what? Uncle Frank's going to coach. He volunteered."

"He did?"

I glanced at my brother as he came through the door. Frank wasn't the volunteering type.

"Yeah, well, you know . . ." he said. "I thought maybe I'd get in some practice."

"Playing basketball?"

Frank's cheeks grew pink. He cleared his throat. "Uhh, no, with kids. You never know when it might come in handy."

The silverware I'd been holding clattered down onto the table. "Frank Turnbull, are you trying to tell me something?"

For a moment he looked confused. Then Frank realized what I meant. "No!" he practically shouted. "Good God, Mel, bite your tongue. I'm just planning ahead, that's all."

I retrieved the fallen knives and forks. "You're sure?"

"Positive. Really positive."

"About what?" asked Bob. He hopped up the steps two at a time and closed the door behind him. "What'd I miss?"

"Nothing important," Frank assured him. "Melanie was just jumping to conclusions and I was setting her straight."

"Melanie? Jumping to conclusions? How out of character."

"Cut it out, you two." I brandished a fork. "Or I won't invite you to stay to dinner."

Frank wasn't impressed. "It's a little late for threats, considering you've already set four places. What are we having?"

"Meat loaf, mashed potatoes, and glazed carrots." I added pointedly, "If you're lucky."

"Ahhh," Bob sighed, then sniffed the air. "There's nothing like the siren song of a home-cooked dinner. It's been years since I've had meals as good as the ones you used to cook."

This is what's known as laying it on thick.

I headed back to the kitchen. "What about Jennifer?"

Bob and Frank trotted along after me like a couple of well-trained dogs. Davey, meanwhile, grabbed Faith and headed upstairs.

"She meant well. But she did things with spices that you wouldn't believe. Lots of spices." Bob shook his head sadly.

"All together in the same dish. Jennifer's cooking was more in the grin-and-bear-it category."

"She's young. She'll learn."

"Not on my time."

I went to the refrigerator and got out two beers. There were frosted mugs in the freezer and a small wedge of Brie on a plate.

"You're an angel of mercy." Frank didn't wait for a mug. He downed half the bottle in his first gulp. "Those kids ran me ragged."

I pulled out a chair and pushed him down into it. It didn't take much. "And the season hasn't even started yet."

"You've got to get in shape." Bob patted his own flat stomach. My eyes followed the gesture. Unexpectedly, I found my gaze lingering.

Bob had looked good when we were married; he looked even better now. Maturity suited him. The boy I'd known a decade earlier had grown into a man who could hold his own in any company.

His shoulders were broader, the breadth of his chest more pronounced. At the same time, his torso was leaner and he'd shed some puppy fat from his face. Once, Bob had barely needed to shave; now, his jaw was shadowed with stubble. The look suited him.

Feeling suddenly uncomfortable, I lifted my eyes and found that Bob was staring at me with the same intensity I'd been training on him. Slowly his mouth widened into a sexy grin.

Heat plummeted into my belly. I didn't smile back. Instead, I spun away and bumped into my brother.

Frank, head stuck in the open refrigerator and looking for another beer, was blissfully oblivious. Thank God.

"Hey Mel, watch where you're going." His fingers closed

over a cold bottle. He straightened, bumped the door shut with his hip and twisted off the cap. "A guy could get hurt around here."

Abruptly, inexplicably, Bob began to laugh.

I shot him a dirty look. For some reason, it only made him laugh harder.

"What's going on?" asked Frank, looking at the two of us.

I only wished I knew.

19

It's a pretty good indication that your life is in turmoil when getting up and going to work in the morning begins to seem like a restful alternative. On Wednesday, it was a pleasure to pull up to Howard Academy and realize that all I had to do that day was educate the youth of America.

Divine intervention, or something along those lines, had relieved me of my other responsibilities. Certainly I couldn't take any credit myself. But now that Sara had resurfaced—almost—I no longer needed to look for her. And since she appeared to be keeping on top of the plans for Bertie's wedding, I was off that hook, too. The dead body found in Sara's cottage had turned out to be not only someone I didn't know, but someone I'd never even heard of before.

Clearly that was none of my business.

All I had to do was hold that thought, and I'd be free.

My light-headed feeling of liberty lasted until eleven-thirty, when a call was put through to my classroom. As Bertie had found out, the office doesn't forward phone calls except in case of emergency. So when I realized it was an outside line that was buzzing, my first thought was for Davey. I snatched up the receiver.

"Hi, it's Debra Silver."

"Who?"

Quickly, I shifted through the names at Davey's school. Not his teacher, not the school nurse, not the principal.

"Debra Silver. You know, we spoke last week?"

Sara's friend. Indoor tennis. Junior Showmanship. My shoulders sagged in relief.

"Right." I tried not to sound too surprised. I wondered how she'd known to find me at Howard Academy. "How did you get past the office?"

Debra laughed. The sound grated on my ears. "Office help are all alike, no matter where they work. I just threw my weight around and told the secretary it was urgent. And it is. Listen, I have to talk to you."

"I'm teaching a class," I said, amazed that such a thing wouldn't have occurred to her. Considering it was what I did.

Three second-graders were standing at the blackboard, struggling with long division. At the moment, there was more erasing than writing going on.

"How about lunch? I'll come and get you. We'll grab something downtown. There's a new Italian bistro I've been dying to try."

Briefly I considered the offer. Attendance at lunch wasn't mandatory for Howard Academy teachers unless it was their turn to sit in the family-style dining room with the students. I'd served my stint the week before. Today I could probably manage to slip away for an hour or so. To be honest, it wasn't as though I hadn't done it before. And I was definitely curious to know what sort of news Debra Silver would consider urgent.

"Tell me where and I'll meet you," I said. Debra hadn't

struck me as the sort of person who worried about other people's time constraints. I'd feel much better having my own ride back to school.

She named a new restaurant on Lewis Street and told me she'd make a reservation for twelve-thirty.

Parking's a problem in Greenwich and has been for years. The spot I finally found was four blocks away. I was five minutes late for our appointment, but Debra hadn't arrived yet. By the time she did show up ten minutes later, I'd already perused the menu and was sipping an iced tea.

"Thanks for meeting me." She slipped off a soft, butter-colored leather jacket and hung it over the back of her chair. Though Debra was speaking to me, her eyes scanned the room. Who was she hoping to find? I wondered. Kathie Lee Gifford?

Debra slid into her seat. Her imperiously raised hand summoned the waiter. "I'll have a glass of Pino Grigio."

The man hurried away to do her bidding. I've always envied people who have that ability to make waiters sit up and pay attention. If it's genetic, I think I must be missing a few of the pertinent chromosomes.

"So," Debra said casually, "how've you been?"

"Fine." It had only been four days since we'd met. Was she expecting otherwise?

Debra's wine arrived. She sipped from the glass and nodded her approval. "We'll need a minute before ordering," she told the waiter who obediently melted away.

"We can't take too long," I told her. "I have to be back at school in an hour."

"That's right, you work."

I decided to overlook her tone, which did not imply good things about salaried labor. "Speaking of which, how did you know where to find me?"

Debra shrugged. "I just called around."

"Around where?"

"You know how small the dog show world is."

I did. But it was my impression that Debra had left that world behind a while ago. "I didn't realize you were still showing dogs."

"I'm not. But I have friends that do. You're right, we should order. Otherwise, we'll be here forever." Debra opened her menu and held it up in front of her face.

I guessed she was hoping I wouldn't notice the abrupt change of subject. I decided to let it go until after we'd made our selections. Pasta for lunch felt like a luxury to me. I ordered penne primavera and a small caesar salad.

"You're probably wondering why I called you," Debra said after the waiter had come and gone. Her fingers toyed with the heavy silverware on her placemat. "This is a little awkward for me."

"What is?"

"Spilling my guts to a private detective."

I stared at her for a minute. "First," I said finally, "I'm not a detective, private or otherwise. I was looking for Sara because I was trying to do a favor for a friend. And second, I don't know what you're talking about."

"That's good. You're discreet." She took a hefty swallow of wine. "I was hoping we could work this out."

"Work what out?"

"You see . . ." Debra stopped and looked around the room, as though checking to see if anyone was listening.

The notion struck me as slightly paranoid. Though the tables in the bistro were unconscionably close together, the noise level was high. No one seemed to be paying the slightest bit of attention to us, and I couldn't imagine why anyone would.

"I have to consider my position."

I wanted to ask what position that was, but I was afraid it

would make me look as dumb as I was beginning to feel. All I'd done since I sat down was ask questions, and none of them ever seemed to get answered.

"My husband is an important lawyer in town. We're very social. With his job, we have to be. His clients are very important people."

Wow, I thought. I'm impressed.

The waiter brought our salads. Fortunately that gave Debra something to do with her hands. She'd already managed to shred two rolls on her bread plate.

"What I'm trying to say," she continued, "is that I probably shouldn't have spoken so freely to you about Sara Bentley the other day."

"Oh?"

"I know how easily things can get twisted around and taken out of context, and I would hate for that to happen in this instance. I really feel that everything we spoke about should be confidential."

I thought back to what Debra had told me when we'd met on Saturday. It wasn't much. And considering what made news in today's world, it was hardly inflammatory.

"There's nothing to worry about. As I recall, all you did was clarify some facts from an old story."

"Yes." Debra nodded quickly. "That's just what I'm trying to tell you. It *was* old news. It all happened a long time ago. Nothing that happened with Sara has any bearing on my life today."

"Okay." I placed my salad bowl to one side as our entrees arrived. I still hadn't figured out what all the fuss was about. "If you say so."

"Just because Sara and I were friends once . . ." Debra paused to sample a small bite of her lobster ravioli. I eyed the dish covetously, wondering if I should have ordered it myself. ". . . doesn't mean that I want my name to be associated with hers in any way now. Do you see what I'm getting at?"

Finally, yes. More or less. Though something about what she'd said didn't seem quite right . . .

"This is yummy," said Debra. "How's yours?"

"Very good." The fleeting thought that I'd almost grabbed slipped away again. Regretfully I let it go. "Excellent, actually. I'm glad you suggested we come here."

"I'm always on the lookout for new places," Debra confided. "There are only so many times you want to eat at the club, with all those same dreary faces."

I wouldn't know about that, but I was just as happy to take her word for it.

"You haven't heard from Sara, have you? I mean, since we last spoke?"

"No," Debra said firmly. "No, I haven't. Why would I?"

"No particular reason. I was just wondering. I assume you know about the fire that burned down her cottage."

"I read about it in the paper like everyone else. And the fact that there was a body involved . . . how perfectly awful! I guess everyone thought it was Sara for a while."

The correct identification had been reported in that morning's papers. Lower Fairfield County doesn't see many murders, especially not in towns like New Canaan. After four days, this one had yet to move off the front page of the local papers.

"Did you?" I asked.

"Did I what?"

"Assume it was Sara?"

Debra nibbled around the edges of a piece of ravioli. In ten minutes, she had yet to make a dent in the food on her plate. I guessed that and tennis was how she kept her well-toned figure. The Greenwich Matron Deprivation Diet.

"Actually," she said, "I tried not to think about it."

Like hell.

"Must have been hard, considering your past history."

"Not as hard as you'd think." A final gulp polished off her wine.

"What the newspapers haven't reported yet is that Carole Eikenberry, the woman who died in the fire, was a friend of Sara's. I was wondering if maybe you knew her."

"No," Debra blurted. She hadn't even stopped to think. "I didn't. I'm sure I didn't. Sara and I don't travel in the same circles. There'd be no reason for us to have any of the same friends."

One repudiation I'd have bought. Two would have been plenty. With three, Debra was pressing her luck.

"Because you haven't really kept in touch."

"That's right. I'm sure I mentioned that on Saturday. Until all this started, it had been years since I'd even thought about Sara. If you're trying to find out about Carole, you'd have to talk to Sara's current friends, and that certainly wouldn't be me."

So I'd gathered. Repeatedly.

Debra pushed her plate away and caught the waiter's eye. Immediately he came scurrying over. "Everything was delicious," she told him. "We'll have the check now."

"Perhaps a nice espresso?" he offered.

"No." Debra was already reaching for her purse. I was glad I'd eaten quickly. "Just the check."

We split the total down the middle after arguing over the tip. Debra, it turned out, thought twelve percent was more than sufficient. If anyone was going to be cheap, it should have been me. That lunch had cost more than I usually spend on two days' worth of groceries.

"You won't forget what I said?" Debra reminded me as we parted at the door. "Confidential, right?"

"Sure," I agreed. Why not? It wasn't as if I'd been about to alert the media.

She seemed relieved. Debra's stride was long and confident, and I watched the back of that pale yellow leather jacket until she became lost in the crowd.

As she slipped from sight, I realized what she'd said that had been bothering me. The other day, Debra had spoken about Sara as if the two of them had never been anything other than competitors turned enemies. Today, she'd characterized them as old friends.

Which one did she want me to believe? I wondered. More important, which one was closer to the truth?

20

That afternoon I got stuck in traffic on the Merritt Parkway and barely beat Davey's bus home. The big yellow vehicle came lumbering down the street as Faith and I were getting out of the car. While the Poodle sniffed around the front yard, checking to see if any strange dogs had invaded her territory while she'd been away, I walked over to the sidewalk to wait.

When the bus stopped and the door swished open, two seven-year-old boys emerged. Joey Brickman is Davey's best friend. His family lives at the other end of the block, and his mother, Alice, and I had become good friends six years earlier over baby play-dates and gymboree.

"Hi, Joey," I said, grabbing my son's backpack as he ran past me to greet Faith. "What are you doing here?"

"Mom had to pick Carly up at school and take her to the doctor. She might have strep throat. Mom stopped by my classroom and told me to come home with Davey. She said she'd leave you a message about it."

Carly was Joey's younger sister. She'd started kindergarten in September and spent the last two months bringing home every germ and disease that an elementary school could incubate. Alice and I were used to covering for one another. Over the years, we'd made a habit of it.

"Okay." I took Joey's backpack, too. "Let's go inside and get you guys something to eat."

As expected, when we reached the kitchen the message light on the answering machine was blinking. I hit the "play" button on my way to the cupboard to get out some granola bars and a couple of glasses.

Alice's voice filled the room. She sounded frazzled, and the message she'd left was just what Joey had said it would be. The machine didn't click off when she finished speaking, however. Instead, there was a second message.

"Hi, Melanie, this is Maris Kincaid. I know this is short notice, but I'm calling because I was hoping we could get together this afternoon. This whole thing with Sara is really creeping me out. I'm grooming a dog in Stamford not too far from where you live, so I'm just going to stop by and see if you're there. I hope that's okay. See you later."

"Fine by me," I said to nobody in particular.

It seemed to be my day for drop-in guests. And for listening to people talk about Sara. Apparently I was the only person in the whole world who realized that what Sara was or wasn't up to was no longer my concern.

The boys finished their snacks and went upstairs to play. Maris showed up a few minutes later.

"Good, you're here," she said when I opened the door. "Did you get my message?"

"About fifteen minutes ago. Come on in."

"I'm sorry to just drop in like this, but I didn't know who else to talk to." Maris followed me into the living room. Her gaze settled on Faith. "Nice Poodle. Do you groom her yourself?"

"Yes. With some help from my Aunt Peg. She's shown Standard Poodles for years."

"Peg?" Her brow furrowed as she thought. "Peg Turnbull?"

I nodded.

"No wonder she's a good one. What's her name?"

"Faith." Trying to sound like I wasn't bragging, I added, "Champion Cedar Crest Leap of Faith."

Maris sat down on the couch and patted her knee, calling Faith to her. "Since she's still in hair, does that mean you're specialing her?"

"No. She just finished week before last. As soon as it's confirmed, the coat's coming off."

She twined her fingers through Faith's dense coat and rubbed behind the Poodle's ears. Faith leaned into the caress. If she'd been a cat, she'd have been purring. My dog was perfectly content, but I was ready to move things along.

"You said you wanted to talk to me about Sara," I prompted. "Have you heard from her?"

"No." Maris looked up, clearly surprised by the question. "Have you?"

"No, but Bertie Kennedy has. Sara called her yesterday. She wouldn't give Bertie any details about what she's been doing for the last week or where she is, but apparently she's okay. If totally unconcerned about the people who've been worried about her."

Maris shook her head. "That's Sara all the way, isn't it? Stir things up and let other people deal with the consequences. Look, I wasn't entirely honest with you the other day."

"Oh?"

"It's not like you started out being honest with me," she pointed out. "And I didn't know you from Adam. So I didn't see any reason why I should start telling Sara's secrets to you."

"And now?" I asked.

"Now things have just gotten weirder and weirder. A disappearance is one thing. On some level, I could even see how Sara might have enjoyed the drama of it. But then there was the fire. And the body. Carole Eikenberry's body. I know perfectly well Sara's not enjoying that. Nobody would."

I leaned forward in my seat. "Did you know Carole Eikenberry?"

"Yeah. Not well, but we'd met a few times. She was a friend of Sara's. A good buddy, I guess you'd say. I know they'd done a lot of things together over the last few months."

"So she was someone who might have known who Sara's mystery boyfriend is," I mused.

I had no idea whether that made a difference or not. It was just another unsolved piece in an increasingly murky puzzle.

"Actually, that kind of has to do with why I'm here. You asked me before if I knew any reason why Sara might have run away and I said no, but the truth is, there was something. Sara didn't want anyone to know. She made me promise not to tell anyone, so I didn't.

"Not until now, anyway. And maybe it's nothing. Maybe it doesn't have anything to do with the rest of this stuff. But with everything else that's going on, I just figured I ought to talk to someone else so I'm not the only one keeping this secret. In case it *is* important. I had your phone number and I found your address in a dog show catalogue, so here I am."

Maris kept chattering, but I wasn't learning anything new. I wondered if she was going to get to the point any time soon.

"Now that there's been a murder," I said, "the police must be running an investigation. Are you sure you wouldn't rather talk to them?"

"Positive. It's bad enough I'm betraying Sara's confidence to one person. I'm not about to spill the beans to the whole world. Besides, this isn't about the murder. It's personal. It's the kind of news a woman has every right to keep private. Sara's pregnant."

Yikes, I thought. That *was* news.

"Are you sure?"

Maris looked annoyed. "All I know is what Sara told me the last time I saw her. She was trying to get me to take over some of her clients and I was telling her no deal. At first she just said she hadn't been feeling well, but the more she kept talking, the more I began to suspect.

"When I guessed right, she was really irritated. Keeping the pregnancy a secret seemed really important to her. Sara wasn't even two months along, so she wasn't showing yet or anything. Last week when you told me she'd disappeared, I thought maybe that was why she hadn't wanted anyone to know about the baby. Maybe she'd gone away to get rid of it."

Sara wouldn't have had to disappear to do that, I thought, but she might have wanted to take some time to recover in private.

"Didn't she want the baby?" I asked.

"That's the problem," said Maris. "Things don't exactly add up. Because Sara said that she did want the baby. In fact, she was thrilled with the idea. But then I wondered if maybe she'd changed her mind. It's not like she's married or anything, and she isn't the kind of person I could picture wanting to settle down.

"I figured it would be just like Sara to drop out of sight,

fix the problem, and then act as if the whole thing had never happened. You know how women get when they're pregnant, all emotional and unpredictable."

No, that was society's perception of how women behaved when they were pregnant. As I remembered my own experience, I'd been remarkably level-headed. Of course, that was an admittedly biased view. Bob might have had a different opinion.

I sat for a minute and thought about things. Maris's news certainly put a different slant on the situation. But unfortunately it didn't address the bigger question: if Sara had merely dropped out of sight for a few days to ponder or even act upon her options, how had a dead body turned up in her burned-down house in her absence?

"Did Sara tell you who the baby's father is?" I asked.

"No, and you better believe I asked. Having a baby is a big decision, not something you just do on the spur of the moment. Even Sara couldn't be *that* impulsive. But she wouldn't give me a clue. Just smiled and said there was no need to worry about minor details like that."

Minor details? I wondered if that meant Sara wasn't planning to tell the father.

I thought back to the first meeting I'd had with Debra at the tennis courts. She'd said Sara was looking for a lawyer. Could this have been the reason why?

I reached up and rubbed my temples. All this information was beginning to give me a headache. I read plenty of mysteries. I know perfectly well that people are supposed to give you answers. How come everyone I talked to just gave me more questions?

"What do you suppose this has to do with Carole Eikenberry?" I asked.

"I have no idea." Maris nudged Faith gently aside and stood up. "And to tell you the truth, I'm not sure I want to know. Having Sara for a friend is like being on a roller-coaster ride. You're either way up or way down. Well, right now I'm thinking about hopping off."

I knew how she felt; I was about ready to jump ship myself. I stood and walked Maris to the door.

"Would you do me a favor?" she asked as she lifted her jean jacket off the coatrack and pulled it on.

"I'll try."

"You said that Bertie had heard from Sara?"

"Right. Yesterday."

"If she hears from her again, or if you do, would you ask Sara to call me? She still owes me the money for all that work I did for her last week. I want to make sure it doesn't slip her mind."

Cold air billowed in when I opened the door. As soon as Maris had gone through, I pushed it shut behind her. I watched through the window as she got in her car and drove away. Somehow I suspected that the small sum of money Sara owed to Maris was the least of her problems.

Alice didn't bother to knock. She simply let herself in the front door and walked straight back to the kitchen, where she found me with schoolwork spread out over the butcher block table. Faith, gnawing on a new rawhide chip, didn't get up, though she did thump her tail up and down in greeting.

"Grab a seat," I said. "And a soda, if you like."

"Diet?" Alice was already heading toward the refrigerator. Her strawberry blonde hair was pulled back in a messy ponytail, and her lightly freckled skin was makeup free. Jeans, which had been tight a month earlier, were now merely snug.

"No, regular. Sorry. You look like you've lost some weight, though."

"Maybe a pound or two. No time to eat. With both kids finally in school, you'd think I'd have more free time, but somehow it hasn't worked out that way."

"That's what you get for volunteering to be kindergarten room mother. And speaking of which, how's Carly?"

"Asleep in the car out front. Absolutely out like a light. I can only stay a minute. It is strep. They did a culture to confirm." Alice popped the top on a can of Coke, guzzled down a long swallow, and sank into a chair on the opposite side of the table. "I'll sit over here so I don't contaminate you. I'm probably covered with germs."

"Like I'm not." Teachers run that risk every day. "Listen, I have a question."

"Shoot."

"Say you were pregnant . . ."

Alice snorted. "Bite your tongue!"

"Okay." I grinned and started over. "*When* you were pregnant . . ."

"Better."

"Do you think you were overly emotional or impetuous? Did you behave irrationally?"

"Eating patterns aside?" Alice cocked a brow.

"Sure."

"No, I think I was a model of madonna-like stability."

"For real?"

"For real." Alice slouched back in her chair. "Why? Did you go nuts or something?"

"No, not that I remember."

"Shoot up a post office? Sign up for the New York Marathon? Buy a satellite dish and stick it in the back yard? Wear Spandex to the ballet?"

"No," I said, enjoying the mental images. "None of the above."

"So what's the problem?"

"I've been looking for a woman—a friend of a friend—who seemed to have disappeared. While she was gone, her house burned down and someone was killed. Another friend just told me that the woman was pregnant, and implied she hadn't been thinking clearly. I just wanted to get your take on the subject."

"Anyone who's involved in a fire and a murder probably isn't thinking clearly. But it's a stretch to blame either one on pregnancy. Otherwise you'd see a lot more dead husbands running around."

Alice stopped, frowning as she thought about what she'd said. "You know what I mean."

I did, and I agreed.

"Pregnant or not, whatever your friend has gotten herself mixed up in, I bet she went into it with her eyes wide open."

That was what I was afraid of.

21

Thursday I actually managed to make it through an entire school day without any unexpected interruptions. Apparently, this fact was not lost on our esteemed headmaster, Russell Hanover II. We passed in the hallway as Faith and I were leaving that afternoon.

Mr. Hanover characterizes himself as a hands-on administrator, and there isn't much that goes on at Howard Academy that he isn't privy to. Our meeting might have happened by chance, but I suspected it hadn't. The man has a gift for micromanagement.

"Everything going well, Ms. Travis?" he asked, pausing to pat the top of Faith's head. Russell calls all his associates by their last names, even teachers who have been at the school for years.

"Very well, Mr. Hanover," I replied demurely.

"You've been busy this week."

"No more than usual." The lie slipped out with shocking ease. This was what getting involved in murders had done to me: corrupted my need for scrupulous honesty.

"I hear you've had several visitors."

"Only two."

If you didn't count Debra, whom I'd slipped out to meet, I added silently.

Russell nodded somberly. He was probably adding Debra to his list as well.

"As I'm sure you know, we prefer that our teachers handle personal matters on their own time. When you're here, we feel that all your energies should be devoted to your students."

"Of course," I agreed. "It won't happen again."

"On the other hand," Russell continued, "we also expect our teachers to be an integral part of the community at large. Considering the importance of some outside projects, we are prepared to offer a degree of latitude when circumstances warrant. I believe your own activities, such as I've been aware of them in the past, might fall under this umbrella."

"Really?" Even though I'd solved a murder on the school grounds the year before, I was still surprised. "Thank you."

"Don't abuse the privilege, Ms. Travis."

"I won't."

"I suppose it's too much to hope that you haven't become involved in another investigation?"

"Worse," I told him. "A wedding."

Russell's brow arched upward. "Are congratulations in order?"

"No, I'm afraid it's my brother's wedding, not mine."

"I hope you'll pass along my best wishes."

"I'd be happy to."

I started to move on, but Russell had one last comment to make. "I'm so looking forward to a peaceful holiday season this year. You will try to stay out of trouble, won't you?"

"Yes, sir."

Too bad we both knew things didn't always work out that way.

"How fast can you come up with a baby-sitter?" Bertie asked.

Davey and I had just finished eating dinner when the phone rang. As soon as I heard the question, I knew I could forget about my plans for a quiet evening at home.

"Ten minutes if Joanie, the girl down the block, is free. Why?"

"I'm at Frank's," said Bertie. "Find out and call me right back."

She hadn't, I noticed, answered my question.

Nevertheless, I did as she'd requested. Joanie was a teenager with many virtues, not the least of which was her love of children in general, and my son in particular. I'd been using her services since Davey was two, and the fact that she'd be leaving for college in less than a year was going to leave a hole in both our lives.

"Sure, I can come," Joanie said cheerfully. "As long as you're not going to be too late. Is it okay if I bring some homework with me for after Davey goes to bed?"

"Fine," I assured her. The teenager knew my son's routine as well as I did. I quickly called Bertie back.

"Great. I'm leaving Frank's now. I'll be by to pick you up in twenty minutes."

"Where are we going?" I asked.

"Oh, that's right. I forgot to mention that part, didn't I?"

Forgot, my foot.

"We're going to New Canaan," Bertie announced. "Sara's back home. She's expecting us."

My mouth opened and shut.

"Speechless, eh?" Bertie was grinning. I could hear it in her voice. "See you soon."

She hung up and I went to break the news to Davey that he'd be spending the evening with his baby-sitter instead of his mother. He was thrilled.

Sometimes being a parent is a real kick in the pants, you know?

I was waiting by the front door when Bertie drove up.

"Have fun!" Joanie said as I slipped on my coat. Faith was lying next to her on the couch. My son, plotting his next move on the Monopoly board between them, barely looked up. I let myself out, ran down the steps, and got into the passenger seat of Bertie's van. She threw the Chevy into reverse and was already backing out as I fastened my seat belt.

"What do you mean, Sara's back?" I asked, picking up our conversation where we'd left off. "When did that happen? Back from where?"

"I don't know. You can ask." Bertie peered into the rearview mirror as she switched lanes. "That's why we're going, isn't it? To ask Sara a million questions?"

"I wonder if she'll have a million answers."

"Let's hope."

Blinker on, Bertie ran a yellow light and dove onto the parkway on-ramp. I braced myself against door and dashboard as the van swung around the turn.

"I found out something interesting yesterday," I said. "Sara's pregnant."

"Pregnant?" Bertie glanced in my direction. At the speed we were traveling, I'd have felt better with her eyes on the road. "Who told you that?"

"Maris Kincaid. She thought it might have had something to do with Sara's disappearance."

"Pregnant?" Bertie repeated. She didn't sound as though she liked that idea at all. "Who's the father?"

"I haven't a clue. Add it to the list of things we want to know. Should I start writing these down?"

"Pregnant?" Bertie snorted.

"Yes, pregnant," I said for what I hoped was the last time. "With child, knocked up, in the family way."

"I hope it isn't Josh's," Bertie said fervently.

So that was what had her so unnerved.

"I don't think so. Maris said Sara's less than two months along. She and Josh stopped seeing each other last summer, right?"

"I guess so."

I shot her a look. Josh had told me Sara dumped him in August for someone new. Bertie didn't sound convinced.

"Is there something going on I should know about?"

"Damned if I know," Bertie muttered.

All this conjecture wasn't helping matters any.

"Shut up and drive," I said.

Though it wasn't late, the back roads of New Canaan were dark and nearly deserted. No street lamps lit our way through the posh residential area. Luckily, Bertie knew where she was going. All the stone walls and split rail fences looked alike to me; I'd have been lost in a minute.

This time when we swept up the long driveway, Bertie took the right fork, which led around the front of the house. Floodlights, situated strategically among the trees, lit our approach and bathed the mansion in a soft glow. I was entranced by the sight.

Bertie took a more pragmatic approach. "What are you staring at?" she asked as she parked the van in front of a wide set of flagstone steps.

"This place is gorgeous."

"Try telling that to the Shelties in the kennel. I'm sure they'll be really impressed."

"What do you mean?"

"Just that." She got out and slammed her door. "Considering Delilah's reputation as a dog lover, you'd think we should see at least a couple of them running around, but we won't."

"Now that you mention it, I noticed that the last time I was here."

Bertie started up the steps. "No dogs in the house. That's the rule. Not that the kennel isn't a dream facility, but still. When Sara was living here, she and her mother used to fight about that all the time."

I pushed the doorbell and listened as chimes sounded within. "Sara knows we're coming, right?"

"Actually," Bertie admitted, "she knows *I'm* coming. You'll be something in the nature of a pleasant surprise."

Wonderful.

Grant Waring opened the door. A pair of reading glasses was perched low on his nose, and his feet were encased in a pair of scuffed leather slippers. Sara might have been expecting visitors, but clearly her stepfather wasn't. He recovered quickly, though.

"Good evening," he said, peering out onto the porch. "Bertie and . . . Melanie, right? Won't you come in?"

The floor in the front hall was made of marble. A curved stairway, highlighted by a Palladian window, led to the second floor.

"It's okay, Grant," Sara called out. Her voice, sounding exasperated, floated down to us from the top of the steps. "They're here for me."

Hand flying on the polished mahogany railing, she raced

down the wide staircase, each foot placed just so as she bent with the curve for maximum speed. It looked like a move she'd perfected in childhood, and I couldn't help thinking that for someone who'd led us on an exasperating chase, Sara was looking remarkably carefree.

"Can I fix you something to drink?" asked Grant.

"No," Sara snapped, answering for all of us. She clasped my hand and slipped an arm around Bertie's shoulders. "We're going upstairs."

Directed by our hostess, we turned our backs on Grant and walked away. The steps took us up to a circular landing, which led in turn to a long hallway. A door at one end was open and a pool of light spilled out. Sara headed that way.

"What was that about?" Bertie asked.

"What?"

"Grant was only trying to be friendly. You didn't have to bite his head off."

"Yes, I did."

So much for that line of questioning. I hoped the rest of the evening would prove more productive.

Following along behind, I found myself entering a bedroom that looked like a little girl's fantasy run amok. Flower sprigged wallpaper in pink and cream matched a ruffled canopy over the double bed. The wall-to-wall carpeting was a sea of fluffy pink shag. Lace curtains framed two pairs of wide windows and formed the skirt for a vanity table. Even the lampshades were trimmed with it. A floor-to-ceiling bookcase held a collection of ornately dressed and intricately made-up dolls. There wasn't a Raggedy Ann among them.

My eyes widened at the sight.

Sara noted my reaction and grimaced. "It hits most people like that. Delilah did it when I was little. The only time those dolls were ever touched was when the maid came in and dusted them. Is it any wonder I moved out as soon as I could?"

Sara didn't seem to expect an answer. Anyway, before I could decide how to respond, we were interrupted by the sound of nails scratching on wood. Quickly Sara closed and locked the bedroom door. Then she crossed the room and opened another door. Titus burst out of the bathroom, whining softly and bouncing on his hind legs.

"Shh," Sara warned, though the dog had barely made a sound. Taking him with her, she walked into the bathroom. "Come on. There's a sitting room on the other side. We'll be more comfortable there."

Indeed. The other half of Sara's suite was a big improvement over the bedroom. At least everything wasn't pink or made of lace. A love seat and two matching armchairs were grouped around a coffee table piled high with magazines. A television and VCR sat against one wall, and a closet held a small refrigerator and a microwave.

Sara got out three sodas and put a bag of popcorn in the microwave. While she waited for it to heat, she sat down in a chair and drew her legs up beneath her. Apparently sure of his welcome, Titus jumped up into her lap.

Sara lowered her face to his ruff, inhaling the dog's scent and caressing his soft hair with her cheek. It looked as though she'd missed the Sheltie as much as he'd missed her. She glanced up, saw me watching, and smiled.

"I wasn't expecting to see you tonight, Melanie."

"I guess that makes us even. I wasn't expecting to see you either. Where have you been?"

"It's kind of complicated."

"My whole last week has been complicated," I said evenly. Imagine that. Sara thought she was the only one with problems. "Bertie's been really worried about you."

"I know. I'm sorry. I just had to get away."

The microwave pinged. Sara started to get up. Bertie waved her back into her seat.

"You've got Titus. I'll get it."

There was an empty bowl on a shelf above the refrigerator. Bertie opened the steaming bag and poured the popcorn out. She set the snack on the table between us.

"Why did you have to get away?" I asked. Sara might have been able to evade Bertie's questions, but I had no intention of letting her sidestep mine.

"I was afraid," Sara said softly. She clutched the Sheltie to her as if she were holding onto a lifeline. "I had to go. I was afraid of what might happen if I stayed."

22

The words hung in the silence of the cozy room. It was like telling ghost stories at a pajama party. The air around us seemed suddenly charged with menace.

Then Bertie snorted loudly and the spell was broken. "Afraid?" she said, scooping out a handful of popcorn. "Of whom?"

"Like I said, it's complicated."

"That's okay," I told her. "We've got plenty of time."

"And besides, it's none of your business."

"Is that so?" Bertie demanded. "Then why did you leave me that note?"

"What note?"

"The one Terry delivered to me last week at the Hartford show. 'I know I can count on you, blah, blah, blah.' That note."

"Oh, that."

Bertie and I exchanged a glance.

"I didn't want to just go away without leaving word with someone. And you were the first person I thought of, because of the wedding. Believe me, I know how jumpy brides can get about things. I've almost been one myself once or twice."

Sara's light, self-deprecating laugh invited us to join in. Neither Bertie nor I did.

"I thought you wanted me to figure out why you'd disappeared," Bertie persisted. "I thought that's what you were counting on me to do. That's why I got Melanie involved. She and I have been looking for you."

"So Delilah informed me." Sara didn't sound pleased.

As if I cared. I wasn't particularly pleased with the way things had turned out myself.

"Where did you go?" I asked.

"What does it matter?"

"Humor me."

"I was staying with a friend."

"In Westchester?"

A fleeting look of surprise crossed Sara's face. "Yes."

"Why didn't you take Titus with you?" asked Bertie. "Your mother found him wandering around outside. That was one of the reasons we assumed something terrible had happened to you."

"I . . . he . . ." Sara hesitated. Her fingers rubbed along the soft, pink skin of the Sheltie's stomach. Turning in her arms, Titus wiggled in delight. Dogs are such suckers. They'll forgive anything. "The person I was staying with doesn't like dogs. In fact, she's allergic. I left plenty of food and water, and he knows how to use the dog door. I thought he'd be fine."

Sara sounded sincere, but I wasn't buying it. Would I have gone off and left Faith behind, alone and unattended? Not a chance.

"Why were you looking for a lawyer?" I asked.

"A lawyer?" Sara was startled. "How did you know about that?"

"I told you," said Bertie, "I asked Melanie to look for you. She's good."

"I guess," Sara muttered. "You must have spoken with Debra Silver."

"I did."

"I'll bet she had plenty to say about me."

"Actually, she was very circumspect."

"Did she drag you off to some god-awful nouveau chic restaurant and stick you with the bill?"

In spite of myself, I had to smile. "You're half right."

"Don't tell me you managed to get her to pay?"

"No, we split it. But you were right about the restaurant. It was very chic."

"The only kind of place Debra will be seen in," Sara said. Obviously she was hoping I'd continue to let her change the subject.

No dice, I thought.

"Did the fact that you were looking for a lawyer have anything to do with your pregnancy?"

Sara paled slightly. My questions were beginning to hit home. She reached for her soda and took a long drink. When she set the can back down, her features were composed once more.

"My, you have been busy. I guess I should be flattered."

"Or frightened." I was sure I'd hit a sore spot there. I wondered what a little probing might turn up.

"What makes you say that?"

"Your reaction, for one thing. You *are* pregnant, aren't you?"

Sara's hand went reflexively to her stomach. "Yes."

"Is that good news?" asked Bertie.

"In the beginning I thought so. Lately I'm not so sure."

"How come?"

"Among other things, I've been having some problems with the baby's father. He thinks I should get an abortion. That's one of the reasons I dropped out of sight for a few days. I needed some time to think."

"Who is the father?" I asked.

Even to my own ears, the question sounded blunt and nosy. I didn't care. I still wanted to know.

I wasn't entirely surprised, however, when Sara frowned at me and said firmly, "That's private."

"Someone we know?" Bertie prompted.

Sara wasn't playing. "Someone *I* know," she snapped. As if that wasn't obvious.

"What about Grant and Delilah?" Bertie asked. "Do they know about the baby?"

Sara didn't answer right away. "Grant does," she said finally. "I told him because I thought he might take the news better than Delilah. I was hoping he would help me break it to her, but when it comes to my mother, he turned out to be a bigger chicken than I am."

"Let's see if I have this straight," I said, trying to line up what she'd told us so far. "You found out you were pregnant. You decided to go away for a few days to think things over. You left your dog behind in your house and sent a note to Bertie so she wouldn't worry."

A trace of sarcasm overlaid that last sentence, but Sara, who was nodding in agreement as I spoke, didn't seem to notice.

"And then while you were gone," Bertie contributed, "all hell broke loose."

Sara's lower lip began to tremble. Her head dipped into

the Sheltie's luxurious ruff. Once again, she was using Titus as a shield.

"Do you have any idea who might have set the fire that burned down your cottage?" I asked.

"None," Sara whispered. Tears welled in her eyes. Her voice was unsteady. "Who could have hated me that much?"

"You said you were having problems with the baby's father—"

She didn't even let me finish the thought. "Not problems like that!"

"I'm sure the police will want to know—"

Sara shook her head and interrupted again. "I've already spoken to the police. Delilah had them here this afternoon. I answered all their questions."

The police had no way of knowing about Sara's pregnancy, I thought. Maybe they hadn't known the right questions to ask. She was walking a slender tightrope if she thought she could hide information like that during a murder investigation.

"Did they ask where you were on Saturday night?"

"You mean, did they check my alibi? Yeah, they did. And I had one, too. I was at a club in Manhattan with a couple of people I know."

"All night?"

"Late enough."

Bertie stepped in and turned the conversation in a new direction. "Carole Eikenberry was a friend of yours, wasn't she?" she asked.

Sara sniffled loudly. Tears spilled over and ran down her cheeks. Out of the corner of my eye, I saw Bertie frown. There was a box of tissues on a table near the door. She got up and brought it over.

"Carole was a good friend," Sara said softly. "Someone who was always there for me."

"I don't think I've ever heard you mention her before."

"So?" Sara pulled out a tissue and blew her nose. "I don't tell everybody everything. I probably never talked about you to her either."

Bertie didn't look appeased. I wondered what she was thinking. When she didn't press the issue, however, I asked a question of my own. "Sara, do you know what Carole was doing at your cottage on Saturday night?"

"I have no idea." Sara's nose was turning red. Mascara smeared beneath her eyes.

"You weren't expecting her?"

"How could I have been expecting her when I wasn't even there?"

"Had you spoken with her recently?"

"Look," Sara said, drawing a ragged breath. "I've already been all through this with the police. I don't *know* what happened."

Blinking back fresh tears, she gazed at us mournfully. "I'm really sorry about all the trouble I caused both of you. If I'd had any idea how things would turn out, I would never have left in the first place. I was only trying to do what I thought was best for me and my baby."

Sara reached up and wiped her face with the back of her sleeve. The childlike gesture made her look unexpectedly vulnerable. She set Titus aside and stood. "I hope you guys don't mind, but I'm really worn out."

Taking our cue, Bertie and I got up, too.

"Are you going to be staying here?" I asked Sara.

"For the time being, until everything gets sorted out, yes."

"So if someone needed to get in touch with you, this is where you'd be."

Sara looked annoyed. "I'm not going to disappear again, if that's what you're asking."

It had been, but I didn't see the need to belabor the point. Sara walked us down to the front door. We didn't see any sign of her parents on the way out. I guessed that was the beauty of living in a mansion the size of a small hotel.

After the warmth of the house, the November air felt shockingly cold. I gathered my coat around me, shivering as I opened the van door, and slid onto a chilly leather seat. Bertie glanced at me as she fastened her seat belt and put the key in the ignition.

"It'll only take a minute to warm up. Then you'll think you're in a sauna. Best thing about this truck is the heater."

Neither of us spoke until we reached the end of the long driveway. It had only taken a minute, but the interior of the van was already toasty. I stretched out my legs and settled back in my seat.

"So what did you make of all that?" Bertie asked as she pulled out onto West Road.

"I'm not sure," I replied honestly. "I think Sara knows more about what's going on than she's willing to admit."

"Tell me about it," Bertie agreed. "For the most part, all she did was confirm what we already knew. And there's no way I bought that act of hers."

"What act?"

"Puleez." Bertie pursed her lips. "That whole crying jag. One minute we're both pushing her pretty hard for information and the next, she bursts into tears. Give me a break. I've never even seen Sara cry before. I doubt if she'd know an honest emotion if it came up and bit her on the butt."

"I don't know," I said slowly. "I thought Sara seemed genuinely upset about what happened to Carole."

"That's what she wanted us to think, anyway. Sara's not

the type of person who really gets involved in her friends' lives. And how close could she and Carole have been? She didn't even know the woman was planning to show up."

"You're looking at it backwards. I think they must have been very close. Close enough that Carole didn't feel the need to call ahead before coming over."

"There is another possibility," said Bertie. "Maybe Sara's good buddy, Carole, is the one who set the fire. That would explain what she was doing there Saturday night *and* how she managed to get caught in the blaze."

"A scenario like that pretty much assumes that Sara was lying to us," I pointed out.

"It wouldn't be the first time." Bertie sounded disgusted. "Like when she said she left that note to make *me* feel better. I don't believe that for a minute. Sara had to know she'd stir things up. That's probably what she had in mind all along."

"Here's something else," I said. "When you spoke with Sara on Tuesday, didn't she tell you that she'd been away for the weekend and just gotten back and heard the news?"

Bertie thought for a moment. "That's right."

"Then tonight, when I asked her where she was on Saturday night, she said she'd been in Manhattan with friends. I imagine she was telling the truth about that because she's probably expecting the police to check on it."

"Which means she was lying to me earlier," Bertie said grimly.

"It looks that way."

I sat in silence for a while, pondering the evening's events. "I think Sara's still afraid of something," I said after a few minutes had passed. "Or someone."

Bertie didn't look particularly sympathetic. "Maybe she ought to be. The way things are shaping up, the next person likely to do her harm is going to be me."

"Hey," I said, spreading my hands innocently. "You were the one who wanted her back."

"Just shoot me now," Bertie muttered, "and put me out of my misery."

"It's going to be a beautiful wedding."

"If nobody else dies in the meantime."

Good thought.

23

Be careful what you wish for, the Chinese proverb advises. Because you just may get it.

Bertie had wished for Sara to be found, and look how that had turned out. I had wished for a father for Davey—thinking Sam, Sam, Sam—and now Bob was back in the picture. Maybe this was God's way of playing some giant cosmic joke.

If so, I wasn't laughing.

What I was doing was putting all those matters temporarily aside and enjoying a day off. Davey was at school and Bob had promised to meet the bus at our house that afternoon. The two of them would see to Faith. I was on my way to the Tuxedo Park Poodle Specialty in Tarrytown, New York to watch Aunt Peg perform her first, provisional judging assignment.

Whoopee!

Specialties are dog shows where only a single breed is judged. The Poodle Club of America is the governing body for Poodles and it recognizes several dozen affiliate clubs in various parts of the country. The Tuxedo Park Poodle Club was a new organization whose membership had grown steadily. I knew Aunt Peg had been enormously pleased and flattered by their invitation.

While hiring judges for an all-breed show can be a delicate juggling act, with dozens of considerations that must be taken into account, specialty clubs have only one mandate: get the best. Aunt Peg not only had superb credentials in the Poodle breed, but she also had the benefit of being an unknown quantity as a judge. Every potential exhibitor would feel that he or she had an equal chance.

Poodle breeders in the Northeast would come to the show because they'd known and admired the Cedar Crest dogs for decades. Owner-handlers would come to support one of their own and hope she supported them in return. And the pros would come because they couldn't afford not to. Someone of Aunt Peg's stature figured to move up quickly in the ranks of important judges, and they wanted to scope out her preferences and technique.

Though I'd pretended otherwise, I could understand why Peg was nervous. In her place, I'd have been nearly catatonic. But when I reached the civic center, walked in, and found her sitting by herself in a small side room with a book and a cup of tea, Aunt Peg appeared perfectly serene.

"Hello," she said, glancing up and setting her book aside. "What are you doing hiding in here?"

"Has the Sweepstakes started?"

Still standing in the doorway, I looked back out into the main room. "The Minis are in the ring already."

"Good. That's what I'm doing here. Not watching."

Of course. I'd forgotten the rules Aunt Peg had explained to me. She obviously had not.

In order to avoid any appearance of impropriety, the

A.K.C. sets guidelines that govern judges' behavior. Aunt Peg was not supposed to watch the judging prior to her own assignment, and she was prohibited from fraternizing with the exhibitors. There were close to two hundred people in the outer room. Due to her long association in the breed, Aunt Peg knew every one of them—which was why she'd deliberately sequestered herself.

"I probably shouldn't have come so early," she said. "But I allowed extra time for traffic, or in case I got lost on the way. And what if I'd had a flat tire?"

None of those seemed a viable concern to me, but I nodded anyway. It was what she needed.

"When I got here, they were still setting up the rings. The show chairman very kindly volunteered to baby-sit me—not that she put it quite that way, of course—but I've done her job often enough to know that she had a million better things to do, so I sent her off and came in here by myself."

Good old Aunt Peg, self-sufficient to the core.

"Nice corsage," I mentioned.

A carnation the size of a small grapefruit had been pinned to the lapel of her suit, just above the small blue ribbon that identified her as the judge. It was obviously a gift from the show committee. In the ring, the sweepstakes judge was similarly adorned.

"They meant well." Aunt Peg lowered her head and took a sniff. "And it does smell rather nice. I only hope it doesn't scare the baby puppies half to death."

"Let me just get a cup of coffee." I'd passed the kitchen area on the way in. "I'll be right back to keep you company."

As I waited my turn in the food line, I gazed around at the show. The venue the club had chosen was roomy and bright. As was usually the case, half the main room had been set aside for grooming. The other half was comprised of two large, fully matted rings. In the front one, the puppy sweeps was in progress. The ring behind that featured an obedience trial, Poodles only.

The most notable difference between this specialty and the many all-breed shows I'd attended was how quiet it was. As a general rule, indoor dog shows tend to be noisy. Dogs left in crates bark from boredom or excitement. And as soon as one or two get started, others are only too happy to join in.

Not Poodles, however. Trained not to bark on their tables or in their crates, they don't. Other than conversation, the only sound in the room was the persistent hum of the big free-standing blow-dryers and an occasional smattering of applause from ringside.

"You'll never guess where I was last night," I said when I'd gotten my coffee and rejoined Aunt Peg. "Bertie and I went to the Warings' house in New Canaan. Sara's come back home."

"It's about time. Is she all right?"

"She certainly appears to be. But there's something else. She's pregnant."

"No!" Several emotions played across Aunt Peg's face as she calculated the effect of that news. "Delilah doesn't know that, does she?"

"No, but Grant does. He was supposed to break the news to her but hasn't."

"I can imagine he wouldn't look forward to that task," Peg mused. "Telling Delilah that her unmarried daughter is about to make her a grandmother? It's not something I'd jump at the chance to do."

Sipping my hot coffee, I recounted the highlights of the previous evening's conversation. Not surprisingly, Aunt Peg was annoyed by how few questions Sara's reappearance had managed to clear up.

"So that's it?" she asked incredulously. "The girl is back and now we're all just supposed to go on with our lives as if nothing happened?"

"Well, except for Carole Eikenberry, presumably."

"Sara must know more than she's telling. I can't believe the police haven't gotten more answers out of her."

"Maybe they did. She said she'd spoken to them. And there was one other idea that occurred to me. . . ."

"What?" Aunt Peg pounced.

"Not yet." I shook my head firmly. "I may be way off base with this. I'd rather do some checking before I say anything."

Promptly at eleven o'clock, the steward called the first class into the ring. Aunt Peg's judging assignment began with Toy Poodles, Puppy Dogs, 6-9 Months Old. Three tiny, adorable Poodle puppies came prancing through the gate, scampering on the rubber mats and playing at the end of their ribbon-thin leads.

Aunt Peg, who had spent the previous ten minutes arranging the tables in her ring, picking nonexistent bits of fluff off the mats, thumbing through her judge's book, and standing, stiff-shouldered, in what hardly looked like joyous anticipation, now took one look at the three small entries that awaited her attention, and smiled blissfully.

Standing ringside, I let out the breath I'd been holding. Everything was going to be just fine. Aunt Peg, who had dedicated the majority of her life to the betterment of the Poodle breed, was about to have a ball. She raised her hands, sent the trio of puppies around the ring, and got down to work.

I spent the rest of the morning watching her judge. By the second class, Aunt Peg had hit her stride. Her touch on the smallest variety of Poodles was deft, her fingers gentle but sure. Unlike some judges, who are put off by the hair and the spray, Aunt Peg thrust her hands eagerly into the coats, feeling for the correct bone structure beneath the beautiful trims.

When the big Open Dog class took command of the ring, I watched as Aunt Peg deliberately kept one entry on the table longer than the others. The little white dog sported a topknot of gargantuan proportions. Peg flipped the hair to one side, taking a long and careful look at the rubber bands that held the ponytails in place. Then she lifted her gaze and stared hard at the dog's professional handler, who was doing his level best to look entirely innocent.

Aunt Peg wasn't fooled and neither was the ringside. As soon as she declined to place the otherwise deserving Toy, her theatrics had the intended effect. Within minutes, word circulated throughout the grooming area. Fake hair—also known as wiglets and switches—was quickly removed from entries undergoing the final stages of preparation for the ring. The A.K.C. makes the rules, but it's up to each judge to enforce them. Aunt Peg was serving notice, right from the start, that she wasn't about to tolerate any shenanigans in her ring.

Best of Variety in Toys went to a beautiful silver champion, whose Japanese handler had brought a string of Poodles all the way up from Maryland for the show. While Aunt Peg posed for win pictures, I grabbed some lunch from the food stand. Peg would be served an elegant sit-down meal with the club president and the other judges, and I wouldn't see her again until the end of the hour-long break. In the meantime, there was something I wanted to do.

Crawford Langley's large setup was near the front of the room in a sunny area beside two wide windows. More than a dozen Standard and Miniature Poodles, in varying stages of readiness, were sitting out on their grooming tables. (The

Toys, having already been judged, had been put back in their crates.)

Crawford was scissoring a tall, black Standard dog whose ears and topknot were still done up in aqua-blue plastic wrappers. At the other end of the aisle, his assistant, Terry, was blow-drying the legs on a brown Mini puppy. His dryer, hooked to the wall by a bright orange electric cord, hummed as he worked.

"Hey, doll," Terry said as I approached. "Is Peg doing a fabulous job or what?"

I knew he'd be pleased. Crawford had been Winners Bitch and Best of Winners in Toys. The bitch's owners were probably already planning a celebratory ad to crow about the five-point major win.

"Fabulous," I agreed. The effusive word sounded better coming from him. "Better still, I think she's having fun."

"I should hope so," Terry sniffed, "considering we're working our fingers to the bone making everyone look absolutely gorgeous for her."

There was an empty grooming table behind me. I pulled it over and scooted up to sit on top. "You and Crawford make your dogs look gorgeous even when you show to Ed Huntly," I pointed out.

Huntly was a Bulldog man, and pretty was a concept entirely lost on him. That never stopped Crawford from trying, though.

"What can I say?" Terry preened. If there'd been a mirror handy, he'd have checked his reflection. "Being beautiful is a curse some of us just have to bear."

"Luckily, you seem to be holding up well."

"At my tender age, I should hope so. You, on the other hand . . ." His baby blue eyes passed critically up and down over my outfit: navy corduroy pants, wool turtleneck, and

comfortable loafers. ". . . could use some work. I don't mean
to pry, dear, but have you ever read a fashion magazine?"

"No," I said, just to goad him. Ever since Terry had
started cutting my hair a year earlier, he seemed to think that
gave him license to comment on any aspect of my life he
found lacking. "But I do have the last three issues of *Dogs in
Review* sitting on my coffee table at home. Does that help?"

"Mais oui. If you're aiming to look like an Irish Setter."

Terry paused to turn the brown Poodle over: pushing the
nozzle aside with an elbow, lifting the Mini with one hand,
deftly slipping the damp towel out from beneath it with the
other, then replacing it with a dry one and resettling the
puppy on top. Terry made the adjustment look easy. The Mini
was snoozing again in no time.

"So," he said casually, "what have we heard from Sam?"

I felt a pang, just like I always did, just like I probably always would, whenever someone mentioned his name.

"Nothing." I forced a smile. "You?"

Terry had had a crush on Sam since the first time they'd
met. The fact that Terry was gay and Sam straight had never
deterred Terry from enjoying his infatuation.

"Not a word." He looked at me and his voice softened.
"He will come back, you know."

I shrugged. It took everything I had to hold my expression steady. "I guess. When he's ready."

"I'm no expert on relationships, but I think you ought to
work this one a little harder."

"Work it?" Outrage stiffened my shoulders. "What is
there to work? Sam left me."

"Did you go after him?"

"No. Would you have?"

"Probably not." Terry shrugged. "Plenty of fish in my sea.
The trouble with you is, I don't see you baiting your hook.

You're in limbo, doll. And that ex of yours that just showed up?" He rolled his eyes. "Don't even get me started."

"Bob? I didn't know you two had met."

"He was at Hartford, right? Taking the child around, showing him the sights. Or vice versa."

I nodded, relaxing. Bob was much easier to discuss than Sam. "What's the matter with him?"

"Nothing, I suppose, if you're old enough to remember *Urban Cowboy.*"

"Bob lives in Texas."

"As if *that's* an excuse."

Terry finished the puppy's second hind leg and turned off the dryer. I'd grown so used to the noise, the quiet came as a surprise.

"If you're finished with that puppy, Marla hasn't been brushed yet." From the other end of the aisle, Crawford slanted a critical look in our direction.

Crawford Langley was an imposing figure, and he knew it. Since teaming up with Terry, he'd let his hair go gray; now it matched the steely shade of his eyes. His posture was impeccable; his taste in clothing, superb.

He was the top Poodle handler in New England, an enviable position that he'd held for as long as Aunt Peg had been showing dogs. In the ring, Crawford never underestimated an opponent. Outside it, he was unfailingly gracious and always discreet.

Unlike his flamboyant partner, who enjoyed good dish more than anything. Thanks to Crawford's vast network of connections, Terry had sources everywhere. A situation I hadn't been above exploiting from time to time.

Someday Crawford may figure out how to get me to stop pumping Terry for information, but it hasn't happened yet.

"Marla?" I asked.

"Open Bitch." Terry sighed. "Big hair. Bad hair. Pouf it up and it just falls flat. That's why we always save her for last."

"Can you talk and brush at the same time?"

"Do pigs eat truffles?"

Terry opened a large wooden crate, reached in and cupped his hand around the muzzle of a white Standard Poodle bitch with a stunning head and tight, arched feet. As soon as I saw the face, I recognized Marla; I'd shown against her with Faith last year when Marla was in the puppy class. Even then, her limp, wispy coat had been a liability, and I didn't think Crawford had managed to put many points on her.

"Aunt Peg will love that head," I said, sliding off the table-top as Terry hoisted the bitch up onto the other side.

"And her front." Terry took my hands, placing one on the bitch's withers, the other on her chest, and let me feel for myself.

It's considered exceedingly bad manners to touch some-one's dog without asking. Not only are you likely to muss the hair, but you also might discover secrets about poor structure that the handler was planning to use that hair to hide. The fact that Terry invited me to verify his claim meant that the bitch's front assembly had to be above reproach.

"Teeth?" I asked.

Terry nodded and I lifted Marla's top lip. The Poodle's tail wagged as I had a look. All were there, with the correct scissors bite.

I remembered Marla as an exuberant puppy with consid-erable reach and drive. The lack of coat—considered to be of paramount importance by that all-too-common breed of clueless judges who don't know what else to look for—wouldn't mean a fig to Aunt Peg.

"She'll love her," I said to Terry.

He glanced in Crawford's direction and was relieved to see that the handler hadn't overheard. Crawford, like Aunt Peg, is superstitious enough to believe in jinxes.

"We're hoping," he replied.

The dog show mantra.

24

Terry placed Marla on her side on the grooming table with her right side up. The left side—the side that faces the judge during competition—is always brushed last. He then sifted through the arsenal in his tack box, selecting and laying out an array of tools.

Finished with the Standard dog, Crawford came sauntering down the aisle to check on his assistant's progress. "If you're going to hang around," he said, handing me a pin brush and greyhound comb, "you might as well make yourself useful. That brown puppy's head and ears need to be brushed out."

A pro like Crawford would never let anyone touch his trims, his topknots or his spray jobs. But brushing, once you knew the routine, was idiot work. Presumably, I qualified.

"Don't let Terry give you advice about your love life," Crawford counseled. His hearing must have been better than we'd thought. "He doesn't know what he's talking about."

"No?" I grinned. Crawford and Terry had been partners

for more than a year. "It looks to me like he's doing pretty well."

"Sure, *he* is," Crawford grumbled fondly. "But what about me?"

"You've got the best looking boy on the block," Terry announced immodestly.

Crawford's only answer to that was to lift one brow. Then he pointed his comb at me. "Exes are always trouble. Tell yours to take a hike."

Just what I needed, another mother.

"I didn't know you'd met Bob, too."

"I didn't have to meet him. I heard about him."

"What is he, famous?"

"Word gets around." Crawford's calm, direct gaze nailed me. "And you never come by my setup unless you need help."

"Not with Bob. Him, I can handle."

"Then who?" Terry asked curiously.

"Sara Bentley."

Crawford shook his head. "I should have known." This time the comb pointed at Terry. "You—keep working." It swung back to me. "You—try not to get him in too much trouble."

He turned on his heel and strode away.

"I think Crawford's getting used to you," said Terry.

"Resigned is more like it." I popped the rubber bands out of the puppy's short, spikey topknot and began to brush.

"What about Sara Bentley?"

"This is kind of delicate," I said.

"Perfect," Terry cooed. "I'm good with delicate."

"I might be totally wrong about this, but I had an idea— an inkling really—and I wanted to see what you thought."

"I don't mean to complain, doll . . ." Terry glanced up.

"But at the rate you're going, you'll have to e-mail your questions to me after the show."

He was right, I was stalling. In truth, I'd been stalling ever since I came over. I might as well just blurt it out.

"Here's what I was wondering about. Is Sara Bentley gay?"

Terry tipped his head to one side, considering me with a bemused expression on his face. "Is this one of those gaydar things? Like I should know because I'm gay? Honey, in case it hasn't occurred to you, that's not the way it works. I check out men. Or maybe you figure that if we're gay, we'd all hang out together, common bond and all that—"

"Quit it!" I wasn't sure whether I wanted to laugh or blush. "Just shut up. That isn't what I meant and you know it."

"Okay." He was prepared to be placated. "What did you mean?"

"I came to you because you know everyone's secrets." His tone was playful. "I don't know yours."

"Terry, you cut my hair. You know everything there is to know about me."

"Maybe you're right." He reconsidered. "Crawford thinks you have hidden depths, but maybe you don't."

"He does?" I focused on what Terry had said at the beginning, rather than the implied insult at the end.

"Of course he does. That's why he worries about you."

"Crawford worries about me?" This conversation was turning out to be full of surprises. "I thought he just found me annoying."

"That, too," Terry admitted.

Right. It was time to get back to the topic at hand. "Sara?"

"Yes."

"Yes, what?"

"Looking at things in your narrow, compartmentalized, hetero way, I guess you might say that Sara is gay."

It was also turning out to be full of insults.

"How about if, just for a minute, I was able to shed the inhibitions of my conventional life and look at things from your ultra-hip, free-spirited homosexual viewpoint?"

Terry smiled. My sarcasm had hit home. "Then you'd probably say she's bi."

That wasn't such a hard concept to accept. In fact, it made a lot of sense.

"So Sara likes men and women both?"

"So it seems." He made a new part in Marla's hair and continued to brush. "Does it matter?"

I nodded. "I'm pretty sure it does. I'm just not sure how yet. How well do you know Sara?"

Terry shrugged, an answer that was pretty much what I'd expected.

"You wouldn't happen to know who she's been seeing for the last few months, would you?"

"Does this have anything to do with her house burning down?"

"I think so."

"Then why don't you go ask Sara herself?"

"We're back to that delicate thing again. There's some stuff she doesn't want to talk about."

The brown puppy squeaked and looked at me reproachfully as my comb caught in a small tangle in his ear hair. I soothed the ear leather with my fingertips and teased the knot apart.

"Then I guess we'll just have to talk about it for her," Terry agreed. "But to tell you the truth, I don't keep tabs. Wasn't she seeing some yummy guy who was related to Bertie?"

"Last summer. But there was someone after that. Some-one who was important to her."

Important enough to be the father of her unborn child, I thought but didn't add.

"Sorry, can't help you there."

"That's all right. Actually, you've been a big help."

"Of course. Aren't I always?" He leaned closer and whis-pered, "Want to pay me back? I could use some influence with the judge."

"Baloney," I said loudly.

"Oh, well, it was worth a try."

Crawford reappeared to put in the brown puppy's top-knot. My job was done, and the lunch break was ending. Aunt Peg, looking well fed and eager to get back to work, was once more in her ring.

The rest of the afternoon careened by. There's something about playing hooky from school that makes time pass with unseemly speed. Aunt Peg sorted out her Miniature Poodle entry with dispatch, then turned with great enthusiasm to her Standards.

By the time the dust had settled at the end of the day, the Mini puppy I'd helped to brush out had been third in a class of three, but Marla had gone Winners Bitch to secure her first major. A beautiful black Standard champion from Pennsylvania had won Best of Variety, with the silver Toy beating both him and the Miniature for Best of Breed.

At any dog show, there will always be more losers than winners. Aunt Peg had quieted much of the usual grumbling, however, by declaring herself available to discuss her deci-sions at the end of the day. I'd hoped to have another chance to talk to her, but in light of her pronouncement, Peg became a much sought-after guest at the wine and cheese party after the show. I wasted half an hour trying to get her alone and watching as none of my twenty raffle tickets won a prize. Finally I gave up, grabbed a couple of cubes of cheddar, and headed home.

Even though I was heading mostly against the rush-hour traffic out of White Plains at five-thirty on a Friday afternoon, I wasn't going to get anywhere quickly. Half of New York's residents seemed to be in their cars, and every one of them wanted to be somewhere other than where they were. I was afraid Bob might be annoyed by the delay—I'd told him I'd be home early and he could go ahead and make plans for Friday night—but when I called from the car, he sounded curiously acquiescent.

"Just have a safe trip," he said. "Whenever you get here, Davey and Faith and I will be waiting."

Give me a break. Who did he think he was, Mr. Donna Reed?

Just for the heck of it, I asked Bob to put Davey on the phone.

"Hi, Mom," my son chirped happily.

"Everything okay?"

"Sure. It's great. Dad and I are making a surprise."

"A surprise?" I gulped. "What kind of surprise?"

Davey didn't answer, but I did hear him giggle. A moment later, Bob was back.

"See you soon," he said cheerfully.

"Bob?" I braked abruptly in the bumper-to-bumper traffic, paying too much attention to the phone and not enough to my driving. "What's going on?"

There was no answer. I was talking to dead air.

When I finally reached home, everything looked normal. Still, I sat in the Volvo for a minute before going in. Excited as Davey had sounded, I couldn't quiet the nagging thought that my son and my ex-husband were up to no good.

Presently the front door opened and Bob peered out.

"There you are," he said, squinting into the darkness. "Faith told us you were here, but you didn't come in, so I came to check. Need any help?"

"No, I'm fine, thanks."

As I got out of the car, I realized what Bob had said. *Faith told them I was there?* When had my ex-husband started listening to my dog? More important, when had he started understanding her?

Bob came down the steps and walked over to the driveway. "Long day?"

"The day was lots of fun. It was the traffic on the way home that nearly did me in. How about you guys? Have you been entertaining yourselves?"

Bob shut the Volvo's door and looped an arm around my shoulders. "We went shopping."

"Shopping?" That was hardly the answer I'd expected. "For what?"

"Umm . . ."

Bob hesitating was never a good sign. I pulled away.

"I told Davey we had to get your permission first," he said.

"What are you two up to?"

"Basketball. Davey wants a hoop."

"He has a hoop."

A small one, set on a plastic stand and base that sat in the backyard. Though now that Bob mentioned it, I realized Davey had had that child's version of the real thing since he was three.

Bob slanted me a look. "He wants a real hoop, regulation height, with a backboard. Something that doesn't fall over if the ball hits it too hard."

I stopped and looked around at the short, narrow driveway that connected my house to the street. Between Bob's Trans Am and my car that was now parked behind it, the paved area was nearly full. And installing a hoop off to one side would either block our front door or encroach on the neighbor's property.

"There isn't room for a full-sized hoop," I said. "Where would it go?"

"If it's all right with you, I could nail the backboard to the garage. That way, we wouldn't need to install a pole and the whole thing would take up a lot less space. As long as you park inside the garage, Davey will have plenty of room to dribble and shoot."

"Inside the garage?" Lately I'd been letting things pile up, which was why the Volvo had been spending nights out in the driveway. "I guess you haven't taken a look in there recently."

"Actually, I did. This afternoon." Bob grasped the handle on the door and raised it. "Davey and I saw you had some work to do, so we did it."

He walked inside and turned on the light. I stared, dumbfounded, at what was surely the most pleasant surprise I'd had in a long time. The single car space, which that morning had been so cluttered with junk I could barely open the door, was now neat and clear. One might almost say pristine.

I hate cleaning the garage, which is why I do it as seldom as possible. In the spring and summer it's easy to ignore the problem. But with winter coming, I'd been steeling myself for the task. And now, just like that, it was done. Six months' worth of debris and neglect—gone. Knowing what Bob had had to work with, the transformation bordered on miraculous.

Slowly I walked over to stand in the pool of light that flowed out onto the driveway. "Where did you put everything?"

"Some of it was just a matter of organization." He

sounded smug. A man, Bob's tone implied, would never let such valuables as tools and lawn mowers come to such a state. "And we took the recycling to the dump. The rest of it, the stuff that looked like junk, Davey and I piled outside around the corner. Once you've had a chance to look at it and make sure there's nothing you want, we'll load it up and haul it away."

It was all a little much to take in.

"Who are you really?" I asked. "And what have you done with my ex-husband?"

Bob moved over to stand beside me. "I hoped you'd be pleased."

"Pleased? I love it. You're a lifesaver. . . ."

His hand slid up my arm to my shoulder. He turned me to face him and I realized how close he was standing. The soft, indirect lighting threw muted shadows over us both.

"I'm going to kiss you," Bob said.

"Yes."

It was just that simple. And just that good.

My fingers went up to tangle in his hair. His warm breath mingled with mine. It wasn't until several minutes had passed and I began to feel frustrated by the bulky layers of clothing between us that I remembered we were standing outside, in the cold, in full view of the neighborhood. Damn.

The realization was enough to make me pull away.

With obvious regret, Bob let me go. "To be continued," he said.

My heart, already thumping hard in my chest, gave a little leap. Did I want this? I wondered. Could I handle this? I had no idea.

A large box tucked in the back corner of the garage caught my eye. Grateful for the distraction, I went to see what it was.

"Backboard and hoop," Bob said, following me. "Davey and I were hoping you'd say yes. If not, we can return it tomorrow."

"It's fine. Better than fine. It's a great idea. Of course Davey's outgrown that little hoop. I should have thought to do something about it myself—"

Bob's hand reached up, fingers pressing against my lips. I knew he wanted only to silence me, but the move felt unbearably erotic. For a moment, I not only couldn't speak, I couldn't breathe. I had to force myself to concentrate so I could hear what Bob was saying.

"It's harder for you to see these things because you have him every day and the changes come so gradually." Bob sighed. "He's growing up so quickly. And you're doing a wonderful job, Mel."

"Thanks." I exhaled slowly. It felt as though I'd been holding my breath for a week. "He loves having you here."

Bob flipped off the light, then reached for the overhead door. I stepped back out of the way as he pulled it down into place.

Over the rumble of castors rolling through the grooves, I could have sworn I heard him say, "Maybe I should stay here, then."

"What?"

Bob straightened, turned, and smiled. "Nothing."

Nothing indeed.

25

Inside, Davey and Faith were waiting for us.

"What took you guys so long?" my son complained.

"We were looking at your new basketball hoop," I said.

Davey's eyes lit up. "You mean it's all right?"

"Fine by me. You and Dad are the ones who are going to do all the work. And speaking of work, thanks for straightening up the garage."

Davey's small frame swelled with pride. "We cleaned for *hours*."

"It looks like it. You did a terrific job."

I looked through the living room into the dining room and saw that the table was set for two. In the center, pale pink roses were floating in a low vase. They were flanked by a pair of polished candlesticks, holding new ivory-colored tapers.

"What's up?" I asked.

Davey giggled. Bob closed the front door. Was I the only one who noticed that nobody answered?

"Remember our deal," Bob said in an undertone to Davey.

I have mother's ears, teacher's ears. Nothing sneaky gets past me. "What deal?" I asked.

Davey lifted his hand to his mouth and yawned lustily. "I'm really tired," he said. "I think I'll go to bed."

"Now? It's barely seven o'clock."

"G'night!" Davey scampered up the steps. Faith trotted along behind him.

That left just the two of us, and all at once, my ex-husband's ears were looking a little pink.

"Bob?"

His smile was hesitant, tentative. "Surprise."

I gazed once more toward the dining room, considered my options, and decided that I quite liked the notion of being cosseted. "You cooked dinner, too?"

"Too?"

"I thought the clean garage was my surprise."

Briefly, Bob looked taken aback. "The garage? What's romantic about that?"

Little did he know.

I walked through to the dining room and stopped beside the table, lowering my face to inhale the roses' heady scent. "Is that what you were aiming for, romance?"

The color in Bob's ears spread to his cheeks. "Umm . . . I guess. Is it working?"

"It's working." I turned to face him. "Thank you."

"You're welcome." He looked like a man who needed desperately to find something to do with his hands. "I have some wine chilling in the refrigerator. Would you like a glass?"

"Sure."

Why not? I thought. This was Bob's show. He could run it

any way he liked. I followed him out to the kitchen. Whatever he had in the oven smelled wonderful.

"What's for dinner?"

He pulled out a cold bottle of chardonnay and attacked the cork with a corkscrew. "You know I don't actually cook."

"Still?"

When Bob and I were together, hamburgers, charred on the grill, had been the limit of his culinary expertise. But he'd had years since then—most of them bachelor years—to rectify that situation.

"Still." He eased the cork out of the bottle and filled two wine goblets. "Frank told me about a little catering shop in Greenwich."

"Not Fabulous Food?"

"That's the one. He recommended the veal piccata."

"I love veal piccata."

"I know."

Bob handed me a glass, then held his own aloft. "How about a toast?"

"To what?"

"Old friends." He cocked a brow. "New beginnings?"

I found myself hesitating. "Are you sure this is a good idea?"

"Are you so sure it isn't?"

"No."

Bob reached over and gently raised my arm. "Then let's just go with that for now."

The older I get, the more I've realized there are some things in life that maybe we aren't meant to understand. Or to examine. Or to rail against. Sometimes you just have to let go and let fate take you for a ride. So I didn't have all the answers. Maybe, for once, I could just stop asking so many questions.

I lit the candles while Bob served the food. The veal piccata was indeed fabulous and we both dug in hungrily. Neither of us mentioned a word about sublimation. And since Davey kept whispering instructions to Faith to be quiet, we both realized that our son was eavesdropping from the top of the stairs.

Some day when I look back on my life and think about the times I shared with Bob, I'm sure I'll remember that night as one of the best. Even now, I'm not sure how the evening would have ended if we hadn't been interrupted. Was the shrill ring of the telephone a kindness or a curse? A calamity or a good excuse? I'll probably never know.

Dishes piled in the sink for later, candles burned halfway down, we were lingering over coffee when the call came.

"Leave it," said Bob, reaching across the table to take my hand as I started to get up. "Let the machine get it."

I sat back down, but I was listening. So was he. Hearing the quick beep, I tensed slightly.

"Melanie? It's Bertie. If you're there, pick up. I have to talk to you. It's important."

I heard Bob sigh, felt his reluctance as he released my hand. I was already rising.

I headed out to the kitchen and lifted the receiver. "I'm here. What is it? Is everything okay?"

"I'm fine and so is Frank." Bertie sounded relieved to have found me. "Bob, too, I think, though I don't know where he is."

"He's here."

"There?" Her voice squeaked. "With you?"

"Yes, with me. We were eating dinner."

"Isn't it kind of late for that?"

I shrugged at Bob, who was frowning, and leaned back

against the kitchen counter. "Is that what you called me about?"

"No, of course not . . . sorry. It's Josh. You know, my cousin? He's in trouble."

"What kind of trouble?"

In the dining room, Bob pushed back his chair and stood. I guessed he'd heard enough to realize that I wouldn't be returning to the table any time soon. He carried my coffee cup over and set it next to me on the counter. I nodded my thanks.

"Actually," Bertie reconsidered, "it's worse than that. I should have started at the beginning. Sara's stepfather is dead."

I straightened abruptly, the last vestiges of my mellow mood slipping away. "What happened?"

"He was murdered."

"When?"

"I think around an hour ago. I just heard about it from Josh."

"What does he have to do with it?"

"That's the thing, he says nothing. But he was there."

"Where?"

"At the Warings', when Grant was shot. There was an intruder and a struggle. Grant was shot in the throat. He died almost instantly."

"Where was Josh while this was happening?" I asked. "Where were Sara and Delilah? And what was Josh doing at the Warings' to begin with?"

"I'm not sure." Bertie's voice was tight. "There are a few holes in what Josh told me. He called from the Warings' house a few minutes ago. The police are there, and they've detained him for questioning."

"He called you and you called me?" I asked incredulously. "Bertie, are you nuts? You should have called him a lawyer."

"I thought of that, but Josh said there was no need. He's just going to tell the police everything he knows about what happened. Josh said he'd come over here when he was done. I thought maybe you could come, too."

"I'm on my way." A sudden thought struck me. "Bertie, did Josh mention if Sara was there?"

"Yes, I guess so. He said that Delilah was nearly hysterical and Sara was trying to find a doctor to come and sedate her."

"So she hasn't disappeared again or anything?"

"I don't think so."

That was a relief.

"You're going out," Bob said as I hung up. The statement was devoid of censure, but he didn't sound happy.

"I'm sorry. I have to." I slipped my arms around his shoulders and pulled him close for a hug. I *was* sorry. I knew how hard he'd worked to make the evening perfect. "Everything was wonderful."

"For me, too," said Bob. "Do you want me to stay with Davey?"

"Can you?"

"Of course." His smile was wry as he glanced toward the sink. "Besides, I guess I've got some more cleaning up to do."

If he was trying to make me feel guilty, he was succeeding. Unfortunately I didn't have time to indulge Bob or the emotion. I grabbed my purse and keys off the counter and hurried out the door.

* * *

It took me twenty minutes to reach Bertie's place in Wilton. I sped most of the way. Murder is a rare occurrence in lower Fairfield County. Right then, I figured the New Canaan police had bigger things to worry about than whether or not I was breaking the traffic laws in their jurisdiction.

Bertie's house was in north Wilton, almost on the Ridgefield border. She was lucky enough to have a piece of land that was tucked in alongside a nature preserve, and due to the demands of her job, she usually had about a dozen dogs in residence. The basement of her home had been converted into kennel space to accommodate the lodgers.

When I pulled up to the small frame house, all the outdoor lights were on. Bertie met me on the porch. She must have been waiting by a front window.

"Thanks for coming," she said. "I apologize for dragging you all the way over here, but I couldn't think who else to call. Josh just phoned. He should be here any minute."

Bertie's living room was cluttered and comfortable. Her furniture was overstuffed and often covered with animal hair. Bertie didn't give a damn. She usually had a dog or two loose in the house, but that night they'd all been put away in their pens. As I sat down, a gray striped tomcat with white paws and a bushy tail sauntered into the room and hopped nimbly onto my lap.

"Beagle, cut that out," Bertie grumbled as the cat began to rub its head back and forth across the front of my sweater. Being a cat, Beagle ignored her.

"That's all right, I don't mind."

Actually I thought their association was rather funny. Bertie, whose first love was dogs of all shapes and sizes, had found the scrawny, scrappy kitten abandoned by the side of the road, and nursed him back to health. Initially loathe to admit that she'd become a cat owner, much less a cat lover, she'd named Beagle after a favorite breed of hound. As if that somehow lessened the sting.

"As long as he doesn't try to sharpen his claws on me."

Bertie grinned. "He'll work his way around to that once he gets you softened up."

We both heard the sound of an approaching car, and Bertie hopped up to open the door again. Josh walked in the house looking pale and tired, and more than a little shell-shocked.

"Are you okay?" Bertie asked.

Josh shrugged. He pulled off his leather jacket and wool muffler and handed them to his cousin. Since he didn't seem surprised to see me, I figured Bertie had told him I'd be coming. He walked into the living room and slumped onto the couch, automatically lifting both feet and placing them on the scarred chest that served as a coffee table.

"What happened?" I asked.

Josh raised a weary hand and rubbed it across his eyes. "Grant Waring's dead. Shot."

"Do the police know who did it?" Bertie walked over and sat down beside him.

"No. Right now, they probably don't know a whole lot more than I do."

"Tell us about it," I said.

"According to Delilah, she was reading in the library. Grant was in his office. She heard some sort of crash, then she thought she heard someone yelling but she couldn't make out any words. Next thing she knew, there was a shot. She went running into the office and found Grant bleeding on the floor."

"Where were you while all this was going on?"

"In my car, heading down the driveway. I'd stopped by earlier to see Sara. She and I had talked, and I left. She called me on my cell phone as I was driving away.

"At first I couldn't make out a word she was saying. I thought we had a bad connection, but then I realized she was screaming and gasping for breath. She told me someone had broken into the house and shot Grant, so I immediately turned around and went back."

"So you weren't actually in the house when it happened?"

"No. I just told you that, didn't I?" Josh's voice held steady. "Nor did I see anyone outside. The police already asked me about that, too."

"Did Delilah have any idea who this intruder was?" Bertie asked.

"Delilah wasn't . . ." He stopped and shook his head. "She wasn't really coherent. Not when I got there, and not for the police either. She and Sara both had blood all over them. Sara said they'd tried CPR, but I don't know why. One look and anyone would have known—"

"You saw the body?" Bertie's eyes were wide.

"What choice did I have? I went tearing back up to the house and ran inside. Sara and Delilah were both frantic. I didn't know how bad things really were. I thought maybe I could help. . . ."

Josh's voice trailed away. He looked down at his hands. His fingers were clasped tightly in his lap.

"I couldn't help. Nobody could have at that point. Sara had already called 911, so we sat down and waited for them to come."

"Weren't you worried that the killer might still have been around?" I asked.

"To tell you the truth, I didn't think about it. Looking at Grant, it just felt as though the worst had already happened. Besides, the French doors in his office were standing open like someone had just gone running out. We all noticed that right away because of all the cold air that was blowing in."

"Don't tell me you closed them," said Bertie.

"Sara did," Josh admitted. "The police weren't happy when they found out. But at the time none of us was thinking straight. It didn't occur to us that we ought to be preserving a crime scene."

The phrase rolled off his tongue quite handily, I thought, for someone who claimed not to have been thinking about it. These days the police weren't the only ones familiar with investigative techniques. Almost anyone who watched TV quickly became well versed in what was important and what was not when a crime had been committed.

"What about servants?" I asked. "Where were they?"

Josh looked blank, but Bertie had an answer. "There's never anyone there after early evening. The Warings like having their privacy. Aside from the kennel manager, the only other live-in is a housekeeper who has an apartment above the garage."

"What about Sara?" I asked Josh. "Where was she when all this was going on?"

"She said she was still upstairs. I'd left her in her room five minutes earlier."

I thought back to Bertie's and my visit the evening before. "Sara didn't walk you out?"

"No. Why would she? I could find my own way perfectly well." He sounded defensive; I wondered why. Even Bertie noticed the subtle shift in his tone.

"I thought you and Sara were over," she said.

"We are." His gaze skittered away.

"So what were you doing going to visit her?"

"We had something to discuss."

Bertie went very still. "I knew it," she said softly.

That didn't sound good.

I looked back and forth between them. "Knew what?"

26

In the time we'd been talking, Beagle had made his way over to Bertie's lap. She stroked the cat's long, warm body and plucked absently at his bushy tail. Beagle responded by swatting at Bertie's fingers with dainty white tipped paws.

"After I got home last night," Bertie said slowly, "I called Josh and told him about Sara being back. I guess I also mentioned that she was pregnant."

"You were right to tell me." A hank of wheat-colored hair had fallen down over Josh's eyes. Irritably he reached up and brushed the strands back. "Sara should have told me herself. I had a right to know."

"I thought you stopped seeing Sara last summer," I said.

"I did. But it's not like we lost each other's phone numbers, you know?"

I supposed I did. It turned out I wasn't the only one having a hard time setting physical boundaries on a relationship that should have been over.

"So you thought you might be the baby's father?"

"I figured there was a chance. Enough of one that I needed to check it out, anyway."

"And?" Bertie demanded.

"Is this something you need to know?"

"Apparently so, since I seem to have put myself in the middle of all this."

It was petty of me, I know, but I enjoyed watching a family squabble that didn't involve my own family for once.

"Sara said the baby isn't mine."

"Sara *said* it isn't?" Bertie asked. "Or you're sure it isn't?"

"I'm sure." Josh let out a windy sigh. "First, because if she's right about the due date, the timing doesn't work; second, because we always used birth control; and third, because . . ."

"Because?" I prompted when he didn't seem inclined to continue.

"Because when I tried to make her tell me who the father was, Sara blew up. She seemed really annoyed that I even knew about the baby. Like it was supposed to be a big secret. She said the only person she'd told on purpose was the baby's father and that it was nobody else's damn business."

"She has a point," I said.

"Like hell."

He seemed awfully upset for a man who'd claimed that their relationship had never been very serious. I wondered whether it was his heart that had been wounded when Sara dismissed him, or his ego.

"So you went to talk to Sara and ended up fighting with her instead."

"Right," Josh said glumly.

I supposed that explained why Sara hadn't walked him to the front door. It also gave her time to sneak down the back stairs, shoot her stepfather, go out the French doors, wait for

Delilah to raise a fuss, and then call Josh as he was reaching the end of the driveway. If she'd been so inclined . . .

Call me a cynic, but I tend to be skeptical of nameless, faceless intruder stories. There'd been three other people in the house around the time that Grant was shot. I had to assume that the police would check them out before doing anything else. For all Josh's purported lack of concern, I knew Bertie was right to be worried.

"How well do you know—did you know—Grant?" I asked.

"Not well. We'd met once or twice when I was with Sara. You know, out by the pool or something. Sara used to talk about Delilah a lot, but she hardly ever mentioned Grant."

"So you wouldn't have had any reason to be angry with him?" I probed carefully.

Bertie glanced over in surprise.

"None." Josh was firm. "Why would I? I hardly knew the guy. My beef is with Sara."

"How about Carole Eikenberry?" I asked. "Did you know her?"

"The girl who died in the fire? Yeah, sure. She and Sara met last summer, and right away they were good friends. When I was still seeing Sara, the three of us ended up spending a lot of time together. Sara's idea, not mine." He held up his hands as if absolving himself from blame. "Carole and I did *not* get along."

"How come?" Bertie asked.

"She just wasn't my kind of person. I don't know, it's hard to put my finger on the reason why. For one thing, Carole was really bossy. Always telling Sara to do this or do that, and Sara would." The look of consternation on Josh's face was almost comical. "I mean, it's not like Sara ever listened to anyone else."

His words confirmed what I'd begun to suspect.

Perhaps Sara had listened to Carole because, for the first time, she'd found someone whose opinion she cared about.

"Toward the end," Josh continued, "Sara was probably with Carole more than she was with me. Half the time when I'd call her, Carole would pick up and then it was a hassle getting through. She was always telling me Sara was in the shower or something. Come on, how many times am I going to believe that?"

As often as it took, I thought, for Carole to drive a wedge between you. Or maybe it was Sara who'd been playing the two of them off of each other. Whichever guess was right, Josh had clearly been the only one of the trio who hadn't fully understood what was going on.

"Where did Carole live, do you know?"

"Down in Westchester somewhere. Sara used to go over to her place, but I never did. I think it was in Armonk."

Just like the exchange Patricia had sent her fax to. That probably cleared up the question of where Sara had gone when she'd left home.

Bertie and I had been operating under the assumption that Sara had been running away from something when she disappeared. Now, looking at things from the other side, it seemed equally likely that she'd been running toward something—a relationship that was important to her, but one that she wasn't yet ready to expose to the whole world.

"Josh, do you have any idea what Carole might have been doing at Sara's cottage last Saturday night?"

"No. She and I didn't talk about Carole. Why didn't you ask her when you were there?"

"We did," said Bertie. "She said she didn't know."

Josh shrugged. "Carole probably just stopped by. She did that sometimes."

Not if my guess was correct and Sara had been staying

with Carole in Armonk. But if Sara had been club hopping in New York with friends, as she'd told the police, why hadn't Carole been with her?

I didn't bother to ask Josh. At this point, I was willing to bet he knew less about Sara and Carole than I did. And if I was feeling baffled, Bertie's cousin was looking tired. He was leaning, eyes closed, against the back of the couch. Even Beagle, who'd stood up to stretch and seemed to be considering hopping over onto Josh's legs, thought better of the idea and lay back down. I turned the discussion back to that evening's events.

"What about the murder weapon?" I asked. "Did the police find one?"

Josh opened one eye. "No. Delilah said the intruder must have taken it with him. Sara told the police that Grant kept a gun in his office. They had her look for it but she couldn't find it, so maybe Delilah was right."

"I don't like this at all." Bertie sounded equal parts annoyed and worried. "And I still think you should get a lawyer."

"What for?" Josh braced his hands against the couch and pushed himself upright. "I'm a witness, not a suspect. And I'm not even much of a witness since I wasn't there when the shooting happened."

"That's your story," I said. "The police may believe differently. Why would anyone want to break into the Warings' house and kill Grant?"

"There could be lots of reasons," Bertie said stoutly. "Maybe he was having business problems—"

"Grant was retired," I said.

"Someone he sent to jail got out—"

"He wasn't that kind of lawyer," Josh felt duty-bound to point out.

"Robbery!" Bertie tried.

Good thought.

"Was anything stolen?" I asked Josh.

"The detective asked Sara about that and made her look around. She said she didn't think so, but Grant's office was a real mess. She showed the police where there was a safe in a cabinet behind the bar, and it hadn't been touched."

"But Grant's gun was missing, so he must have gotten it out for some reason," I said, thinking aloud. "Why would he have done that unless he meant to use the gun for self-defense? And if he was armed, how did he end up dead?"

"Don't look at me," said Josh. "I have no idea."

My gaze shifted to Bertie. She shook her head.

Three reasonably intelligent people and not a decent answer among us.

Good thing we didn't do this for a living.

By the time I got home, Bob was asleep on the couch. I let Faith out back, then stood in the arched doorway leading to the living room and watched for several minutes as his chest rose and fell with each deep breath he took.

The television was on, tuned to a sports channel where, improbably, a giant slalom was being shown. Bob, who won't even drink a soda if it has too many ice cubes, must have nodded off before skiing came on. He'd removed his shoes and tucked his feet beneath the end cushion. His arms were crossed over his chest.

It was amazing, considering how much turmoil he'd caused in my life, just how peaceful my ex-husband managed to look. And while part of me was sorry that Bob hadn't waited up, hoping to continue the evening where we'd left off, on the whole I realized I was relieved.

Images from our life together flitted through my mind, like a series of postcards from a long-ago trip. I'd spent some of the best times of my life with Bob. And some of the worst. He would always be my first love, the man with whom I'd experienced the giddy high of feeling my heart open to all life's possibilities.

He would also always be the man who'd deserted me when the going got tough, left me flat without even a remorseful backward glance. In the span of our time together, I'd felt both the glory and the cruelty of love. I'd learned to trust, and I'd felt betrayal. And I'd grown up.

For better or worse, Bob's actions had had everything to do with the woman I'd become. I'd always feel the connection to our shared past; not to mention that tug of physical awareness. But flattered as I was by the attention he'd paid to me, tempting as it would be to slip back into something that would come together so easily, I had to let Bob know that my answer was no. I couldn't go back to where I'd been years earlier, nor would I want to.

My ex-husband might have changed, but I had, too. And it was time to move on.

I let Faith inside, then went upstairs and got a blanket and pillow out of the linen closet. Bob stirred when I lifted his head and slipped the pillow underneath.

"Don't tell me it's morning," he mumbled groggily.

"It isn't." I brushed my hand along his brow. In this sleepy state, he looked just like his son. "You've got hours yet. Go back to sleep."

Rather than take my advice, he fought to rouse himself. "Is everything okay?"

"Fine. I'll tell you about it tomorrow."

"Tomorrow," Bob murmured, losing the battle. "There's always tomorrow."

"Right." Because I could, because he wasn't awake to read something into it that I didn't mean, I leaned down and kissed him gently on the lips.

A soft caress. A heart-felt good-bye. Funny how life works sometimes. The decisions that ultimately mean the most are, in the end, the easiest to make.

27

I arose the next morning to an almost empty house and a note on the kitchen table. *Gone fishing,* it said.

Like that made sense. Nobody went fishing in November, did they? And where in Fairfield County would you go to go fishing, anyway?

I had no idea.

Nor did Faith. I know because I asked her. When I came downstairs, she was lying on the kitchen floor, her nose resting on the rim of her empty food bowl in what I'm sure she thought was a charmingly subtle gesture.

"What's up?" I asked.

The Poodle pricked her ears and woofed softly.

Hungry! That answer was easy enough to decipher.

But when I moved on to the bigger questions, like where were Bob and Davey, what were they planning to use for poles and bait, and what, by the way, was the meaning of life, Faith was annoyingly noncommunicative. Of course, by then I'd put some dried kibble in her bowl and she was busy chewing. That probably had something to do with it.

I poured myself a cup of coffee, added a dollop of milk, and sat down to ponder Sara's situation. What the heck? For once, it wasn't as if I had anything else to do.

What had started as a puzzle had ended with a murder. Usually, in my experience, things work the other way around.

Maybe, I decided, I should start with Grant's murder and work my way back to Sara's disappearance. I'm not a big believer in coincidence, so I was pretty sure the two things had to be related. What did I know about Sara and Grant separately? And what did I know about the two of them together?

Item one: Grant was Sara's stepfather. Though her relationship with her mother had been seriously strained for most of her life, by all accounts, Sara and Grant got along well.

So what, I wondered, thinking back, had they been arguing about at the dog show two weeks earlier? Something important enough for them to air their grievances in public. Maybe something upsetting enough to cause Sara to disappear the next day.

Hmmm.

Item two: Despite all the men that she had previously and publicly enjoyed flings with, there was a good possibility that Sara had, for the last several months, been involved in a romantic relationship with Carole Eikenberry. During that time, she had become pregnant.

Item three: Feeling pressured by the baby's father, Sara had run to Carole for refuge. That led me to believe that although Sara's pregnancy was a secret, Carole must have known about it.

Big deal, I thought. None of that brought me any closer to figuring out what Carole had been doing in Sara's cottage on Saturday night. Or who had set the fire that took her life. Or what had happened to Grant's gun and why he hadn't used it to defend himself.

I sipped my coffee, nestled my bare toes in Faith's thick coat as she lay stretched out beneath my chair, and let my thoughts drift. Sometimes I solve problems better when I'm not trying so hard to find an answer. And when a possible solution came moseying into my mind, I didn't sit up and shout eureka! but I might as well have. Because all at once I realized what I should have seen earlier.

I'd been thinking back to Thursday night when Bertie and I had gone to visit Sara at her parents' house. Bertie had asked Sara whether or not her parents knew she was pregnant. And Sara, who'd insisted to Josh that the only person she'd informed was the baby's father, had said, "Grant does. I told him."

For a moment, the revelation seemed so stunning, so unexpected, that it was all I could do to process the ramifications. I'd been assuming that Carole was Sara's mystery beau, the partner she'd kept so carefully concealed. But Carole was only half of Sara's explosive secret; her stepfather, Grant Waring, had been the other half.

I was so astounded by the direction my thoughts had taken that I barely even heard the doorbell ring. Faith, of course, was quicker on the uptake. Especially since, as it turned out, one of our visitors was a dog. Eve, to be precise.

Aunt Peg was standing on the front step beside her, holding a box of doughnuts. "Breakfast," she announced when I opened the door. "Have you eaten yet?"

"No, I . . ."

Aunt Peg wasn't listening. She thrust the pink box into my hands, marched past me, and peered up the stairs. Eve, meanwhile, was dancing circles around Faith in the hall. Not much seemed to be required of me—Peg was now poking her nose into the kitchen—so I opened the box, helped myself to a glazed doughnut, and took a bite.

"Looking for something?" I inquired as Peg circled back through the living room.

"Bob."

Oh. I chewed and swallowed.

"He isn't here."

"He was last night."

"So he was," I said agreeably. "Isn't that allowed?"

"Don't be fresh," said Peg.

So help me, I couldn't see why not. Wasn't this *my* life we were discussing?

"I got the impression he might be staying over." Aunt Peg threw down that verbal gauntlet on her way back to the kitchen. This time I followed.

"Is that what you're doing here so early? Checking up on me?"

"Certainly not." Aunt Peg is one of the smoothest liars around. It's a gift. Unfortunately for her, it's one that I've long since stopped being fooled by. "I came by to drop Eve off for the weekend."

"Thank you."

"You're welcome."

She was now putting a kettle of water on the stove to heat for tea. Since the professed goal of her visit—dropping the puppy off—had already been accomplished, I guessed we were now getting ready to move on to phase two. I took a seat at the table.

"Anything else?"

"Have a doughnut," said Peg. "The sugar will cheer you up."

"I'm already about as cheerful as I get." I hoped that didn't mean that she was setting me up for bad news.

Instead Aunt Peg changed the subject. "I brought lots of doughnuts. Chocolate ones, too. Where's my nephew?"

"Gone fishing, apparently."

"Fishing? Where?"

I'd managed to surprise her. Of course, Bob had managed to surprise me, too.

"I have no idea. Bob took him. The two of them were gone when I got up this morning."

"Aha!" cried Peg.

I reached for my mug, dragged it over, and took a sip. The coffee was now cold. "Bob slept on the couch."

"You should have sent him home."

To Texas? I wondered. Or to Frank's place? Shoulda, woulda, coulda.

"Actually, I was out when he fell asleep. How did you know he was here?"

Aunt Peg carried over her tea and sat down. The two Poodles were playing tug-of-war with a length of thick, knotted rope. In a minute, Peg would probably remember that the game was bad for Eve's newly emerging adult teeth, but for the moment she had other things on her mind.

"I called, of course. Just as soon as I heard about Grant. The story made last night's news. Bob told me you were off getting the scoop from Bertie."

I nodded. "Her cousin Josh was there when it happened."

"When *what* happened? The news report was annoyingly vague about the details."

Today being Saturday, Bertie would already have left for the first of the weekend's shows, which was probably why Aunt Peg was grilling me rather than going directly to the source. On the other hand, even though we'd just seen each other the day before, I had plenty of news to bring her up to date on.

Aunt Peg managed to polish off two jelly doughnuts in the time it took me to recount what Josh had said, throw in what I'd learned at the specialty from Terry, and finish by airing my own speculations about what was going on. When I got to my guess that Grant was the father of Sara's baby, Aunt Peg began to shake her head in denial. It was hard to tell whether she was more horrified or intrigued by the possibility.

"He must be thirty years older than she is! Not to mention married to Sara's mother. That's almost incest."

"They're only related by marriage," I pointed out.

"But they've been living in that house together since Sara was a child. Are you trying to tell me that there's been hanky-panky going on all that time?"

Hanky-panky. Only Aunt Peg could come up with a phrase like that. But her question put another new spin on things. I'd been thinking of Sara as the aggressor in the relationship, going after Grant the same way she'd gone after so many other things she'd wanted. Once again I was forced to consider that I might have been looking at things backward.

"I don't think so," I said finally. "Sara's friends talk about the troubled relationship she had with her mother. Nobody seemed to think Grant was a problem."

"Then what's your explanation?"

"I think Sara made it happen." It was conjecture on my part, but it made sense. "I think she met Carole Eikenberry and fell in love. Sara's getting to that age where the biological clock starts ticking. I'm betting that she and Carole decided to have a baby together."

"But why Grant?"

"Revenge," I said simply. "Everything I've heard suggests that Delilah was a terrible mother. Maybe after all these years Sara decided to strike back, to hit her mother where she knew it would hurt.

"Sara planned to tell Delilah what she and Grant had

done, but then she lost her nerve. She had told Grant about the baby, however, and he was pressuring her to have an abortion. That's why she ran away from home."

"And the fire that killed Carole?"

"I'm still guessing," I said.

Aunt Peg lifted both hands and beckoned with her fingers, impatient for more information, even if it was only speculation.

"I think Grant set it hoping that the fire would flush Sara out from wherever she was hiding. Remember, he knew how attached she was to Titus and that she'd left the Sheltie behind in the cottage. I'm betting he thought that was the one thing that would be sure to get her attention.

"Grant desperately needed to get Sara back home so he could change her mind about having the baby. Don't forget, he was under a serious time constraint. If Sara was going to have an abortion, she had to do it soon.

"Not only that but Delilah was still in the dark about what he'd done and I'm sure Grant wanted to keep things that way. Once Sara left, Grant lost all control of the situation and he knew it. Compared to the alternative—having his wife find out that her daughter was pregnant and by whom—I bet setting that fire didn't seem like such an awful thing, especially if it could accomplish what he needed it to do."

"Except that in the process, he ended up murdering Sara's other lover."

"Right. But I've been thinking about that and I'm almost certain that Grant had no idea Carole was in the house. After all, what would he have stood to gain by killing her?

"Remember how the newspaper article said that the body was near an upstairs closet? Well, Bertie and I were over at Sara's house right after she disappeared. We opened that closet and the door stuck terribly. Imagine this: it's Saturday night and Carole's in the cottage—"

"Why?" Peg demanded.

"I don't know," I said impatiently. "Maybe nobody knows. But she was there, we know that for a fact. Now suppose Carole heard someone coming and didn't want to be seen.

"She could have gone upstairs and hidden in that closet, never dreaming that the cottage would be set on fire and she'd be trapped. Later, after the roof caved in and the cottage was reduced to rubble, the door might have sprung open. Or maybe it was destroyed. But by then, it was too late."

"Not bad," Aunt Peg said, considering. "Not perfect, but not bad."

Noticing, finally, what the two Poodles were up to, she deftly slipped in a hand and removed the rope toy, substituting a pair of rawhide chews in its place. The switch was made almost before the dogs knew what was happening. If I'd tried that, I'd have started world war three. Instead, both Poodles settled down on the floor to chew contentedly. Sometimes you just have to marvel at her talents.

Aunt Peg turned her attention back to me. "So Grant killed Carole," she said. "Who killed Grant?"

So much for taking a few minutes to bask in the glow of what I'd accomplished so far. As usual, Aunt Peg wanted me to have all the answers. But while I was fairly certain of the deductions I'd already outlined, I was less sure of my next theory.

"See what you think about this," I said. "Sara's been having problems with Grant for weeks. Now Carole is dead and he's responsible. Burning the cottage brought Sara home all right, and the next day Grant was shot. There was no intruder in that house, just Grant, Delilah and Sara. And I think Sara shot him."

Voicing the idea out loud seemed to give it credence. As

did the fact that Aunt Peg wasn't arguing with me. Maybe I hadn't filled in all the blanks but I'd assembled enough bits and pieces to emerge with a creditable picture.

"We ought to go tell this to the police," I said.

Aunt Peg frowned. "When have the authorities ever paid the slightest bit of attention to anything you've tried to tell them?"

That was the problem with being a nosy amateur. Not surprisingly, the professionals I'd run into tended to want me to do nothing more than keep quiet and stay out of their way.

"Have you got a better idea?"

"For starters, I should think we'd better warn Delilah. If she's living in that house with a murderer, she certainly needs to know about it."

Good point.

Leaving Peg with the rest of the doughnuts, I ran upstairs and got dressed in a black wool pants suit. It was time to pay another condolence call.

28

"I hope we're wrong," Aunt Peg said. "I hate to say it, but I hope there really was a mysterious intruder at the Warings' house last night and we're running off on a wild goose chase."

We were in my car speeding toward New Canaan, having left the Poodles behind along with a note explaining where we'd gone in case the fabled fishing trip didn't turn out to be an all day excursion.

I shifted my gaze from the road ahead and glanced at my aunt. "Do you really believe that?"

"No." Peg sighed. "And that's what has me so worried. Lord knows, Delilah can be a difficult woman. But when I think that she's very likely harboring a murderer in her own home and having no idea of the danger she's in . . ."

Listening as she spoke, I did the only thing I could do and pressed my foot down harder on the gas pedal.

"If Sara has snapped, there's no telling what she might do next. She always was rather unpredictable, even as a child. And that incident at Westminster is proof that she doesn't respond well to stress. Knowing what we did about Sara's past, we should have guessed—"

"We *did* guess," I said. "That's precisely why we're on our way to New Canaan."

"We should have guessed sooner!"

Aunt Peg wasn't happy and neither was I, though for an entirely different reason. Sound as our theory seemed to us, it was just that: a theory. Bearing that in mind, I had no intention of bursting into the Waring house like a pair of Rottweilers with a mission. Instead I was hoping we'd be able to hang back and make a quiet assessment, then pull Delilah aside for a private chat.

"Do you suppose Sara's still got the gun?" Aunt Peg mused.

"The police didn't find a murder weapon. Or at least they hadn't by the time Josh left. He said he and Sara figured the intruder must have taken it with him."

"Or snuck it back upstairs for safekeeping," Peg muttered darkly. "Maybe we should have called ahead, just to make sure that Delilah was okay."

I put on my turn signal, zoomed off the exit ramp, and headed left on Route 106. "We're almost there now. Five minutes, max."

Mid-morning on a Saturday, I'd have expected West Road to be nearly empty. It wasn't. Instead, we joined a line of cars that all turned into the Warings' driveway. News of Grant's murder had obviously spread through the quiet town. Delilah's friends and neighbors were gathering to pay their respects.

"See," I said as I wedged the Volvo into a small spot along a box hedge. "I'm sure everything's fine. With this many people around, Sara wouldn't dare try anything."

"Let's hope not."

Aunt Peg hurried up the wide front steps. She lifted the

heavy brass door knocker and let it fall. A moment later, the door was opened by a housekeeper wearing a plain gray dress and a weary expression. Circles under her eyes attested to the fact that she'd probably been up most of the night.

"Miss Bentley is receiving visitors in the living room," she said.

Aunt Peg and I exchanged a glance.

"We came to see Mrs. Waring."

"You'll have to talk to Miss Bentley about that." The woman took our coats and draped them over an arm that already held two others. As she waved us toward the living room, the door knocker sounded again.

"Come on," I said to Peg. "Let's go see if we can find Delilah."

Like the driveway out front, the living room was jammed. The throng of callers spilled over into the dining room, where a buffet brunch had been laid out on the table. A maid in a uniform that matched the housekeeper's was serving orange juice and coffee.

Conversation was muted, voices were hushed. People gathered in small groups, looking properly somber. Though many of the faces were familiar to me from the show circuit, I didn't see Delilah anywhere.

"There's Sara," Aunt Peg said, grasping my shoulders and turning me so I could see through the crowd.

She was sitting in a low chair beside the marble fireplace. Her eyes were puffy and red, and her hair was gathered into an untidy knot at the nape of her neck. As we made our way across the room toward her, Sara caught my eye, stood up, and held out a hand.

"Melanie, Mrs. Turnbull, thank you so much for coming. I appreciate your support." The line sounded rehearsed, but I could hardly blame her. Sara had probably had occasion to use it a dozen times in the past half hour.

"We're so sorry about what happened—" I began, but Aunt Peg elbowed me aside.

"You poor, dear girl," she said. "What *did* happen?"

"I wish I knew." Sara's bottom lip quivered. "As I'm sure you can imagine, this has all been a terrible shock. Everything feels like a blur to me right now. The police keep asking me questions and I can't seem to get anything straight in my mind."

"There, there," Aunt Peg said soothingly. "That's a natural reaction to the trauma you've been through. You must try to take it easy until everything settles down. Melanie and I were hoping to pay our respects to your mother, but we haven't seen her."

"No, I'm afraid Delilah is indisposed. She isn't receiving visitors."

"But surely she'd be comforted by the presence of an old friend. . . ."

"I'm sorry," Sara said firmly. "As I'm sure you can understand, Delilah is quite overwrought. She isn't seeing anyone."

"Is she here?"

Sara didn't answer. Instead, she looked past us into the crowd. "Please help yourself to some food. If you'll excuse me, there are some people I must see."

"Baloney," Peg said heartily when Sara had gone. "So much for doing things the easy way. Now where do you suppose Delilah is?"

"I can't imagine she'd have gone far. She's probably upstairs somewhere."

"I don't like that at all." Aunt Peg was frowning. "If you'll pardon the expression, Delilah Waring is tough as an old boot. I'm sure she's upset. Under the circumstances, who wouldn't be? But even under adversity, she's not the type of person to willingly hide herself away.

"Don't forget, I was here last week when we all thought that Sara had died in the fire. What could be worse than believing your only child had been taken from you in such a horrible manner? But Delilah was very much in evidence then, greeting her guests, giving orders, running the show, just as she's always done. I find this sudden disappearance of hers highly suspicious."

"Me, too," I agreed. "Let's go find her."

Aunt Peg looked delighted by the prospect. "You mean search the house? Do we dare?"

"I don't see why not. Who's going to stop us? Sara? With all this going on, she'll probably be too busy to even notice."

Since the downstairs rooms were easy to gain access to, we split up and gave the bottom half of the house a surreptitious sweep first. Five minutes later, Aunt Peg and I met back in the front hall.

"Nothing," she said.

"Me neither."

I'd just seen Sara, though, and knew she was busy in the living room. The housekeeper had disappeared. Aunt Peg eyed the wide stairway.

"Up we go, then," she said.

Heads high, shoulders back, looking as though we had every right to explore the rest of the house, Aunt Peg and I marched up the steps. To my enormous relief, nobody paid any attention to us.

The only other time I'd been on the second floor of the Waring home, Sara had led us directly to her rooms. Now, as we paused on the landing, I was dismayed to realize how many doors led off of the spacious hallway. Not only that, but most of them were closed. Despite all the activity below us, the second floor of the Waring house had the hushed stillness of a tomb.

I hung back for a moment, but Aunt Peg wasn't deterred.

"Nothing ventured, nothing gained," she said determinedly. Marching over to the nearest door, she grasped the knob and drew it open.

"Linen closet," I heard her mutter as I crossed the hall and started on the other side.

I'd half expected the doors to be locked, but none were. Instead I found myself peering into one beautifully furnished bedroom after another. Considering how few people lived in the house, I found myself wondering what was the point of having so much space, not to mention owning all that furniture. Just the curtains alone must have cost a small fortune—

Behind me, Aunt Peg cleared her throat loudly. I turned and looked. Though most of the rooms I'd seen had been bright and cheerful, the one whose doorway she was standing in was only dimly lit. Its shades had been lowered to block the morning sun.

"This is a surprise," I heard Delilah say. Her voice sounded hoarse and cranky. "Is that you, Peg?"

"Me and my niece, Melanie."

I went to stand beside my aunt. She moved over so that Delilah could see both of us in the doorway.

"Go away."

"We need to talk to you."

"I don't feel like talking."

"We're sorry to bother you," I said, "but it's important."

Delilah was reclining on a chaise longue on the other side of the room. Though Sara had said her mother wasn't receiving visitors, the woman was fully dressed, right down to stockings and a pair of polished Ferragamo pumps. A small table beside the chaise held a glass filled with a clear liquid. The scent of gin lingered in the air. Delilah was staring off into space.

"Nothing's that important anymore."

"That's not true," Aunt Peg said gently. "I know things seem bleak now—"

"Bleak?" Delilah very slowly turned her head so that she was facing us. Even so, her gaze seemed to be turned inward. "Bleak doesn't begin to describe the depths I've sunk to. Please close the door."

Of one accord, Aunt Peg and I stepped forward. We shut the door behind us.

"So you're staying." Delilah frowned. She didn't look as though she had the strength to argue with our decision. "You're braver than my daughter, I'll give you that."

"Actually," I said, "it's Sara we wanted to talk to you about."

"We're afraid you might be in danger," Aunt Peg added.

"Danger?" Delilah cocked her head to one side as though considering the notion. Watching the studied cadence of her movements, I wondered if her doctor had given her a sedative, and if so, how many extra pills she'd taken. "No, I don't think so. Sara's a disappointment to me on many levels, but she hasn't got the guts to be dangerous."

"We think she may have a gun," said Peg.

Delilah didn't respond. She didn't look surprised either.

"There was no intruder in this house last night, was there?" I asked.

"There was death and destruction." Delilah's voice shook. "Isn't that enough?"

"Destruction?"

"Yes, destruction. That's the only way to look at it. Everything I loved, everything I believed in, was destroyed in an instant. After that, there was no turning back.

"I'm not a forgiving woman. Nor am I an easy one. The only thing I can say in my own defense is that I'm just as hard on myself as I am on everyone else."

"Delilah," Aunt Peg said smoothly, "no one's blaming you for what happened."

"Then you're a pair of fools, both of you."

Uh oh.

"Are you . . ." I stopped, swallowed, tried again. "Are you saying that you're the one . . . ?"

Delilah's hard eyes nailed me. "For someone who fancies herself a detective, you're rather out of the loop, aren't you?"

Apparently so.

"I'm just surprised," I said. "I can't imagine why you would have wanted to burn down Sara's cottage."

"Oh, that."

Delilah waved a hand and her fingers smacked against the highball glass on the table. She peered at it owlishly for a moment, then picked it up and took a long swallow.

"I'm having a drink," Delilah announced. "Would you like one?"

"No," Aunt Peg and I replied in unison.

"Suit yourselves."

" 'Oh that,' as you call it," Aunt Peg said grimly, "resulted in the death of an innocent young woman."

"Bad luck." Delilah shrugged. "And you two needn't look so disapproving. As it happens, I had nothing to do with that stupid fire."

"Who did?"

She lifted her glass again. Her perfectly aligned white teeth played along the rim. "That was Grant's doing. Imagine. I had no idea. I was right in the house, living with both of them, and I didn't have a clue."

She seemed to have shifted topics. I grabbed on and tried to go with her. "About Grant and Sara, you mean?"

"Grant and Sara, Sara and Carole, Grant and Carole . . ." Her voice faded away, then came back. "I suppose I must have been rather obtuse."

"Grant and Carole?" Now she'd lost me.

"Bound together by death, you might say. Murderer and victim."

"So Grant set the fire that killed Carole?" Aunt Peg repeated, hoping to confirm what we suspected.

Delilah stared off into a distance that only she could see. "He seemed to think he had his reasons. I don't suppose I'd have agreed, but there you are. The girl's death was an accident. Grant swore that was so. He'd never have set the fire if he'd known she was there."

"When did you discuss that with him?" I asked. "Did you know about it at the time?"

"No-o-o. . . ." Delilah drew the word out, letting her lips and tongue linger over the denial. "They say the wife is always the last to know, don't they? I guess I'm proof of that. It was all going on right under my very nose, and I had no idea."

"But you do now," said Aunt Peg.

"Yes, I do," Delilah agreed. "Rather unfortunate, isn't it?" Her hand slid gracefully beneath the cushion of the chaise and reemerged holding a small gun. "I've seen too much. I've done too much. And I'm quite certain that I know much more than I ever wanted to. I'm afraid there's only one thing left for me to do."

29

Aunt Peg's gasp seemed unnaturally loud in the quiet room. "Delilah," she said reprovingly, "you aren't threatening to shoot us, are you?"

"Oh dear, you must really think I've taken leave of my senses." Delilah laid the gun down in her lap, but kept her fingers twined around the grip. "Of course I'm not going to shoot you. I'm going to shoot myself."

It was amazing how civilized the two of them sounded discussing what was, essentially, a very uncivilized topic. The only thing I could think to do was to keep everybody talking until I came up with a plan.

"So you're the one who ended up with the gun." I matched my conversational tone to theirs.

"Ended with it, began with it, used it." Delilah sighed. "It was all a terrible mistake, of course. I knew that right away. It wasn't as though I'd made a decision to act. The whole thing just sort of . . . happened.

"I hadn't even tried to pull the trigger and the gun went off. I never imagined it could happen just like that. But you can't say that I don't learn from my mistakes. If it was that easy to use the gun once, it will be just as easy to do so again."

Delilah's fingers toyed idly with the weapon. "That's all I'm left with now, isn't it? One final act to bring the whole sad story to an end."

"It was an accident," said Peg, sounding relieved. "You shot Grant, but you didn't mean to."

"In truth, I'm not sure what I did or didn't mean. I was certainly very angry. It wasn't so much the act itself, but the betrayal. My husband and my daughter together, I could never have forgiven that. I'm sure Sara knew it. I'm sure that's why . . ." Delilah shook her head wearily. "It doesn't make much difference now, does it?"

"Of course it does," Aunt Peg said stoutly.

Delilah didn't seem to hear her. "My husband is dead. My daughter hates me, she's made that clear enough. There's nothing left for me anymore."

A sudden flicker of movement caught my eye—a brief flash of blue in a doorway that led to . . . what? A bathroom? A sitting room? I stared at the opening for a minute but didn't see anything else. Maybe I'd only imagined it.

In the meantime, Aunt Peg was trying to get my attention. Behind her back, her hand was cocked in my direction, fingers beckoning, gesturing for me to do something. To do what? I wondered.

"This isn't the end, Delilah," Aunt Peg was saying. "You can get help."

Her hand was flapping now. Urging me to act. As if she had a plan. As if she thought she was a mime and I could understand what she was trying to convey.

"All of us, all your friends will pull together—"

"And what?" Delilah's tone was bitter. "Hire me a good lawyer? Find a psychiatrist willing to testify that I'm crazy?

I am, you know. I must be, don't you think? Otherwise, why would I be sitting here with a gun in my hands?"

"This has all been a tragic misunderstanding," said Peg. "Grant killed Carole by accident, you killed Grant by accident. There were mitigating circumstances; anyone can see that. I'm sure something can be worked out."

"Worked out?" Delilah snorted.

As she reached for another sip of her drink, I began to inch slowly toward her. If Aunt Peg expected me to grab the gun, she needed to come up with a better diversion than she'd managed thus far. Delilah was staring into space again. Though she was speaking aloud, it was almost as though she'd forgotten anyone was listening.

"Worked out?" she repeated. "That's just what I kept telling myself every step of the way. When I found out Sara thought she was gay. When she told me Carole was her—what was that term she used?—life partner. When she said she was pregnant and that she and Carole were planning to raise the child together.

"Every life has its ups and downs, I told myself. We'll get through this. Everything can be worked out. And then Sara told me who her baby's father was." Tears gathered in Delilah's eyes and began to trickle down her cheeks. "At first I thought she was lying. Then I thought my whole world had come to an end. Do you have any idea what that feels like?"

"No," Aunt Peg said softly.

"The worst thing was that Sara was happy about what she'd done. Defiant. So filled with satisfaction in the face of my despair. She wanted to destroy me and she succeeded."

"So you went and got Grant's gun," Aunt Peg prompted, trying to keep Delilah talking. Three more steps and I'd be there.

"It was in his office. Loaded, and locked in his desk for emergencies. We all knew where it was kept. I'm not sure what drove me to take it out. I know I never meant to use it. I was just going to threaten Sara with it—"

"Sara?" I gasped.

Delilah turned and looked at me, standing so close. Too close, she could see that right away.

"Do step back," she said, lifting the gun and pointing it in my direction. "I'm afraid I don't have to tell you that I'm perfectly capable of using this."

I retreated a step. The gun wobbled in Delilah's grasp. I stepped back again, and over to one side. The barrel of the pistol didn't follow and I relaxed slightly. It was much easier to breathe when it wasn't aimed in my direction.

"Where was I?" Delilah asked Peg. Under the circumstances, her steely composure was more unnerving than hysterics would have been.

"You went to get the gun. . . ."

Aunt Peg's tone was mild, but she shot me a glare. I'd blown the best chance we were going to get, her eyes said. I hoped she wasn't right.

"Well, yes, I did, didn't I? That's how things went. I was only going to use it to show Sara that I meant business. She was to leave this house and never return. Leave Grant and me in peace to see what we could salvage of our marriage.

"It had to be done. The break had to be made. There's always been something the matter with my daughter. I've known it from the time she was small. She's always been weak, unfocused. Well, frankly, I'd had enough."

"What about Grant?" I asked.

"Grant." Delilah sighed as she said her husband's name. "He must have heard us yelling. Sara'd had a visitor in, some young man. I don't mind telling you that they'd been shouting, too. Somehow, the fact that someone else was angry at her strengthened my resolve. As soon as he left, I went to Sara's room.

"You can't imagine the things my daughter said to me—horrible, hurtful things. I couldn't stand to listen anymore. No mother could. I left and went down to Grant's office to get the gun. He must have heard the commotion, because he followed me there. Grant tried to take the gun away. . . ."

Delilah's voice faded as she relived the horrible moment. Or so it seemed at first. Then abruptly I realized she'd stopped talking because she was listening to something.

Some sort of disturbance was going on downstairs, accompanied by enough noise that it was audible through the closed bedroom door. I heard the sound of dogs barking, several startled shrieks, and pounding footsteps.

"What on earth . . . ?" Peg muttered, glancing toward the door.

There was more barking, followed by a series of excited yips. Delilah's lips curved in a small smile. An odd reaction, I thought, but at least she hadn't lifted the gun again. Instead she was listening, her expression intent. If she'd been a dog, she'd have had her ears pricked.

I strode to the door and opened it, intending to look out onto the landing. Instead I found myself jumping back as a horde of galloping Shetland Sheepdogs came flying up the stairs and racing down the hallway. There must have been at least a dozen of them—sables, blue merles, tricolors, in a happy jumble of wagging tails and lolling tongues—and Sara was leading the charge.

The dogs came pouring into the bedroom like a herd of stampeding buffalo. They scattered across the carpet, jumped up on the bed, then finally found Delilah on the chaise and leapt up into her welcoming arms. Deftly Aunt Peg navigated through the melee, reached around the wriggling bodies, grabbed the gun, and slipped it into her purse.

"My babies, my babies," Delilah crooned, surrounded by her beloved Scotchglen Shelties.

The throng of eager dogs vied for position on her lap, their tongues licking away her tears as soon as they appeared. Delilah spread her arms wide and tried to gather them all in. Her voice, soft and sweet as a lullaby, murmured each one's name.

On the other side of the room, Sara stood perfectly still in the doorway and watched the scene. I tried to read her expression but couldn't quite decide what emotion I saw there. Sadness? Relief? Pity? Perhaps a combination of the three.

She was wearing a blue sweater, I realized, the same shade as the flash of color I'd seen in the doorway. Sara had overheard what Delilah was saying, had seen how despondent her mother was, and had gone to get help. Delilah might not have known her daughter very well, but Sara clearly had understood exactly what her mother needed.

"You saved her," I said.

Sara's mouth was a flat line. When she spoke, her voice so low I almost couldn't hear her.

"Some women should never have children," she said with a small sigh. "Only dogs."

30

I went down and asked the housekeeper to clear the house of guests, while Aunt Peg used the phone in the bedroom to summon the police. When she was done, Sara called the family lawyer. Surrounded by her cherished Shelties, Delilah seemed almost oblivious to our actions.

If she noticed that her weapon had vanished, she didn't mention its loss. Maybe she'd been hoping all along that we would talk her out of using the gun. Or maybe seeing her dogs had reminded her that she did have something to live for.

Sara, Aunt Peg, and I closed the bedroom door and went downstairs to wait.

"Good work," Aunt Peg said to Sara. "That was quick thinking. Melanie was supposed to be providing a diversion, but she wasn't getting the job done *at all*."

Nothing like having your own relative call you useless. Hadn't I come up with the information that had brought us hurrying over here in the first place? I didn't see Aunt Peg mentioning *that*. Of course, that would mean admitting to Sara that we'd thought she was a murderer.

"That part was easy to figure out," Sara said quietly. "No matter how much pain Delilah might cause other people, I knew she'd never hurt her dogs. She loves those dogs more than anything. She always has."

"Did you know she was the one who shot Grant?" I asked.

"No, not until I heard what she said upstairs. Maybe it was stupid on my part, but I when I ran down last night and Delilah told me someone had broken into the house and shot him, I believed her."

"It *was* an accident," said Aunt Peg. "Delilah didn't mean to shoot him."

"Yeah." Sara's tone was grim. "She meant to shoot me."

"Not exactly," I corrected. "She meant to intimidate you."

"It's not as if she needed a gun for that. Delilah's been intimidating me my entire life. And the one time I decided to fight back, look what happened."

Sara hadn't just fought back, I thought. She'd launched an offensive whose sole intent had been to cause real damage to everyone around her. Not that I could see the point in bringing that up.

We stopped at the foot of the wide staircase, waiting, I guess, for someone to arrive. There was no sign of anyone yet, however. Sara turned and wandered toward the dining room, where an assortment of finger foods had been set out on the table. Aunt Peg and I exchanged a glance and followed.

"Do you mind if I ask you a few questions?" I asked as Sara perused the offerings, snagged a jumbo shrimp, and dipped it into a bowl of cocktail sauce.

"Go ahead." Sara sounded resigned. "I guess this will all be out in the open soon anyway."

"Why did you leave home the week before last?"

Sara nibbled on the end of her shrimp. "Two reasons. One, because Grant was hassling me about the baby and I figured if I just disappeared, that would show him I was serious when I said that he couldn't push me around."

"And the second?" asked Aunt Peg. Like me, she didn't seem to have much of an appetite.

"I did it for Carole. Up until that point, we'd kept our relationship a secret, which for some reason gave Carole the idea that I was ashamed of her. I wasn't, not at all, but I also wasn't ready to make any big announcements either. My moving in with her, even for a little while, was my way of showing her that I was totally committed, even if I wasn't ready to go public yet."

"But if you were staying at Carole's place, what was she doing in your cottage last Saturday night?"

Sara paused a moment before answering. "That's the stupid part," she said finally. "Carole's death was just a horrible, unnecessary waste. She was trying to do something nice for me, and she ended up dying because of it."

Aunt Peg looked just as baffled as I knew I did. "How?" she asked.

"Carole and I had had an argument earlier on Saturday. We were supposed to see some friends in the city that night and Carole wanted to tell them about the baby and about us being a couple. I wanted to hold off. We both blew up and said things we shouldn't have.

"Carole was so upset she said she was going to call and cancel our plans, and that made me mad all over again. I told her she didn't own me and she couldn't tell me what to do, and that I was going to New York without her.

"I guess after I left, Carole began to regret our fight as much as I did. She left me a note telling me she'd gone to New Canaan to fetch Titus. I'd left him here because she was so allergic she could hardly breathe when he was in the same room, but Carole knew how much I'd been missing him. Apparently she was going to make this wonderful gesture to make me feel better at her own expense."

"But Titus wasn't in the cottage," I pointed out.

"I found that out when I got back, but I didn't know it at the time. Nor did Carole. I'd left Titus overnight before, and he'd always done okay. I had no reason to think that this time would be any different."

Aunt Peg was scowling and I knew what she was thinking. Unless I jumped in, Sara was about to be treated to a lecture on the responsibilities of dog ownership.

"So Carole went to your cottage to look for him?"

"I assume that's what happened. Carole must have been there when Grant, that sneak, went out to do his dirty work. She knew what had been going on between Grant and me, and I'm sure she didn't want to answer any questions. She probably hid, figuring she'd come out again when he was gone. Obviously she had no idea of what he meant to do, or that she'd never have a chance to escape."

Sara stepped over to a window, brushed back the curtain with her hand, and looked out. I wondered if she saw anyone coming up the long driveway.

"One last thing," I said. "Debra Silver?"

"What about her?"

"What is she afraid of?"

Sara glanced my way. She let the curtain drop. "The truth, mostly. And something she did a long time ago."

"When you were competing against one another?"

"Yes, although one thing had nothing to do with the other. At least not directly. Debra and I were teenagers at the same time, both of us growing up, trying things out, experimenting with our sexuality, I guess you might say."

"Did you and she have a physical relationship?"

"Briefly. It was the first time either one of us had ever done anything like that. For me it was a revelation, an awakening. You know how kids are. I was so excited, I just assumed Debra felt the same way."

Sara frowned. "Well, she didn't. As far as she was concerned, it was just a one-time thing, a drunken experiment on New Year's Eve that got out of hand. When I called her the next day, she seemed almost angry about what we'd done. She informed me there was no way we'd ever be getting together again."

"That would have been a month before Westminster," said Aunt Peg. "Is that why you poisoned her dog?"

"I never tried to poison Kadu," Sara said firmly. "All I wanted to do was put him out of commission for a day. Debra had hurt me and I wanted to hurt her back. I certainly wasn't afraid to compete against her, even though that was the story she told everyone.

"Debra couldn't afford to make a big stink about what happened, because she knew if she complained to the A.K.C. I'd tell everyone why I'd done it. She's always been terrified that someone would find out about us and think she was a lesbian."

Sara snorted in disgust. "Debra Silver with her perfect manicure, her perfect tennis game, and her perfect husband. Even after all these years, she's still afraid that I'll spill the beans and ruin everything. I can't imagine why she thinks I'd even bother."

Probably because she knows you well enough to see what a bitch you are, I thought. Considering that Sara had been the catalyst for much of the mayhem that had transpired, she seemed to be feeling amazingly little remorse.

Out in the hallway, the doorbell chimed. The police had

arrived, or maybe Delilah's lawyer. I didn't much care either way. I'd had just about enough of the Waring/ Bentley family. Sara and Delilah deserved one another. I was happy to leave them to deal with the consequences.

31

Despite all the turmoil that had preceded it, in the end, Frank and Bertie's wedding came together beautifully. The tiny church on Round Hill Road provided an utterly charming setting. The bride glowed. The groom, not surprisingly, alternated between looking enormously proud and scared half to death.

This was a huge step for my brother. I'm not sure he realized how huge until he stood before the altar and watched Bertie walk toward him on her father's arm. As his sister, I recognized the fleeting look of panic that crossed his face. So did his ex-brother-in-law. Standing beside him, Bob reached out and gave Frank's arm a reassuring squeeze.

Frank's nervousness receded. His smile grew wider as Bertie neared. By the time the two of them were standing together in front of the priest, the couple's pleasure in each other was palpable.

Davey made an adorable ring bearer, and Bob, like the rest of the groomsmen, looked sharp in a dove gray morning suit. With Christmas only a day away, the church was decorated with garlands of pine boughs in addition to jonquils, roses, and the yellow tulips that Bertie loved. The scents mingled in the air—a fitting metaphor, perhaps, for the union that was being blessed.

The ceremony was brief. Though given the opportunity, no one objected to the marriage, for which we were all profoundly grateful. Not that we were expecting problems, but with my family you never know.

The couple recited traditional vows, but their first kiss as man and wife was passionate enough to earn them a raised eyebrow from Aunt Peg. Seated behind us in the polished mahogany pews, Terry was grinning. Crawford, like Peg, looked miffed. I figured it was probably a generational thing.

A reception followed at the Greenwich Country Club. Our procession of cars drove slowly up the long driveway, winding between two holes of the golf course and passing the paddle-tennis courts before coming to a graceful roundabout in front of the white-pillared clubhouse. Despite all the distractions, Sara had done a wonderful job with the arrangements.

Ironically she wasn't there to enjoy the event she'd planned. A week earlier, Sara had suffered a miscarriage and was home, resting in bed. Bertie had promised to send Josh by afterward with a piece of wedding cake and a full report on the proceedings.

The ballroom decorations were tastefully lavish. I know that because even Terry approved. Ice sculptures adorned the long buffet table, and Patricia had managed to find yellow tulips for the centerpieces, too. But lovely as everything was, I couldn't help feeling a lingering sense of sadness.

It was hard not to remember that at one time I'd thought Sam and I would be the ones having a Christmas wedding, a public celebration of the love I'd thought we shared. Instead, this joyous occasion belonged to somebody else, and I'd neither seen nor heard from Sam in months.

When the music started and the dance floor filled with happy couples, I found an empty table in a quiet corner and sat down for a few minutes of solitude. Frank was squiring Aunt Peg sedately around the dance floor while Bertie and Terry made an impossibly dashing duo. Even Davey had found himself a partner among Bertie's younger relatives and was twirling in time to the infectious beat. As I settled back to watch, I found my toes tapping beneath the hem of my gown.

"Mind if I join you?"

I looked up to see Bob, wonderfully handsome in his formal attire, standing behind me and waiting for permission to sit.

I nudged out the chair closest to me. "Sure, go ahead."

"As I recall, you used to love to dance."

"I still do. I just thought I'd sit for a minute."

"Thinking."

"Yes."

"About weddings?"

I nodded. Even after all the time apart, he still knew me too well.

"You and Sam?"

"I thought it would happen." I sighed. "It didn't."

"You and me?"

I lifted my eyes.

Even though he'd asked the question, Bob seemed to know the answer he was going to get. "I don't want to go back," he said.

"Good."

"But I was thinking we might try going forward . . . together."

I reached over and placed my hand on his knee. "We'll always be friends."

"Ouch."

"I can't lie to you, Bob," I said gently.

"I wouldn't want you to. It's just that . . ." He paused, laying his hand on top of mine. ". . . being around you and Davey makes me happy."

"We like having you here, too."

Six weeks earlier, I'd have been shocked to hear myself say such a thing. But what a pleasant surprise the turnaround had been. I could never fall in love with Bob again, but his visit had turned out to be an unexpectedly welcome distraction. Not to mention the restorative effect it had had on my ego.

My ex-husband watched the play of emotions across my face. "You're still waiting for Sam," he said slowly.

"No." I realized as I said it that it was the truth. I'd never regret one minute that I'd spent with Sam, but it had been his choice to walk away. What I would regret was wasting any more of my valuable time wishing for something that wasn't going to be. "I'm not. Not anymore. Now I guess I'm just working on getting over him."

"Will you give me a call when you do?"

"I might." I smiled. "Who knows? By then you'll probably have hooked up with another Jennifer, or Tiffany, or Chelsea . . ."

"One twenty-year-old is enough, thank you. Think of it this way, I've already had my midlife crisis and gotten it out of the way. That makes me a pretty solid bet for the future. How many men can say that?"

"Not many," I admitted.

"We'll keep in touch," he said.

"Of course we will."

"Just in case you change your mind."

"Bob—"

He didn't let me protest. Instead he took my hand, lifted it to his lips for a brief kiss, then used it to draw me to my feet.

"Let's dance."

"I'd love to."

For the first time that day, my smile felt genuine, not forced to suit the occasion. The band was playing Van Morrison's "Moondance." We walked over to the dance floor and I stepped into Bob's arms.

Davey and his dance partner glided by. She was at least six inches taller than he was and probably three years older. Neither seemed troubled by the disparity. The girl was leading, which was a good thing, because my son's grasp of ballroom dancing is rudimentary at best.

"What do you think?" I asked him. "Shall we dance all night?"

Anything that involves staying up past his bedtime garners Davey's immediate approval. "Yeah!"

Two votes in favor, none against. Everything in life should be this easy.

Christmas Eve passed in a flurry of baking, wrapping, eggnog, and laughter. I don't come from a family of procrastinators. For the most part, we'd all finished our shopping early, which left us with nothing to do but actually enjoy the holiday.

Aunt Peg hosted an open house in the afternoon and early evening. She doesn't entertain often, but when she does, she draws a crowd. Dog show folk mingled with family, friends, and neighbors around a twelve-foot Christmas tree, which, improbably, featured a blinking Poodle on its top branch.

Davey, who'd been excited for a week at the twin prospects of being in the wedding and celebrating his favorite holiday, finally began to wind down around eight o'clock. His eyes were drooping as he kissed his father good night and I loaded him into the car. Back at home, he revived just long enough to hang up his stocking and set out a glass of milk and shortbread cookies for Santa before brushing his teeth and tumbling into bed.

Outside, snow had begun to fall. Flakes drifted through the haloed light around the street lamps and settled softly on the ground. The night air was cold and dry; within minutes the snow began to accumulate.

I let the two Poodles out in the backyard, watching their reactions through the kitchen window. Eve, seeing snow for the first time, turned her face up into the flakes, blinking in wonder. Faith, who already knew how much fun a snowstorm could be, immediately began to tunnel, shoving the white stuff aside with her nose as she scooted around the yard.

I loved her racy new look: the grooming-intensive continental trim had been replaced by a becoming blanket of short, black curls on the day the certificate had arrived from the American Kennel Club confirming Faith's championship. Now she could play as much as she liked, and the Poodle was making the most of her newfound freedom. Out in the yard, both dogs' dark coats were quickly frosted with white.

Davey was sound asleep when I went upstairs to check. I doubted that he was dreaming of sugarplums—more likely the toy truck he'd been eyeing covetously at the mall for the past two months, which was now sitting wrapped in the hall closet. Satisfied that he wouldn't awaken, I began to dig his presents out of their hiding places.

The Poodles, predictably, wanted to help with the arrangements. Each earned a shortbread cookie for her hard work. I drank the milk myself.

Setting things up took longer than I thought it would, but the end result was well worth it. Our Christmas tree wasn't tall, but it was full. White lights glistened on its heavy branches. Brightly colored ornaments seemed to dance on silver strings. I turned down the lights in the living room and stood back to savor the effect. The peaceful hush of the snowy night outside added the perfect final touch.

The gentle sound of someone tapping on the front door was so soft that for a moment I thought I'd imagined it. The Poodles were alerted, though. I grabbed Eve before she could make any noise, then quickly shushed Faith with a wave of my hand. She ran to the door and cocked her head questioningly.

I followed her out to the hall, unfastened the locks, and drew the door open. In that instant, time seemed to stop. All my thoughts, all my emotions, were wiped clean.

I couldn't think what to say. I couldn't even seem to move.

All I could do was breathe. In, out. In, out.

I'd been there before.

Heart pounding, I stood and stared at the man who was standing on my front steps. His head and shoulders were dusted with snow; his blue eyes, shining with love.

"Merry Christmas," said Sam.

Please turn the page for
an exclusive sneak peek at
Laurien Berenson's

HOT DOG

Now on sale!

Davey finished his homework before dinner was on the table; in second grade, you don't get a lot. Sam's spaghetti turned out to be every bit as good as its aroma had forecast. The dachshund puppy and my two Poodles were already halfway to becoming fast friends. In short, despite the strife that had gotten us off to a somewhat shaky start, the evening managed to pull itself together.

Later, Sam and I tucked Davey into bed together, sharing the routine as we'd done so many times in the past, with each of us reading a chapter from Davey's current favorite, *Charlotte's Web*. The cozy, familiar ritual felt exactly right. It reminded me how much all of us had given up due to my stubborn insistence that Sam and I not slip back into our old relationship without first examining how things had gone awry.

Maybe I was wrong to hold out for something perfect, I thought, standing in the doorway to Davey's semi-darkened bedroom and listening to Sam read. Maybe I was asking too much.

After a few minutes, Sam tucked the book away in

Davey's night table. He smoothed the blankets over my already sleeping son. Watching the care with which Sam performed the simple tasks, a sudden, unexpected sheen of tears misted my view. What we shared was something precious and rare—not perfect perhaps, but certainly well worth fighting for.

As Sam headed downstairs, I took a moment to turn off the light and give Faith, who slept at the foot of Davey's bed, a pat. Then I slipped across the hall to my own bedroom. A quick survey revealed at least a semblance of order. Close enough, anyway, for what I had in mind. With luck, Sam wouldn't even notice his surroundings; he'd have other, more important things to concentrate on.

Turning to go, I caught my own reflection in the mirror above the dresser. My cheeks were slightly flushed, my eyes bright with anticipation. I hurried into the hallway and down the steps, only to stop, frowning, at the bottom. I'd expected to find Sam in the living room, or maybe even the kitchen. I hadn't thought to see him standing by the front door with his coat on.

"You're leaving?" I didn't even try to keep the disappointment from my voice.

"It seemed like a good idea."

I couldn't imagine why. It seemed like a terrible idea to me.

I crossed the short distance between us, reached up, and slid my hands beneath the leather jacket that was already growing warm with his heat. Palms flat against Sam's chest, I nestled my body in close, stood up on my toes, and pressed my lips to his.

I felt Sam's mouth curve in a smile. Then he dipped his head toward mine and returned the kiss. His hands went around my waist, molding my hips hard against his. The first kiss turned into a second. Sam wanted this every bit as much as I did. Yet still, he pulled away.

"I think I'd better go."

"Why?" I sounded breathless and confused, which was pretty much the way I felt. My hands reached for him, even as he stepped back.

"Answer me one question," Sam said softly. "Do you trust me?"

Of all the possible questions in the world, I thought, don't ask me that one. How could I answer what I didn't know? Yes . . . no . . . maybe . . .

I wanted to trust Sam. I wanted to believe that he wouldn't betray my confidences to Jill Prescott just as I wanted to believe that he would never leave us again, but how could I?

Sam and I had been engaged once; as far as I was concerned, we'd already made a lifetime commitment. And yet when things got tough, he hadn't turned to me. Instead he'd found his only comfort in solitude. Obviously there'd been something lacking in our relationship; and until we found that hole and patched it, I would always wonder what the next rough spot might bring.

Did I trust Sam to always want what was best for us? Yes. Did I trust him to always *do* what was best for us? Maybe not.

"That's not a simple question." I followed Sam's lead and stepped away as well.

"Yes or no, Melanie. That's all I want to know. Do you trust me?"

I knew what Sam wanted me to say. I knew what he needed to hear. And I was as incapable of building our future on a lie as I was of flying to the moon. In the end, my silence spoke for me.

"That's why I have to go." Sam leaned down and brushed one last gentle kiss across my lips. "I love you, Melanie."

"I love you, too." Those words came easily, truthfully, joyously. But I could see by the look in Sam's eyes that they weren't enough.

He reached for the knob and opened the front door. "I'll see you this weekend, right?"

I blinked my eyes and tried to concentrate. After a moment, Saturday swam into focus. There was a dog show Saturday in New Jersey; Aunt Peg was judging Poodles. Sam and I were both planning to go and watch.

"Right," I said. "Saturday."

His gaze raked over my tousled hair and flushed cheeks. The ghost of a smile played across his lips. "Sweet dreams," Sam said.

Like hell. Two could play this game. I drew the tip of my tongue across my lower lip and exhaled softly. "You, too."

The door slammed behind him as Sam let himself out.

I didn't have sweet dreams or any dreams at all that I remembered. Instead, I fell into a light, restless slumber that left me drifting in and out of sleep. I'd finally begun to nod off when my eyes suddenly flew open and I jerked upright in bed.

My heart was racing. My fingers gripped the covers. I had no idea what was wrong.

The room was dark save for a narrow beam of moonlight shining in through the window. The clock on the nightstand read three thirteen a.m. I gulped in air and sat perfectly still, listening. . . .

For what? I wondered. I had no idea.

Next to me on the bed, Eve was awake as well. Her head was up, her ears pricked. I had pushed Dox's crate against the wall in the corner. Now I could hear him moving within. Was that the unaccustomed noise that had awakened us?

No, I realized abruptly, there was something else. The slight but unmistakable sounds of movement from downstairs. A door swished open. A floorboard creaked.

Davey? Not likely. My son slept like a rock. Besides, if he was up, he wouldn't have gone downstairs, he'd have come to me. Then who . . . ?

My heart froze, even as my brain flatly refused to register the implications. My imagination had been running amok lately. This was nothing more than another symptom of the same problem. It couldn't be anything other than that, could it?

For a minute, I strained to hear something else. Anything else.

And then I did.

Someone was moving in the hallway outside my bedroom. Breath lodged painfully in my throat. My hand went to the night table, searching for a weapon. All I came up with was a book. Paperback, not even hardcover. Big help.

All at once, I heard a soft whine. Faith's black muzzle wedged into the crack I'd left in the doorway and pushed the bedroom door open.

"Oh, it's you." Relief made my shoulders sag.

Of course it was Faith. Who else would it have been? The big Poodle was up and prowling around the house, that was all.

She padded quietly into the bedroom. Her tail, usually carried high in the air, was low and still. Her ears were flat against her head. She looked at me uncertainly.

"What's the matter?" I patted the bed beside me. Faith didn't hop up to join us. "What are you doing up?"

She didn't answer. She didn't have to, because both of us heard the next sound at the same time. It was coming from downstairs. My first, hopeful guess had been wrong. It wasn't Faith who'd awakened us. Whatever had gotten us up had roused her as well.

Shaking, shivering, I slipped from beneath the covers. I heard . . . something . . . But what was it? The swish of material being dragged? The hushed whisper of voices?

Was there someone in my house?

Call 911. That was my first thought. Pick up the phone beside the bed and call. And say what? I wondered. That I was hearing noises? That my old house might be creaking in the night? That my dogs were awake and I hoped I wasn't imagining things?

Jill Prescott would get a good laugh out of this, I thought, nervous tension buzzing through my body like a jolt of electricity looking for a fuse to blow. I could see her lead-in now. *Melanie Travis thinks she knows how to solve mysteries. The only mystery last night was why she brought the police racing on an emergency call to her empty home.*

Faith and Eve were watchdogs, weren't they? If someone was downstairs, surely they'd have sounded an alarm. Maybe, I thought. And maybe not. The Poodles were also creatures of habit, accustomed to sleeping through the night, and socialized to look to me for guidance when they were unsure.

I crept past Faith to the bedroom door. Cautiously I peered through the slender opening. And saw nothing. But still . . . I could swear I heard voices. Was that a good sign or a bad sign? Wouldn't intruders at least have the sense to be quiet?

Faith came up beside me, pressing her warm, solid body against my leg. The comfort she offered was tangible and welcome. Whatever was wrong, my Poodle wanted to help. I reached down and stroked her neck and shoulders.

"What *is* that?" I whispered.

Her tail came up and began to wag slowly. Faith didn't care what was happening downstairs. As long as we were together, all was right with her world. Now I needed to make sure that all was right with mine.

"We'd better go see," I said.

I had no idea if the impulse was brave or foolhardy, but I couldn't spend the rest of the night cowering in my bedroom. Looking around, I saw a bud vase sitting on the dresser. It wasn't much but at least I wasn't empty-handed.

Eve hopped off the bed and came to join us in the doorway. Like her dam, she knew what "go" meant. Like Faith, she was always ready to have an adventure, even in the middle of the night. If we were going somewhere, she didn't want to be left behind.

Slipping out into the hallway, I went first to Davey's room. His door was open; I could see his small form curled beneath the comforter, his head resting on the pillow. His breathing was deep and even.

I reached out and pulled the bedroom door closed. Behind me, both Poodles were waiting expectantly, ready for whatever might come next. Even better than letting these two big dogs accompany me downstairs, I realized suddenly, I could send them on ahead.

"Who wants to go out?" I whispered, my tone urgent, inviting. "Come on, let's go outside!"

Eve yipped and danced her front feet in the air. This was more exciting than she'd hoped. An *outdoors* adventure in the dark!

Together, the Poodles scrambled past me. When I'd only had one dog, the mad dash to the back door had taken place in silence. With two, however, the excitement was multiplied. It had become a competition. Faith and Eve were barking as they ran; the clamor they created seemed to bounce off the walls.

I knew what they were saying. Each was yelling the canine version of "Me first! Me first!" But as I ran along behind them, I could only hope that someone down below would hear their deep-throated bellowing in the darkness and envision a pair of attack-trained Dobermans bearing down upon them.

By the time I reached the bottom of the stairs, the Poodles had already skidded around the banister and headed down the hallway toward the kitchen. I caught my breath, reflecting on the fact that the tone of their barking hadn't changed. That was a good sign. If they'd seen anyone, I would know it by now.

On the other hand, having sent the pair on a single-minded dash to the back door, I'd left the rest of the small house unscouted. Pausing, I reached around and flipped on lights in the living and dining rooms. Both were blessedly empty, just as I'd left them before going to bed.

I was telling myself it was just as well that I hadn't called the police when I reached the kitchen. Eve was standing by the back door, waiting for me to open it. Faith, however, was in the middle of the room peering curiously at the little television set that was a new addition to my kitchen counter.

The TV was on and its screen cast an eerie glow out into the shadowy room. Shimmering colors reflected off the refrigerator, the sink, the shiny tile floor. The effect was spooky, and at the same time, compelling. Faith stared as though mesmerized.

An infomercial was playing. The participants were talking to each other about the incredible value of the product they were hawking. Theirs were the voices I'd heard from upstairs.

"What on earth . . . ?"

I reached for the wall, finding the switch panel and turning on lights inside and out. Eve whined impatiently by the back door. As well she should: I'd told her I was going to let her out.

Automatically I went to flip up the dead bolt. Abruptly, my hand froze in mid-air. The lever was already upright. The door wasn't locked.

I sucked in a breath and spun around, certain in that instant that I'd felt someone creeping up behind me. There was no one there.

Of course not.

This was ridiculous. I snapped off the TV and the room fell silent. Still, my heart was pounding so powerfully it hurt to breathe. I could feel its rhythm pounding in my ears.

I wasn't an idiot. I was a grown-up with responsibilities. And I always locked my doors at night.

At least I thought I did. Unless the argument I'd had with Sam had been a more potent distraction than I'd realized, which appeared to be the case.

Giving up on the back door, Eve went and slurped a drink from the water bowl. The utter normalcy of her actions began to have a calming effect on my nerves. I crossed the room and opened the basement door. Lights on, I stuck my head down the steps.

Like the rest of the house, it was empty. Silent. Undisturbed.

Now that the puppy had had a drink, not to mention this burst of nocturnal excitement, there was no way her bladder was going to hold until morning. I opened the back door and let both Poodles briefly outside.

There was a possibility, I admitted to myself, that I'd forgotten to lock the dead bolt. But had I left the TV on? No. No way. Hadn't happened.

I watched that set in the mornings when I was getting Davey ready for school. And sometimes in the evening while I was cooking dinner. But not last night. Sam had been there and we'd been talking. The set had never been on.

I hadn't touched that TV any more than I'd left on all the lights in the house last Sunday. I had no explanation for any of this. What was going on?

After a short break from crime solving, stay-at-home mom Melanie Travis has not *become boring—no matter what her alarmingly opinionated Aunt Peg says. She still has a nose for sniffing up a good mystery, especially when it involves the life of a legendary dog breeder . . .*

Despite Melanie's domestic demands—a toddler and a house full of Standard Poodles—helping Edward March pen his life story is an opportunity she can't pass up. Of course Edward turns out to be a growly old man who wants his book—*Puppy Love*—to consist mainly of his amorous encounters with women from the dog show community. It's juicy gossip, but not *dangerous* . . . until Andrew, Edward's son, pays Melanie an angry visit to stop her from working on the book.

When Andrew suddenly turns up very dead, the victim of a seemingly intentional hit-and-run, the police are looking at Edward as Suspect #1. There was lots of bad blood between Andrew and his father, but Melanie is looking at the bigger picture. Would some of Edward's ex-trysts have gone after Andrew to shut Edward up? How about all of those husbands and boyfriends with bones to pick? And who is that woman whom everyone is avoiding at the funeral?

Between getting caught up in the bafflingly dysfunctional March family, sorting out two generations of disgruntled ex-lovers, and uncovering a shocking case of secret hoarding, Melanie's running into dead ends almost as fast as she's running out of time. The longer the killer stays unleashed, the sooner she may end up in the dog house for good.

Please turn the page for an exciting sneak peek of
Laurien Berenson's next Melanie Travis mystery
GONE WITH THE WOOF
coming in September!

CHAPTER 1

Life is made up of small moments, most passing by in the blink of an eye, unremarked and unremarkable. But every so often one of those small moments expands and time seems to stop. We're faced with an occurrence so intense, so monumental, that the rest of life's cluttered minutiae simply slip away like a passing wisp of breeze.

What remains is a haze of shock and emptiness, a void that we must somehow learn to negotiate. There's an elemental shift in worldview and a lesson never forgotten: that nothing in life is as permanent as we once believed.

That was how I felt when a murderer whom I'd been chasing stood two feet away from me and looked me in the eye, then lifted a gun to his temple and blew his brains out.

It was an instant when everything changed.

Maybe clarity of vision is a sign of maturity. If so, I earned mine the hard way. But in that fleeting speck of time when I put my own life at risk and watched another life end, I knew with absolute certainty what was important to me and what was not.

I had a new baby, an almost new husband, and an eleven-year-old son, whom I loved more than anything. I also had a houseful of dogs and an extended family whose only goal seemed to be to drive me crazy. The thought that I might never have seen any of them again was beyond unbearable.

And yet in that single moment I had put all of that on the line. What was I thinking? I didn't know.

One thing I did know. I needed a break.

"I just want to say that you've become rather dull."

"Really?" My tone might have been a bit dry.

I was sitting across the kitchen table from my aunt Peg, a woman who in her first sixty-five years has stirred up more excitement and controversy than many South American dictators. Come to think of it, she also runs the members of her family like a small, somewhat unruly junta. Peg stands six feet tall and has iron-gray hair and sharp, brown eyes. Should a brawl erupt anywhere in the vicinity, my money's on her.

"Yes, really. Don't make me say it twice. I shouldn't have to say it at all. You used to be interesting. Now . . ." Aunt Peg stood up, walked over to the counter, and poured herself a second cup of Earl Grey tea. Her gaze slid pointedly to the window over the sink.

It was New Year's Day, and we'd had six inches of fresh snow overnight. Eighteen months had passed since I'd made the decision to try to realign the balance in my life. I'd wanted to attain some sense of normalcy, and I liked to think that I'd achieved that goal.

What Aunt Peg saw in the backyard was my husband, Sam, and our older son, Davey, shoveling the new snow off the deck. From the way the pile was shaping up, I suspected there might be a snowman in the offing.

Younger son, Kevin, twenty-two months old and all but swallowed up by a snowsuit, boots, and mittens, was toddling unsteadily around the yard, accompanied by several big black Standard Poodles. That was what passed for normal at my house.

"Now I'm happy," I said.

"So you think," Aunt Peg sniffed. "You're what? Thirty-five years old?"

I nodded warily. Not because her assessment of my age was wrong, but because Aunt Peg never begins a lecture without a purpose in mind, usually one that involves work for me.

"You need to get back in the game."

"Excuse me?"

"For one thing, you need to figure out what you're going to do with the rest of your life now that you no longer have a job."

Aunt Peg was referring to the fact that after Kevin was born, I had taken a leave of absence from my position as special needs tutor at a private school in Greenwich, Connecticut. A single semester away had now stretched to three.

When Davey was little, I'd been a single mother. I'd had to work. This time around I had a choice. And the thought of leaving Kevin with a nanny or an au pair didn't appeal at all. Even if my son's current favorite word—from an admittedly limited vocabulary—was an emphatic and defiant *no*.

"I have a job," I said calmly. "I'm a mother."

"Oh, please. Hillary Clinton is a mother. It didn't stop her from becoming secretary of state."

"You want me to go into politics?"

Okay, that was immature. The verbal equivalent of sticking out my tongue. But give Aunt Peg the slightest bit of encouragement, and she tends to run roughshod over anyone in the vicinity. Speaking as the person most likely to be trampled, what can I say? Sometimes I sink to my kids' level.

"Don't be ridiculous. I want you to use your brain. I want you to think. I have an idea."

"Wonderful," I muttered.

The back door came flying inward, bringing with it a blast of cold air, five scrambling, sodden Standard Poodles, and three rosy-cheeked, snow-covered men of varying sizes. Davey had his gloved hands cupped together. He was holding a snowball the size of a small globe.

Sam was just behind him, carrying Kevin. Even in chunky boots and a puffy down jacket, with a red nose and snow-tipped eyelashes, Sam looked like the kind of man most women would want to take straight to bed. Even after six years together, I'm no exception.

Sam lowered the toddler into my arms and, having heard my last pronouncement, said, "What's the matter?"

"Aunt Peg has an idea."

"Good day for it," Sam said mildly. He and Aunt Peg are the best of friends. Sometimes that irks me, but mostly I try to rise above it. "New Year's resolutions and all."

Davey, who had pulled open a low cabinet and was rummaging around inside, stood up and spun around. "Are we going to make resolutions?"

"Sure, if you want to. Put that snowball in the sink, okay?"

"I can't. I'm going to report on it for science class."

Davey's tall for his age. He takes after his father, my ex-husband, Bob. They're both long limbed and graceful. But my son's personality is all me. He could argue the spots off a Dalmatian.

Davey turned back to the cabinet and withdrew a large mixing bowl. "How long do you think it will take to melt?"

"It's started already," I mentioned. Between the five Poodles, the three sets of boots, and the water dripping from his hands, the floor was awash with melted snow.

Sam reached over, plucked the snowball out of Davey's hands, and plopped it in the bowl on the counter. Aunt Peg grabbed a towel from the stack near the back door and went to work drying Poodle legs. That left me to get Kevin undressed.

"Who wants hot chocolate?" I asked.

"No!" cried Kevin. I'd unzipped the front of his snowsuit and peeled the top off his shoulders. He yanked his arms free and waved his small hands in the air.

"Gotta love a kid who knows what he wants," Sam said.

"I think he takes after Aunt Peg." I lifted Kevin up and freed his legs. His red rubber boots kicked off and landed in a puddle on the floor beneath my chair.

"And isn't it nice that someone finally does," said Peg.

It took another twenty minutes to get everyone warm, dry, and organized. Amazingly, the floor even got mopped. Once it was dry, the Poodles lay down around us, forming a canine obstacle course for unwary walkers or—if you were Kevin's size—a fluffy stool on which to perch.

The five of them were Sam's and my blended canine family. Faith and Eve were a mother-and-daughter duo, originally Davey's and mine. Faith had been bred by Aunt Peg and gifted to me six years earlier, either as a reward or an assignment. I'd never been entirely sure which. Raven and Casey were two champion Poodles from Sam's breeding program that he'd brought with him when he moved east from Michigan to Connecticut.

The remaining Poodle was Tar, the only male in the group.

Also bred by Aunt Peg, he had been Sam's specials dog: a champion whom Sam had campaigned to numerous Group and Best in Show wins at venues up and down the East Coast. Now retired, he, like the others, wore the close-cropped, easy-to-care-for sporting trim. With two children keeping us busy, both Sam and I were happy to be taking a break from having to "do hair."

"Finally," said Aunt Peg when we were seated around the table once more. "Can we now get back to the business at hand?"

"Certainly," said Sam. "Who wants to begin?"

"Me," cried Davey.

"Excellent. Someone with initiative." Aunt Peg stared at me pointedly over the top of her mug. Peg's sweet tooth is legendary, and her hot chocolate was coated with a layer of mini-marshmallows. "Unlike certain of my other relatives."

"I resolve to eat fewer lima beans," Davey said firmly. "And not to lose my homework. And not to call Kimberly Winterbottom stupid, even when she is."

"Good job," I said. "I don't like lima beans, either."

"Kimberly Winterbottom?" asked Sam.

"She thinks she knows everything." In sixth grade now, Davey was in his first year at Hart Middle School in North Stamford. The move from elementary school made him feel very grown up. "And she doesn't. Not even close."

"Fair enough," said Peg. "Sam, would you like to go next?"

"Not me," Sam said, demurring. He knew better than to get in Peg's way. "I'm not ready yet. Why don't you take my turn?"

"I'll be happy to."

No surprise there. Aunt Peg had been waiting for this opening since she'd arrived an hour earlier. Now she swiveled her seat around to face me.

"You've become boring," she said.

You know, just in case I'd missed that insult the first time.

"There you go," I replied cheerfully. "That can be my resolution. Be less boring."

New Year's resolutions have never been my thing. I just don't see the point of vowing on the first day of the year to read more books, lose ten pounds, or run a marathon. Because if I didn't want to do that stuff before, what are the chances that a change of date is going to make me want to do it now?

"You're stuck in a rut," Aunt Peg persisted. My easy acquiescence didn't even slow her down. "I can help with that."

"Don't tell me," I said. "Here comes the idea."

"As well it should. Somebody has to shake things up around here."

Kevin punctuated that thought with a loud bang. Settled on the floor, next to the cabinet Davey had opened earlier, he was engaged in one of his favorite occupations, stacking pots and pans. The leaning tower he'd been erecting had just lost its battle with gravity. Judging by the building skills he'd displayed thus far, Sam and I were guessing that a career in architecture was not in his future.

Aunt Peg didn't even lose a beat. "Edward March," she said.

Sam looked up. "What about him?"

"He's turning in his judge's license."

"Wow," said Sam. "I wouldn't have thought he'd ever retire. March seems like the type of judge who'd hope to croak in the Best in Show ring at Westminster, as he pointed out the winning dog."

"Don't we all," Aunt Peg remarked. "And Edward does

like his dramatic moments. Nevertheless, I believe health issues have gotten in the way. He's taken very few assignments in the last several years, and now he seems to think that it's time to bow out gracefully and on his own terms."

"Who is Edward March?" I asked.

Aunt Peg and Sam have both been a part of the dog show world for so long that occasionally they forget that I don't have their wealth of experience and insider information to draw upon. Aunt Peg's Cedar Crest Kennel, founded decades earlier with her late husband, Max, had produced some of the top winning Standard Poodles in dog show history. Once a successful owner-handler who'd competed in dozens of shows a year, Aunt Peg still kept up the same hectic schedule, now serving as a much-in-demand dog show judge.

Sam's tenure in the dog show world had been shorter in duration than Aunt Peg's, but he had been no less devoted. His Shadowrun Kennel was a small but select operation. Like my aunt, Sam had spent countless hours studying pedigrees, genetics, and the best available bloodlines. He was also a talented and enthusiastic dog show exhibitor.

Basically, in this group I was the redheaded stepchild.

"Don't worry, Mom," said Davey. "I don't know, either."

I reached over and plopped a few more marshmallows in his mug to thank him for the support.

"You don't need to know." Aunt Peg slanted her nephew a fond glance. "Whereas you"—her gaze shifted in my direction—"could be better informed."

Nothing new there.

I sipped my cocoa and leaned back in my seat. "Why don't you tell me what I'm missing?"

"Edward March is nothing less than dog show royalty."

"Like Prince William?" asked Davey. He had watched the

royal wedding on television, fascinated less by the ceremony than by the vintage cars that transported the royal family.

"Not exactly," Sam explained. "Prince William has a hereditary position. Edward March earned his acclaim. His Russet Kennel was started in the nineteen sixties and soon became the driving force in Irish Setters. He was single-handedly responsible for dozens of champions in that breed throughout the second half of the last century. If there was an Irish Setter in the Group or Best in Show ring anywhere on the East Coast, chances are it was a Russet dog."

"Bob and Janie Forsyth handled all his dogs for many years," said Aunt Peg. "Surely, you know who they are."

Of course I did. The esteemed husband-and-wife team was dogdom's most famous couple. As handlers, they'd all but ruled the sporting dog and terrier rings for decades, before retiring to become highly respected judges. I had shown Eve under Janie Forsyth and had picked up two points toward her championship.

"So he's a man who used to have good dogs," I said. So far, this all sounded like old news.

"Not just good," Aunt Peg corrected. "Some of the very best in his breed. And like his handlers, he followed up by becoming a very good judge. His opinion really meant something, and that's a rare gift. If Edward March put up your dog, you knew you had a good one."

That was high praise coming from Aunt Peg. She didn't hand out accolades lightly.

"And?" I asked.

"And what? Isn't that enough?"

"It's plenty. But what does it have to do with me?"

"Oh, that." Aunt Peg sniffed, as if the change in topic from dog show royalty to her wayward niece was distinctly uninteresting.

"Now you've got me curious, too," said Sam. "So March is turning in his judge's license. Where does Melanie fit in?"

"Apparently, in celebration of his fifty-some years in the dog show world, Edward intends to write his memoirs. Anyone who's ever seen his desk could tell you that organization isn't his strong suit. He's looking to find a coauthor to help him do the job properly. I told him I knew just the right person."

CHAPTER 2

I sat up straight in my chair. "Me?"

"Of course, you. You'd be perfect for the job."

"But I'm not an author. I don't have the slightest idea about what goes into writing a book."

"You used to be a teacher. You tutored children who were behind in English class. It's all the same thing, isn't it? Just grammar and stringing sentences together in a way that makes sense. How hard can that be?"

That was the sort of question Aunt Peg always asked when she wanted to involve me in a project that I knew better than to attempt. The problem is that my aunt has never run from a challenge in her life. So it's never crossed her mind that her relatives don't feel equally invincible.

"It sounds like an interesting idea," said Sam. "From what I know about Edward March, he's quite a character. I'm sure he has some fascinating stories to tell. His life was pretty much dog show history in the making. You could end up writing the definitive record of our sport over the last half century."

It's not as if *that* lowered the intimidation factor any.

"Will there be pictures in your book?" asked Davey.

"I should think so," Aunt Peg told him. "What good is history without illustrations?"

Sam nodded in agreement.

Did you hear that? *My* book," Davey had said. And nobody had argued with him. Not even me.

That thought was enough to goad me back into the conversation.

"Wait a minute," I said. "I'm not even sure there's going to be a book."

"Of course there's going to be a book," Aunt Peg informed me. "That's already a given. With or without your help, Edward plans to write his memoirs. All we're discussing now is your participation . . . or lack thereof."

"Something like that would be pretty time consuming," I mentioned. Was I grasping at straws, or did it just feel that way?

"I'm sure it will be. I'd imagine that Edward would require a proper commitment from you. But since you currently have neither a job nor even a single dog in hair . . ." Aunt Peg swept an eloquent gaze around the room. "Really, Melanie, what do you do with yourself all day?"

Sam, that traitor, was laughing quietly. He'd angled his body away, but I could see his shoulders shaking.

"If I agree to do this, it means that you're going to be spending more time taking care of Kevin," I said to his back.

The threat of extra baby duty wasn't nearly enough to sway him back to my side. Sam just shrugged. "Fine by me."

"Good," said Aunt Peg. "Then it's settled."

"Yay, Mom's going to write a book!" cried Davey.

On the floor, several of the Poodles lifted their heads and cocked an ear, wondering what all the excitement was about.

Nobody seemed to want to hear my vote.

"I guess that means I'm in," I said.

* * *

It all sounded so simple in theory.

Unfortunately, it wasn't long before reality reasserted itself. Less than three days actually, starting when Monday arrived and Davey's school reopened for the new semester. And we got four more inches of fresh snow.

Aunt Peg's call came just minutes after Davey's bus picked him up at the end of the driveway. I hadn't even had time to pour a second cup of coffee. Sometimes I think she must have our house bugged.

"You're all set," she said. "I told Edward to expect you at nine thirty."

"This morning?"

I knew Aunt Peg worked fast, but even for her, this was warp speed. And would it have been too much to ask for her to have checked with me first?

"Of course this morning. Edward's eager to get started. I assumed you would be, too."

Peg tends to be enamored with her own version of the truth. I bet she even said that with a straight face.

"Kevin has Gymboree this morning. We go every Monday."

"He's a baby, Melanie. I'm sure he doesn't know what day of the week it is. You can take him tomorrow instead. He'll never know the difference."

"*I'll* know the difference, and so will the teacher. Our class is today, not tomorrow."

"Really." Peg exhaled in a huff. "As if a baby should even have a schedule."

Yet another reminder that Aunt Peg had never been a mother.

"Gymboree?" Sam stuck his head out of his office door.

He designs computer software and works for himself. Most days that's a blessing. Today, not so much.

Frantically, I waved him off. Blithely, he ignored me. "I can take him."

"That man is an angel," said Aunt Peg. "You don't deserve him."

There were moments when I was quite sure that I didn't deserve either one of them.

Edward March lived in Westport, a cosmopolitan Connecticut town about fifteen miles up the coast from Stamford. Financially speaking, Westport has the same kind of profile as Greenwich, but the money there is quieter. Celebrities move to Greenwich when they want to be seen. They move to Westport when they want to enjoy the pastoral peace and privacy.

March's estate was on the north side of town. I took the Merritt Parkway and followed Aunt Peg's directions from the exit. Luckily, the trip took less than half an hour, because I'd gotten off to a late start.

Trust Aunt Peg to think that in a house with a husband, two children, and five big dogs, a half hour's notice would be enough time for me to get everything squared away before heading out for the morning. I used up ten minutes just folding laundry and emptying the dishwasher.

At least the tight schedule didn't leave me much time to worry about the fact that I was on my way to a new assignment for which I felt conspicuously underqualified, and which also involved working for an eminent person whom I'd never even met.

Sure. No butterflies there.

I navigated the last mile of the trip with care. March's quiet country road hadn't been plowed since the overnight addition of new snow, and a thin sheet of ice coated the shallow ruts left by previous travelers. My Volvo handles adverse conditions like a champ, but having lived in Connecticut my whole life, I've learned to give ice and snow the respect they deserve.

There was a tall, wrought-iron gate at the end of March's driveway, but the intent seemed to be more decorative than functional, since it was sitting open. From the road, all I could see of the house were two brick chimneys, visible in the distance, above the treetops. Acres of rolling meadowland, snow covered and glistening with the soft sheen of the morning sun, extended outward on either side of the driveway and ended at a distant tree line.

The house was a traditional Colonial, two stories tall and built symmetrically square, painted white, with black shutters. It wasn't as large as I might have expected from the grand approach; most likely, it had been built before land values in Fairfield County had soared into the stratosphere.

The driveway circled around in front of the door, and there was a parking area off to one side. I pulled over there, turned off the car, and gathered up my purse and notebook. Really, an actual notebook. The kind with pages.

Running out the door that morning, I'd had no idea what sort of writing tools a potential coauthor might be expected to supply. I hadn't wanted to arrive empty-handed, but I didn't want to appear overeager, either. Just because Aunt Peg had nominated me for this position didn't mean that Edward March was going to agree with her choice.

The deep, sonorous tone of the doorbell had barely finished echoing before the front door drew open. A young woman, dressed in a chunky turtleneck sweater and faded blue jeans, greeted me with a smile.

"Good. You're here. Mr. March appreciates punctuality. Please come in."

After the cold outside, the house felt wonderfully warm.

"I'm Melanie," I said as she shut the door. I was already unbuttoning my coat and unwinding my scarf.

"And I'm Charlotte," the young woman replied. Her handshake was as firm as my own. She hung my coat and scarf on a rack tucked in a corner behind the door. "I'm Mr. March's assistant. He's waiting for you in the library. If you'd please follow me this way."

Charlotte's formal way of speaking was at odds with her college coed looks. Blond hair, straight and shiny, swung around her shoulders as she proceeded down the wide center hallway. Dangly earrings, one to each ear, swayed in time. Her make-up had been applied with a light hand, and her unpolished nails were bitten short.

"I know Mr. March is looking forward to meeting you," she said, stopping in front of a dark wooden door. "This project is dear to his heart, and he's been very anxious to get started."

"I hope I'll be able to help."

"Oh, I'm sure you will. Mr. March can be a little, um . . . disorganized. But he has so many wonderful stories to tell. All he needs is someone who's willing to listen and then figure out how to make order out of chaos. I'm sure you'll do just fine."

Her belief in my abilities was quite touching, I thought. Especially considering the fact that we'd just met.

"Besides . . . ," Charlotte confided in a low voice as she drew the door open. Her hand at my back ushered me forward into the room. "You look like you're made of much stronger stuff than the last two candidates."

Last two candidates? I spun around in surprise, only to find the door closing in my face. Having delivered that unexpected news, Charlotte was gone.

Briefly, I closed my eyes and wondered if Aunt Peg had

been aware that her friend had already attempted—and failed—to begin writing his book with two previous applicants. Knowing my aunt, that was just the sort of incendiary information she'd have been tempted to keep to herself.

"Don't just stand there." Edward March's voice was an imperious growl. "Come over by the light so I can get a look at you."

Once I'd turned and had my first look around, it was easy to see why March had summoned me to join him by the window. The room was only dimly lit, and there wasn't anywhere else to sit down. The expanse of the library between us was impossibly cluttered.

A suite of overstuffed leather furniture was covered with cartons, books, and periodicals. Two file cabinets, a world globe on a massive frame, and a glass-fronted cherrywood cupboard all vied for floor space. I was pretty sure I even saw a wooden rocking horse tucked away behind a couch.

March himself, standing just in front of his expansive desk, was a large man with a stern look that matched the growl he'd just uttered. He had a full head of white hair and broad shoulders that stooped forward, causing his frame to look as though it was collapsing inward. The effect made him no less intimidating. March's left hand, fingers gnarled with age, grasped the top of a wooden cane.

No wonder the previous two candidates hadn't lasted long, I thought. I was half tempted to make a run for it myself. Then my gaze slid back up, and I saw the calculating look in March's eyes and realized that was exactly what he was expecting.

"Well?" he demanded. "How long are you going to keep me standing here? Do I look like I have all day?"

Begin as you mean to go on, I thought and walked with a determined stride across the room.

It was like navigating my way around an obstacle course. I didn't give March the satisfaction of looking down to see where I was going. And I didn't so much as wince when I stubbed my toe on the damn globe.

"My name is Melanie Travis," I said.

"I know that. Margaret called and told me to expect you."

Margaret? I'd never heard anyone call Aunt Peg by her full name before. Intrigued, I filed that tidbit away for further consideration.

He peered at me closely. "You don't look like a teacher."

"Really? What do teachers look like?"

"Skinny. Buttoned up. Like fun is out of the question."

"You don't look like too much fun yourself," I told him.

"You should have known me when I was younger." His laugh was a dry, wheezing cackle. He patted a nearby chair that was angled toward his desk. "Come over here and take a seat. Tell me how someone as pretty as you got to be a teacher."

Wonderful. A man who was twice my age was flirting with me. I wondered if this was why his assistant, Charlotte, had been in such a hurry to leave the room.

"I thought we were going to talk about you," I said. "My Aunt Peg tells me that you want to write a book."

"Indeed I do."

When March moved around behind his desk and sat down, I stepped forward and took the chair he'd pointed out. I folded my hands primly on the edge of the desk and settled down to listen.

"I've lived a long life. I have a lot to say. I need a good scribe, someone with a decent head on her shoulders to write things down for me. Do you think you could manage to do that?"

"Quite possibly," I said. "What happened to the last two people who tried?"

"They were idiots." His hand waved away the question.

"If I don't know what they did wrong, how do I know if I can do better?"

"That's not up to you to decide."

Maybe, maybe not. As far as I could tell, the jury was still out on whether or not March and I were going to be able to forge a decent working relationship. I sat and waited.

March frowned. Then he scowled. He seemed to have an entire arsenal of fierce expressions at his command. Idly, I wondered if he practiced in the mirror.

Finally, he said, "The first one . . . It turned out that she didn't like dogs. Now, how was I supposed to work with that?"

"Probably not very easily," I admitted. Considering the book's subject matter, it seemed like a valid objection.

"You like dogs, don't you?"

"Of course I do."

"You see? I knew any relative of Margaret's would have to be a dog person."

Luckily, March hasn't met my brother.

"And the second candidate?"

"That was a problem right from the beginning. When he took notes, he wrote things down in that horrid shorthand that passes for conversation nowadays. What's it called? Textspeak?"

"Oh my." My inner teacher cringed in sympathy.

"You see? Like I said, idiots. But I can already tell that this is going to work." March leaned toward me across his desk. His hand slid along the polished surface, grasped my fingers in his, and gave them a squeeze. "You and I are going to get along famously."

Gently, I disentangled my hand and put it down in my lap, out of reach.

That remained to be seen, I thought.